Please feel free to send me an email.
filters these emails. Good news is always welcome.

Jasmine Rose - jasmine_rose@awesomeauthors.org

Sign up for my blog for updates and freebies!
http://jasmine-rose.awesomeauthors.org

About the Publisher

BLVNP Incorporated, A Nevada Corporation, 340 S. Lemon #6200, Walnut CA 91789, info@blvnp.com / legal@blvnp.com

DISCLAIMER

This book is a work of FICTION. It is fiction and not to be confused with reality. Neither the author nor the publisher or its associates assume any responsibility for any loss, injury, death or legal consequences resulting from acting on the contents in this book. The author's opinions are not to be construed as the opinions of the publisher. The material in this book is for entertainment purposes ONLY. Enjoy.

Praise for **A Unique Kind of Love**

Great book! I couldn't put book down from the very start! The prologue was a great hook and the storyline is so original and creative. I give this book two thumbs up!

-Amanda Bennett, Amazon

I remember reading it for the first time and falling immediately in love with it. Beautifully written with A Unique Kind of plot.

-Elena, Amazon

After reading this, I was very social and kind to everyone. I love Lena and everything she went through is meant to be because if none of it happened she wouldn't have woken up and she wouldn't have known he was the right one. I absolutely loved it all, wouldn't change a thing.

-Eliana, Goodreads

THIS BOOK IS AMAZING!!! I couldn't help but read it all in one go, so addictive! The plot was amazing, the writing flowed smoothly and it was so interesting that I finished it in one day! But then I read it again! And again! Everyone should read this book, it is so amazing, it deserves to be number one!!!!

-Sapphire, Goodreads

Love this book, the plot and the characters are unique and it makes you think just what the true idea of love is. Every update just made me fall more and more in love with Liam and Lena's relationship. So glad it's being published so more people can read and enjoy this book. Definitely in my top 10 favourite books!

-Hannah Caldwell, Goodreads

I'm so crazy about Jasmine Rose! When I read her book Mars, I just couldn't get enough. So when I found out she had another book, I was ecstatic. Yep, she's definitely like John Green and I'm not even mad. I'm sold!

-Jayme Lane, Goodreads

A Unique Kind of Love

By: Jasmine Rose

BLVNP

ISBN: 978-1680307771

Table of Contents

*To my amazing parents, to Luci, Dana, and my fans
without whom I wouldn't have been able to do any of this*

You didn't go.
You stayed.
It caught me by surprise.
I never had somebody stay before.
It was almost like,
You wanted to stay.
I never had anybody want to stay.
Strangely,
It was like you loved me.
I never had anyone love me before.
What's even stranger is,
It was like you were my best friend.
I never had a best friend before.
Along this twisted path,
I fell in love.
I've never fallen in love before.
And my love,
That's the only thing,
I've ever felt certain about in my life.

~Anonymous~

FREE DOWNLOAD

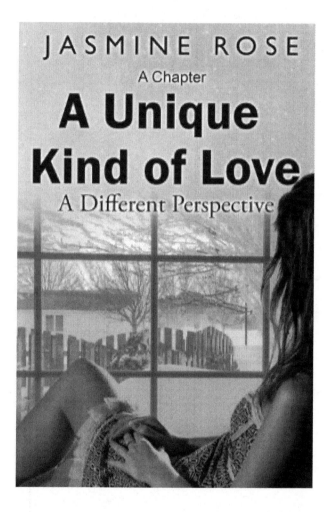

Get this freebie and MORE when you sign
up for the author's mailing list!

http://jasmine-rose.awesomeauthors.org

Prologue

Two light grocery bags in hand, she followed her dad to the bright, white family car that caused them many troubles as they struggled to find it in the middle of snow. The girl opened the front seat door and slipped inside the car, completely oblivious to the look her father was giving her.

He sighed. "Lena?" The girl froze because he never called her by her actual name, unless he was serious about something. He always called her Rosie. "We talked about this. On the way here, you'd sit in front. On the way back, you'll sit behind me."

"Daaad! Please?" Lena pouted and widened her eyes a little. He shook his head and pointed to the back seat. He refused to give in to her, not again. Lena groaned and held out a hand to her dad. He took it and supported her waist as she moved to the backseat. She huffed and put on her seat belt.

"Happy?" she asked.

He gave her a smile. "That's my girl."

The car ride was silent, until her dad put a CD in and played it. Lena grinned and sat up immediately. At the first notes of the song, she made jazz hands. Her ponytail swung as she swayed in her seat to the music.

"Love, love me do. You know, I love you. I'll always be true," they both sang loudly. The Beatles had always been their favorite band, even though Lena's mom didn't like them much.

"I love you, Dad!" cried out the girl, her chestnut-colored eyes shining in exhilaration and excitement.

Her father laughed. "You know I love you too, Rosie."

The next seconds were a blur. Between the music, their singing and the momentary happiness, there was a truck that had passed the red light and was heading towards them. Time froze—this was the moment that would turn the girl's life upside down.

Lena turned just in time to see the truck inches away from colliding with the car. Her dad noticed as well, and his eyes widened. She screamed. The car lurched and Lena was thrown forward violently, the seatbelt biting into her stomach and knocking the wind out of her. The sound of her dad calling out her name was the last thing she heard before the world faded away from her.

"Rosie!"

I could hear a vague sound in the background.

I felt myself crying. For a long moment my upper eyelid seemed glued to the lower one, because I couldn't open my eyes. When I finally could, they hurt from my tears.

My gaze settled on Mom's terrified expression, and I watched as her face slowly softened with relief. She wiped the tears on my cheeks, although that didn't stop them from falling again.

She patted my hand. "Was it a bad dream, honey?" she asked. I took deep breaths to steady myself. I nodded.

"I wish I turned earlier, so I could—I don't know," I whispered, watching as the invisible switch clicked in my mom's mind.

"I wish he was here," she said.

Me too, Mom, I thought. I miss him too. How often had I wished that he was still alive, and that I was the one who had died?

I closed my eyes again and felt myself drift away into another dream.

1

Wonder and Anxiety

"The best is yet to be."
~Robert Browning~

Lena Rose Winter

Sighing, I laid my head down on the unshaven grass. I smiled. Stars glimmered and gleamed at me, assisting the moon's job to light up the sky at night. It seemed to me that there was a snowfall sparkling in outer space and I felt privileged to witness it. With soft, soothing music blasting in my ears, I felt better than I had in a long time. Comfort was something I cherished more than anything. I could feel a slight breeze blow on my neck; it cooled the few beads of sweat that had formed earlier that night.

Mom and I had decided to do a Welcome to the New Home barbecue. We'd eaten until our stomachs were begging for a break. It was always a moment that embellished my relationship with her. She went to sleep about an hour ago, the wine easing the process. So I'd been lying here for what, an hour or two? In those moments, I witnessed the sun disappearing and permitting the moon to rise in the sky; it was a never ending cycle.

Except, of course, for people who lived in the North Pole.

I had come close enough once, though. A few years ago, when I was twelve, Mom's company gave her a post somewhere in Alberta, Canada. We lived there only for about two months, but my, oh my, we had gone there in the middle of January. I still recall fearing that my toes were going to fall off because I couldn't feel them.

Thank God that this time, we moved into a place that wasn't too horribly cold, hopefully. Albany, NY seemed like a pretty cool place so far. I took a walk around yesterday and there was a gigantic park, Ridgefield, where I was sure to spend more time throughout the year. Myrtle Avenue was a considerably calm street and I was content about the small house we rented for the year. Since it was senior year, Mom promised that we could stay here long enough so I could finish my year and do all of the senior celebrations.

I was never one to fear new beginnings, considering this was the seventh home I lived in. In the span of four years, I had gone to seven different schools, met different kinds of people, and lived in unique types of houses. I was aware of what was waiting for me tomorrow.

Pressure.

Questions would be asked and answers would have to be given. I'd have to walk away from the spotlight and fade away from the minds of students who loved the "new girl." I would go back into the turtle shell I built myself.

A particular star in the sky winked at me and it got me thinking about Dad.

I often wondered why life could be so fair, yet cruel. Growing up without a father for the past seven years was hard. I saw my mother cry on his birthdays and, of course, I also carried around the memory of my fellow 4th grade 'friends' practically engraving the idea that I murdered my dad in my mind. Mom often said that I wasn't to blame, that it was his fate to die. Still, it wasn't something anyone can just forget.

A shooting star shot through the sky, and I closed my eyes.

I wish that this year brings me happiness, I thought.

***

I forced a big smile as I looked at myself in the mirror, my reflection looking ecstatic. Letting go of the strain I was feeling, my lips fell back into a straight line. I gave the rest of my features a cursory look. My long, dull chestnut brown hair flowed to my waist, and not even the sunlight hitting it could make it appear any more special than it was.

I wrapped a silver bracelet around my wrist. "Let's do this," I murmured.

"LENA! YOU'RE GOING TO BE LATE!" called Mom, disturbing the moment of peace I was having and making me jump in fright. I shook my head, chuckling absent-mindedly.

You'd think that after 17 years of living with her, I would've gotten used to her yelling that I was going to be late— which I never was—but I could swear that her screaming gets louder every time. I slipped my comfy, soft jean jacket on and hopped down the stairs.

I placed a kiss on her forehead. "Good morning," I said.

I mentally pinched my nose as I did so; I hated the smell of coffee. Mom gave me a small smile, sipping on her black, steaming drink. Her onyx black hair was in an elegant bun and she was in her business clothes, which meant that she was going to work.

"Good morning, sweetheart," she said, checking something on her phone. She looked up at me and gave me a small smile. "You ready?"

I nodded, pouring myself a cup of apple juice.

"Oh, I just remembered," said my mom, lifting her eyes from the magazine. "One of my co-workers' daughter goes to this school. Look for her. Stacy Hennings. Okay?" I noticed the familiar kindness and worry in her gaze. Noticing my absence of response, she prodded, "Okay, Lena?"

I rolled my eyes. Mom always had a fear of me being friendless. But what she didn't understand was that sometimes, I wanted to be alone. I'd gladly choose re-reading Looking for Alaska on a Saturday night than partying with a bunch of stuck-up teenagers. I was just that kind of person.

Saluting like a soldier, I replied. "Yes, mother." She looked at me, raising an eyebrow.

"What?" I exclaimed, feeling self-conscious all of a sudden. She walked over to me and stuffed a waffle in my mouth.

I immediately removed the oversized waffle from my mouth and glared at her, both of us extremely amused.

"I was just wondering what I've ever done to deserve a daughter like you." She winked, poking my nose.

I folded my arms over my chest and pouted. "Is that a compliment or an insult?"

"A little bit of both," she answered, putting her now empty cup in the sink. She pointed at it and I nodded.

"Hey! And I'll do them, I know."

After a few minutes of the daily teasing and fighting, I walked out the door, blowing her a kiss.

"Love you!" I exclaimed, taking a red apple and walking to our front door.

"Take care! Watch out for cars and don't forget to smile and be happy!" shouted Mom. I closed the door behind me and took a deep breath. I felt a smile appear on my face, making me feel just a little bit better.

Sure, it was autumn, but the weather was extraordinary. The sun was out, perfectly shining, but there was a breeze cooling the slight heat. The leaves of the trees surrounding my neighborhood were red, orange, and yellow, making the view breathtaking. I wished I had my camera to capture this moment. My dream has always been to become a photographer, to save every moment of every sunrise, sunset and every scene that takes my breath away.

I began my route to my new school, Albany High School. During the summer, I had walked by the school so many times—I knew the way by heart. I plugged my earphones on and put them in my ears. Lego House was playing, and that was because it had been on replay for a few days. I hummed its tune softly as I walked to the high school where I'd spend my senior year.

It was time to pick up the pieces and build a Lego house.

***

After about 15 minutes, I arrived at my new high school. Unlike all those summer days when there was no one, it was now packed with teenagers. And seriously, it was chaos. As my eyes scanned the scene before me, all I could see were footballs being thrown around, making any path to the main entrance impossible.

Jocks these days.

There was a girl leaning her back against a giant tree, absent-mindedly smiling as she gently rocked her head. I could see ear buds in her ear and I figured she was listening to the music she loved.

A group of girls were gossiping about something, concentrating on that subject. I frowned upon seeing one of them dressed in underwear, or as they called them, short-shorts. It was autumn for God's sake! If you needed to get lustful gazes from guys, you should've done it during summer, instead of risking hypothermia.

I headed to the main entrance, eager to get my schedule. I muttered a few "Excuse me's" along the way. Some students looked at me, as if analyzing me with their eyes.

Why wouldn't they?

I was the new girl.

Out of nowhere, something hard hit the back of my head. Black spots clouded my vision and I felt my body fall to the ground as I lost consciousness.

Well, gosh diddly darn, what a great start to the new school year!

2

Surprise and Meetings

Lena Rose Winter

I felt reality come rushing back to my head—which ached painfully, by the way.

I opened my eyes. I blinked several times to clear the hazy view in front of me.

"Thank god!" exclaimed a worried-looking blonde, gorgeous girl. "You're okay. She's okay, everybody! Now, go away, shoo!"

Shockingly, every single person who was around me a second ago, dispersed like they were bees and the girl was their Queen.

Lifesaver Barbie extended her hand towards me. "Thanks," I said, brushing whatever dirt there was on my pants. I momentarily felt relieved that I hadn't chosen to wear white skinny jeans today.

"Hi, I'm Stacy. Are you okay?" Lifesaver Barbie asked kindly.

Great. My first potential friend's initial impression of me was that I was a clumsy, fainting freak.

"Uh, hello! I'm Lena," I said, giving her a smile. "Are you the Hennings' daughter? I think our parents work together." I clutched the back of my head, feeling a bump forming. The pain still thudded against my skull.

"Yeah, that's me! Sorry about that. Ryan and the rest of the boys can just be so stupid sometimes!" And she giggled. I mentally flinched. Giggles were like laughs sent from fairyland.

Then again, why would anyone deny Stacy Hennings a giggle? She was the epitome of beauty. She had long, cascading blonde hair that made her look as if she wore a golden cloak of silk over her head. She had bright blue eyes and simple, yet delicate features. She was wearing shorts and a blue t-shirt that showed a little too much cleavage.

I let out a small laugh. "It's fine. After all, what's a first day of school without a little bit of fainting?"

***

Looking at my schedule, I felt content.

Pre-calculus

Art

AP World History

AP Biology

(Lunch)

French 4

AP English Literature

Stacy peeked at my schedule and let out a small squeal. A shudder ran through my body, but I hid it quite well. This was the fifth time she'd squealed so far in the day, and it was only 9:25 am.

Oh, god. This was going to be a long day.

"We have French together!" she exclaimed. "And it's first period too!"

I took a deep breath and gave her a smile as I motioned for the heavy bag I carried. "I've gotta go put my stuff in my locker. I'll see you in class!" I said, already walking away.

She furrowed her perfectly plucked eyebrows in confusion. "But you don't know where it is?"

"I'll figure it out!"

Breathing a sigh of relief, I walked towards the hall where my locker would be.

Okay, so here are the five hundreds.

After a bit of walking, I finally found mine. I put my bag on the ground and started emptying its contents into the locker. I was humming Wonderwall beneath my breath. My locker was right beside the drinking fountain and there appeared to be a small leak because there was a small puddle of water spreading on the ground beneath it.

I sang softly, not giving it further thought. I put the French book on one of the wooden portable shelves I brought with me. "'I said maybe, you're going to be the one that saves me. And after all, you're my wonderwall...'"

Suddenly, I mistakenly stumbled on the bag behind me and almost fell. My heart stopped for a second. I regained my balance by clutching on the locker door. "Oh, god."

Apparently, I'd underestimated the ability of water expanding because at that moment, I slipped on the puddle of drinking water. I let out a scream and mentally braced myself to fall on the already wet ground.

Instead, a strong arm steadied my waist. I opened my eyes and met blue, ocean-like ones. They were unlike any other color I'd ever seen. They were soft, yet sharp at the same time. A boy, probably a senior as well, saved me from the fall.

He was extremely attractive. But not in the hot way; it was a simple, handsome attractiveness. He let go of my waist and gave me a small nod and walked away.

My eyes widened for a second. "Thank you!" I called out after him. I wasn't even sure that he heard me. I looked down at my wet shoes and grimaced. My favorite red Converse was partly soaked. I could feel the water penetrating into my socks.

I let out a frustrated groan just as the bell rang, signaling that we have to go to class. I took my French book, L'Apprentissage de La Vie.

Taking a look at my schedule, I headed to my first class with—Mme Lapointe. I suddenly remembered an old French quote I had read somewhere when I learned French in California. It reminded me of the boy who'd saved my life:

"Les yeux d'une personne sont la porte à leurs pensées, leur sentiments et la pureté de leur cœur." (A person's eyes are the doors to their thoughts, feelings and the purity of their heart.)

3

French and Chicken

Lena Rose Winter

So, are there more chickens than eggs in the world? Or is it vice-versa? I wondered, twirling a new pencil in my hands.

Theoretically, every chicken lays an average of 300 eggs every year. If multiplied by the number of hens, which was 16 billion, there would be a lot of eggs.

Therefore, a lot of chickens.

Mr. Johnson, our fabulous English teacher, had been gibbering and jabbering about Shakespeare's works and the ingenious way the playwright always chose to end them: in tragedy. Unfortunately for me, he was so absorbed in his subject that all the other talking going on in the class was ignored.

"And then she, like, totally told him to shut up, but he kissed her and now they're back together. Isn't that cute?" blabbered Stacy, not waiting for an answer.

She simply continued on and on and on. It seemed like Stacy felt the immediate need to fill me in on the lives of every single person in this school. I swore, if she had a slightly higher

IQ, she'd be perfect for the FBI. Her researches were thorough and precise, even though they were completely futile. It was like every moment of her life was dedicated to knowing every piece of information there was about a human at Albany High School, from the first outfit they wore in freshman year to their latest lip gloss.

Okay, maybe I'm exaggerating.

You have no idea how much I want to tell you to shut up and go live on Mars, but I'm polite, I thought, pursing my lips. I closed my eyes and willed myself to ignore her. I opened them again and glued them on the professor. I admired how absorbed he was in what he was talking about even though three quarters of the class weren't even listening.

Stacy suddenly poked my shoulder. "Lena!" whispered the blonde girl, a tone of urgency in her voice.

Ignore.

"Shakespeare's plays are now presented by every single theater in the world!" said Mr. Johnson, admiration written across his wrinkly face. I felt warmth enter my heart at how much passion the old man displayed.

"Lena, turn around!"

Poke me one more time, I dare you, I mentally threatened, keeping my eyes on the cursive, perfectly written Shakespeare titles on the white board.

At the jab in my side, I turned around. "What do you want?" I asked, in a hushed voice.

"Jonah has been looking at you," she informed me flatly, jealousy beaming from her. Confusion flooded over me.

You see, moments like these apparently made Stacy's top ten gossip lists. This was my third day at school and I had absolutely no clue who in the world she'd been talking about. So

I nodded at her in the same manner a dad would pat his son's head and promise them chocolate, but they really just want their sons to go away.

"Cool," I said, averting my attention away from her.

This time, she grabbed my arm. I flinched and turned towards her again. "Jonah Walter is the hottest boy in school," she clarified, as if that was supposed to change anything. Her eyes threw daggers at me.

I gave her a smile. "And I should care because?"

I suddenly noticed the silence in the room, quickly broken by the sound of a clearing throat. Stacy and I both looked at Mr. Johnson. His lips were pursed and he seemed deeply perturbed by us interrupting his lesson. Beads of sweat formed on his forehead.

If looks could kill, Stacy and I would've died the second he looked at us.

"Miss Winter and Miss Hennings. Was fantasizing about Mr. Walter so important that it couldn't wait until after my class?" drawled Mr. Johnson. A few chuckles and hoots were heard across the room.

Face getting red? Check.

Palms getting sweaty? Check.

Getting embarrassed on my first week here? Double-check.

"Yeah, Lena, are you fantasizing about me?" asked a deep voice. I could feel the cockiness dripping in his words. Turning towards the source of the voice, I gave its owner a glare.

Stacy was not wrong when she had said that he was attractive. Green eyes twinkled in amusement. Not a hair on his head was out of place and his clothes looked designer-worthy. I found myself comparing him to the boy who'd saved my life earlier that week.

I chose not to answer his taunt and simply raised an eyebrow.

He winked. "Well, that makes two of us."

I grimaced at the way he'd said that. He fits perfectly in the player/asshole category of guys. My first date, when I was fifteen, was with someone of that type. To put things simply, it was the worst date of my life.

"For your information," I told him, "I wasn't fantasizing about you. I barely even know you and frankly, you're not worth fantasizing about at all." I gained some satisfaction from the bewildered look on his face. I gave him a smile and shrugged nonchalantly.

Jonah was about to answer, but Mr. Johnson gave him a look that could've frozen Hell over. "This is an English class, not a high school flirting class. Continue like this, and you'll get a detention."

My eyes widened and I clenched my teeth together. I turned around and looked down at the empty notepad in front of me. I began copying what was on the board, not paying any attention to my surroundings.

It was incredibly unnerving that I had just been on the point of getting a detention. And because of who? A boy I didn't even know. Despite the fact that I wasn't the typical, utter nerd, it still annoyed me to almost get a detention on my third day of school.

Class ended soon enough and I stormed out. I could hear Stacy calling me, but I couldn't bother to turn around and answer her.

I stuffed my books in my locker, grumbling gruesome words under my breath. The boy drinking from the water fountain looked up at me suddenly, and I recognized him faster than you could say idiot. He was smiling at me cheekily. I gave him a glare and continued taking my stuff for Art class. He leaned against the locker beside mine, the strong scent of Axe making me scrunch my nose in disgust.

I refused to acknowledge his presence. "Hey, Len," he said. I took my sketch pad and special pencils.

"Sorry about the whole almost-detention thing."

I never looked at him when I replied, "You're not sorry."

"So I take it you don't forgive me, then?"

I turned my back to him and started walking away, but he grabbed my arm and in a sudden motion I was facing him again. The bullets my eyes were shooting at him were enough to start and end a war.

"Would you forgive me if I take you out on a date?"

I snorted in a way that was the opposite of ladylike. "Absolutely not," I answered firmly. "Never going to happen."

"Oh, come on!" He pouted. "I'm a nice guy! You won't regret it."

I rolled my eyes at him. "I have no reason to like you." I tried to shake my arm from his grasp.

"But you have no reason not to like me either. I apologized for the whole almost detention thing."

He has a point.

"I don't want to go out with you then."

He put his hand on the spot where his right lung would be and feigned a disheartened face. "That hurt."

The bell rang, signaling that I was late for class.

"Not going to happen, that date, all right?" I slipped my arm from his grip and started running towards the Art studio, which, sadly, was on the first floor of the school. And where was I? On the third.

I heard footsteps behind me as I ran, but I didn't turn around. I sprinted down two flights of stairs, not sparing a moment to catch my breath. What I didn't notice was the extra step I had to take on the landing. I felt myself starting to fall and the rails seemed to be too far away for me to hold on to. I fell to the ground, feeling my rear end and my knees send messages to my brain: I was hurting.

I looked up at the other person who had been running behind me. He wore an expression that was between worried and amused.

"You okay?" He offered me a hand.

Groaning, I took it and stood up. "No, I am not okay."

"I've got to admit, no girl has ever run away from me when I asked her out on a date," said Jonah, snickering. I gave him a glare that made the smile disappear. I started walking towards my class. He walked beside me.

"Lena, come on. Please? I won't eat you."

"You never know."

He laughed. "I'm serious. Would it really hurt you and step on your pride to go out on one date with me?"

"Yes. Don't you have a class to go to?"

"The teachers love me. You don't take me seriously."

We stopped beside my classroom and I grimaced at the sight of Mrs. Pilon already teaching the class something. I had to get rid of Jonah and fast.

"I give up, fine. I'll go out with you on one date. Only one," I said, my expression tight. He leaned in so close I could feel his hot breath on my ear. I could feel goose bumps on my arms—I shivered. This made me extremely uncomfortable. The ounce of acceptance that had just begun to form towards him was slowly fading away.

"I'll pick you up at six, Saturday night."

Then he walked away.

4

Dates and Insults

"You will get lost before finding the right path."

Lena Rose Winter

Some parents don't like the concept of their daughters going out with boys, leading to teenagers either sneaking out or suffering formal and strict meetings with the boy. Other parents couldn't care less. They acknowledge the boy with a nod and simply cry out, "Bring her home by ten!"

Mine, however, acted like a teenage girl best friend. The fact that she was a designer made my mother want to make me look absolutely stunning for any event, important or insignificant.

"Oh, baby girl! You look gorgeous! Now turn around, you should see how beautiful you look like right now! That guy, Jones, is going to melt at your sight!" exclaimed Mom dramatically.

I'd been sitting in this chair for almost 2 hours, getting "pampered" for my date by my mom. I stopped bothering to correct her way of saying my date's name about an hour ago.

I stood up and turned around to face myself in the mirror. I smiled. My makeup was simple, it was almost unnoticeable.

I was wearing a pale pink, strapless dress that reached my knees. It was simple, cozy, and serene. My definition of perfect. Luckily, my mom lent me her black high heels. To top it all, my mom placed a gorgeous necklace on me.

"Family tradition," she whispered, then winked.

"Thank you."

My mom hugged me and suddenly turned serious. "Be careful. Take the pepper spray with you, just in case." At my raised eyebrow, she added, "You never know if he's a pervert."

I started laughing hysterically and answered, "Mom, we're just going to a restaurant and then watch a movie."

"Still. Who knows what's on boys' minds these days? Let's hope that Noah is a good guy," she warned me, pointing a finger in my face.

"Jonah, Mom. It's Jonah."

She rolled her eyes and muttered something about weird boy names. She walked out and closed the door.

Well, she's my mom, so that explains why I'm weird.

I took a peek at the bedroom clock; it displayed 7:00 sharp. Jonah was supposed to be here by now.

Would he bail on me?

Tick.

He wouldn't, would he?

Tock.

He wouldn't dare.

Tick.

Oh, yes he would.

The doorbell resounded in the whole house and I jumped.

"Lena! Your date is here!" my mom shouted.

I took a last look in the mirror and grabbed my black Guess purse on the way out the door. I put my cell phone, my lip gloss, a little packet of tissues and…the pepper spray. Who knew?

I technically sprinted down the stairs, but near the end, I walked elegantly. Per se.

Then, I saw him.

Jonah was dressed in dark blue jeans, a white V-neck shirt, and a matching dark blue jacket. His hair looked perfect, his cologne made my nose tingle and, overall, he looked like a movie star playing the supposed bad boy.

When he saw me, his mouth dropped a little bit, but he recomposed himself quite fast.

I giggled at his reaction.

He smiled kindly and said, "You look amazing, Lena."

For a moment, I was so mesmerized I'd forgotten my mom was there.

She was smiling mischievously

"Well, you take good care of her, boy." She winked playfully. Even if I was annoyed by her, I was ecstatic. This was the happiest I'd seen my mom in days.

Jonah chuckled, then took my hand and placed a gentle peck on it. Like a feather.

"Don't worry, ma'am. She's in good hands," he replied smoothly. "I'll have her back by 11, is that all right?"

I could see my mom swooning at his attitude.

"That's marvelous. I'll go work on some designs now, bye!"

And with those words she turned around and headed for her room.

Jonah looked at me and smirked. "What a mom you have. Now I know where you get the weirdness from!"

I blushed a little. "Oh, shut up."

He opened the front door and ushered me to come, in a gentlemanly way.

"I must admit, I had a feeling you would've run away from me by now."

I groaned. "Now, why didn't I think of that?"

***

"No, no, no!" I said stubbornly, crossing my arms. "There's no way I'm getting on this... this thing!"

Jonah whined, "Why? Come on!"

I was currently standing on my lawn, in front of a black motorcycle with red flames all over it.

"No."

"Lena. Come on!"

"Absolutely not!"

Before I could process what was happening, I felt myself being carried, bridal style. I started hitting Jonah on the chest but that did nothing to stop him. He just smirked at my efforts to get free. But there was something else, something weird. I don't know. A strange feeling nagged in my chest. A bad feeling. I didn't feel like I was supposed to be in his arms. I shook that feeling away, determined to have a good night. I closed my eyes.

When I opened them again, I was sitting on the motorcycle, a helmet on my head, Jonah comfortably sitting in front of me. I put my arms around him tightly and reclosed my eyes.

***

"Babe, you can wake up now, it's over. And you're cutting off my circulation."

I hesitantly opened my eyes and immediately let go of my grip on his strong, muscular waist. I got off the motorcycle, stood up, and brushed invisible wrinkles on my dress. I unbuckled the helmet and handed it to Jonah.

"Oh, will you stop smirking!" I said, annoyed a little.

I looked to the place we were standing in front of and frowned. It was a fancy, Italian restaurant.

Jonah slid his arm around my shoulder and we walked to the entrance. He opened the door for me and bowed, making me laugh.

We sat on a table for two and after about 10 seconds, a blonde waitress came towards us. Her shirt was a little too low for my taste, but Jonah didn't seem to mind at all. Her caked face was showing a wide, flirty smile. I already disliked her. Her eyes were glued on my date.

"Hello there, Jonah! Long time, no see! Do you want the usual?" she asked in a 'seductive' voice. Jonah's eyes didn't lift up for a second from her busty chest

"Hey, babe. Yeah, the usual. A lasagna, but don't make it too hot. At least, not as burning as you are right now." He winked and showed his famous smirk.

I coughed.

She turned to me, and immediately scrunched up her nose. "What do you want?"

"Baked potatoes and the chicken, please," I said, not paying any attention to the way she greeted me.

Her eyebrows lifted a little in distaste and said, "Wow, I know she's not the usual. She looks plain. What happened to you, Jonah?"

Frustrated by her attitude, I looked at Jonah expectantly, but he stayed motionless and silent. On the inside, I was punching her. On the outside, I stayed calm and collected. Her name tag read: Heather.

It's on.

"You, know, Heather," I said, making eye-contact with her, "it's not really in your job description to flirt or tell any lies. If there's anyone unusual here, it's actually you. Plus, looking like a freaking slut won't help you get him; he likes real girls, not dolls."

I was pretty sure I was burning holes through her. She snorted, twirled a strand of her hair and turned away. Jonah smiled a little and wasn't very discreet when he checked her out as she walked off.

When she was completely out of sight, he looked at me with a bewildered expression. "What was that all about?"

"She was being impolite," I simply replied, giving him a small smile. He laughed a little and we kept on talking. I couldn't stop thinking about the way he refused to defend me. It hurt a little.

He was funny, I had to admit. A little cheeky, but in an amusing way. He talked to me about how his friends were and about his football matches. He never seemed to stop talking about himself, or how he was the pride of the family. I chose to ignore his comment about the waitress being "burning hot." To be truthful, he was slightly boring. Normally, a conversation was supposed to engage two or more people, not just one guy.

Heather came back, the food in her hands. She put the plates down and grazed her fingers against Jonah's coat. He shivered and smirked.

She gave me a smile that could freeze the Sahara over when she said, "Anything else?"

"A less slutty waitress, please."

Heather turned towards Jonah, her eyes wide. "Jonah! Do something!"

He cleared his throat and played with the fork in his hands. "Babe, don't be like that. Heather isn't slutty. Be nice."

I've had enough of this damned date.

I stood up and looked at Jonah. I took two full glasses of water in my hands.

SPLASH.

In a split second, Heather and Jonah were drenched in freezing water. His green eyes were blazing with anger. I gave him a sweet smile.

"And Jonah, don't bother talking to me again. I don't go out with assholes who don't respect their dates and treat them like dogs. So, no, I won't be nice. Have a good night with Heather here, babe."

I winked, turned around, and walked away.

***

Damn, I felt proud of myself.

Walking out of the sucky restaurant, I noticed a boy coming in with an elderly woman. My heart started feeling weird. The boy raised his head up and our eyes met. Those blue eyes, they were no stranger to me.

Why does he look so familiar? I thought, racking my brain for a response.

I walked carefully towards him and tapped his shoulder. He and the old lady turned towards me.

"Excuse me, have we met before?" I asked.

His eyes widened slightly in recognition but he continued walking. He was almost entering the restaurant. The elderly woman stopped him.

"Liam, it's impolite to walk away from people talking to you." She turned to me, untangled her arm from the boy's, and extended a hand. "Hello, dear, I'm Darla Black."

I shook her hand. "I'm Lena. Sorry for interrupting, I just thought I saw him"—I nodded towards Liam—"somewhere before."

Darla looked at him. He shrugged. "Maybe he's in one of your classes, Lena."

I nodded, knowing now that was partly true. We had French, Art, and Math together. "Maybe. Goodnight, ma'am, sorry again. Sorry, Liam." I waved at him.

"Call me Darla," said the elderly woman. I smiled at her.

I backed away a little and tripped over something. A dirty bucket of water was behind me; someone must've forgotten to take it away after they were done sweeping the floor.

Liam's arms stopped me from falling, but that felt familiar too. The feeling of safety…

It suddenly clicked in my head. This was the mystery guy who saved my life on the first day of school.

Before I could dwell on it, his grip on my waist was nonexistent. I straightened up and smiled. He stayed expressionless. There was something about him that concealed secrets. It intrigued me.

"Well, Liam. Thank you for saving my life, again. Bye ma—Darla."

He stayed silent. He gave me a soft nod before turning away and going inside the restaurant with his grandmother.

I turned and walked away. I recognized the street and felt relief wash over me. The restaurant was extremely close to my house.

I took off my heels and held them in one hand. I walked and walked, a million thoughts running through my head.

That was why I didn't feel good when Jonah carried me. It was because I'd already experienced a feeling of safety elsewhere. With Liam. When I'd almost fallen—twice now—and he caught me, I felt safe. With Jonah, I did not.

On another note, how clumsy could I possibly get? I was tripping and falling everywhere these days.

5

She Said, He Said

"A little crazy is good."

Lena Rose Winter

Two weeks later

My stomach grumbled. I clutched my abdominal muscles to stop the noise of a dying whale. The bell rang, signaling lunch time. I was happy dancing, from the inside.

"Go on, run, you little whore."

The words made me freeze. I turned around, toward the owner of the voice. My eyes widened.

A group of boys were huddled around me, and... Jonah? He was lazily leaning against a locker, a huge smirk plastered on his face. My eyebrows pulled up. What was this, some kind of a joke?

"What did you say?" I asked slowly, as if I was talking to a child.

"Didn't you hear me? I said you were a whore. I bet your car accident made you just a little bit deaf."

His words made me gasp loudly. How did he know? I clenched my teeth. "Oh, so that's what happens when a girl loses interest in you, Jon-ass?"

He ignored me. "Or is it the fact that your daddy died? Poor little Rosie."

My breath caught in my throat.

Rosie.

He used the name my father once called me. How did he know that? To begin with, how did he know about the accident? Everything was known during elementary school but now, years later and far away, it was more of a secret. And the look of pity that used to be in people's eyes was now nonexistent.

Jonah took his time walking towards me and before I knew it, he was just inches away. I stayed silent, not knowing what to expect. I observed him. His face was full of malice and hate. I felt the bubble of dislike and annoyance form into something much stronger. Almost, hate.

His hands reached out to tuck a strand of my hair. I flinched and stepped away from him.

"Don't you dare touch me! How the hell do you know about my accident?" I cried out.

Now, I felt like the whole school was surrounding us. Every eye was glued on Jonah and me.

"Let's say I have my sources."

"Oh, so you stalked me?"

He winked, and I wanted to puke. "I call that investigating, babe."

He kept advancing towards me, and I kept backing up. I felt so alone. No one was there to defend me. I felt anger boil in my veins. It was time to practice my black belt karate skills.

Crack.

I punched him in the face.

The whole crowd gasped and then they started cheering for me. I felt my heart smile in satisfaction. But my face stayed expressionless. I could already feel a bruise forming on my fist, although, this was the least of my worries.

"This will teach you not to mess with me, or my family, you freaking douche bag."

With that, I let my spit land on him.

***

It was funny how easily people could abandon you.

Stacy had been ignoring me all week and when I talked to her, she put her head down, as if she was ashamed of me. I gave up on her and simply ate my lunch alone now.

Having decided I wasn't going to mope around all weekend, I decided to go to the park. I put a huge hoodie, my favorite comfortable sweats, and my Ugg boots. My hair was in a messy braid and my face was make-up free. I couldn't care less about how I looked. I had my camera around my neck and that was all that mattered.

"Mom! I'm going to the park!" I shouted, hoping she'd hear me.

"Okay, darling!" she replied, shouting louder than I had. "Love you!"

I stuffed my phone in my pocket and put the headphones in my ear. I walked as far as my feet could take me. Then I arrived at Ridgefield Park.

It was my own personal heaven.

Many golden hues formed the color of the leaves that lay scattered all around. Young laughter rang out everywhere. Some passed time as they jumped on a heaped pile of discarded leaves. I was walking, admiring the view, oblivious to the sound of crunching under my feet as I walked a well-trodden path. A slight breeze whispered along the trees and teased more leaves into releasing their tentative hold. Deeply engrossed in feeding a little bird, an old woman didn't notice a wayward leaf on her head.

I smiled, something that was rare to me during the last couple of days. I felt happy, so happy.

I tried to capture every fleeting moment. Everything. From the flock of birds flying to a warmer place, to children playing tag. From the beautiful trees releasing their hold on the orange, red, and yellow leaves, to an old couple holding hands, concentrating only on each other.

I remembered what Dad had said at one point.

"Every single piece of life needs to be remembered. Every moment, sadness or joy, in this big world can never be forgotten. Everything has its own remarkable beauty, it has to be captured. This is a photographer's job. If you do this, you have the whole world in your hands. In your camera."

My eyes welled with tears and I felt my knees go wobbly at the thought of him, so I sat under the biggest tree in the park. I protectively put my arms around my knees and placed my head over them.

I cried, and cried.

I blew on all 10 candles happily. I was ecstatic. Everyone cheered and gave me a hug. After eating the delicious chocolate cake, my dad told me to put on my snow wear. I was confused, but I obliged. He took my hand and we went to the backyard where snow was everywhere. In his hands were small bags.

Out of nowhere, he lifted me up and spun me around. I giggled, joining my father's resounding laughter. He put me down and then squatted to be on my level.

"Happy birthday, Rosie! You're a double-digit number now, do you know what that means?" he asked seriously.

"No, daddy, what does that mean?" I said, curiosity building inside me.

He took the package and gave it to me. I hastily opened it to find a brand new Canon camera. I gasped and looked at it as if it was the most beautiful thing in the world. I gave my dad a tight hug, as his eyes beamed with excitement.

"Thank you, thank you, thank you! I love you so so much, daddy! I'll treasure it forever and ever," I told him.

He smiled at me in admiration.

I closed my eyes at the memory.

This was the first time I felt weak in days. But I was tired of having to hold it all in, to seem so strong all the time. Hot tears kept flowing down my cheeks; they seemed unstoppable. I tried to wipe them away, but that only made them fall harder.

Everything was because of me, everything.

After what seemed like a lifetime and I'd cried all the tears in my body and let them dry on my face, I was pretty sure I looked like a zombie. I quickly untangled my braid and let my hair loose on my head. I lifted up my gaze and let my eyes scan the scenery in front of me. Everything seemed normal, yet something caught my eye.

There was a boy, sitting underneath the tree across from mine. He was holding a sketchbook and…Drawing? Every once in a while, he would look up, directly at me.

He seemed handsome, with a face practically begging for his picture to be taken. I took a quick shot of him and then looked away. I studied the photo closely.

It was Liam.

I didn't know why, but my feet dragged me towards him. His eyebrows pulled up a little when I arrived, as if I was interrupting him from doing something important. I sat beside him.

Silence filled the air. Although, it wasn't an awkward silence, it was comfortable. I took a peek at his work. There was a girl, looking sad, her head was on her knees. There was a messy, yet perfectly drawn braid. Beside her, a camera was lying on a heap of leaves. Under the drawing, there were two perfectly written words. I gasped.

Intrigued and shocked, I looked at him. His blue eyes were observing me, waiting for my reaction.

"I-Is that me?" I asked, hoping the answer was yes.

His head bobbed down.

I immediately felt stupid after the next question I asked. "I'm Lena, and you're Liam, right?" The head action repeated.

"How's your grandma?"

He nodded again.

Why wasn't he answering me? "Did I do something wrong?" I inquired, fearing his answer.

He put his head down and shook his head. Was he embarrassed about something?

On the spur of a moment, it clicked in my head. He was mute.

My eyes widened and I apologized. "I'm so sorry; I didn't mean it like that."

Something flickered in his eyes. He scribbled down: No pity, please.

I nodded, understanding. I knew how he felt.

"No, I hate pity too. Do you mind if I join you?"

He instantly relaxed and shook his head as a "no." I felt relief flood me.

I leaned my head on his firm shoulder. My head fits perfectly along its contours. He was warm. He continued drawing, it was a new one.

I closed my eyes and savored the moment. A million thoughts were running through my head. And his, if what I felt was right. My heart kept screaming something, but I ignored it. All I could think about were the scribbled words under his drawing. A drawing of me. Two words that made me feel confused, yet strangely happy:

True Beauty.

6

Freedom

"The meeting of two personalities is like the contact of two chemical substances: if there is any reaction, both are transformed."
~Carl Jung~

Lena Rose Winter

Sleeping has always been one of my all-time favorite things in the world, but how comfortable I was at the moment was unreal.

I opened my eyes and regained my memory of what happened. I gasped at the realization that I had fallen asleep beside Liam. I touched my cheek, was there any drool? I breathed a quiet sigh of relief. There was no drool. I was okay.

"Liam? You fell asleep? Oh god, oh god. I fell asleep."

His eyes were closed and he looked so peaceful. I admired him a bit. Beautiful, was all I could think. His eyelashes were long. Maybe he wasn't sleeping? Hell, even I fell asleep. His eyes fluttered open. He smiled when he saw me. I laid my hand on my hair, self-consciously. Did I really look that bad?

He had a childlike appearance. His hair had managed to get messy. "Good afternoon, sleepyhead," I said, my lips tugging a bit.

He scribbled something on his sketchbook and then showed it to me: if anyone slept here, it was you.

I felt a blush rise to my cheeks and put my head down. Why did I have to sleep? Really. It seemed as if embarrassment followed me everywhere, especially whenever he was there.

"What time is it?" I asked, changing the subject.

He pointed at his wristwatch, which displayed: 7:00. I let out a curse in shock and fear. My mom was going to be worried. Hell, knowing my mom, she might have already called the police. I got up and started jumping up and down anxiously.

He stood up and looked at me like I was a freak. He waved his hands up and down as if to say: calm down, woman. He took a deep breath and pointed at me, so I could do the same.

I imitated him; my nerves felt like a needle popped their balloon. I smiled gratefully; he bowed. I giggled a little.

Suddenly, his eyes got big, and his smile reached his ears. There was a twinkle in his eye.

"What is it? What?" I asked, intrigued. He made a twirl with his index finger. So, I turned around.

It was sunset time. In my mind, it was camera time.

"Wait! I'm going to call my mom, so she doesn't get worried." He nodded, in comprehension.

I took my phone out of my back pocket and checked for any missed calls. None.

Huh, weird.

I called my mom's cell phone. After two rings, my mum picked up.

"Lena Rose Winter, where are you?" Her shrill voice was coated with worry and fear as she started screaming at me.

I winced and pulled the phone away from my ear. Liam rolled his eyes at me. When the shouting stopped, I spoke to her: "Mother, breathe. I'm at the park, I just fell asleep." I heard a huge sigh of relief on the phone.

"Okay, okay. Good. I assume you want to stay to take pictures of the sunset?"

I grinned; my mom knew me better than anyone. "Please?" I said, knowing her answer.

"Fine. But be back by eight, okay?"

"Sure, Mom. Thank you!" I blew a kiss to the phone and we said our goodbyes.

Liam grinned at me, his pearly whites showing. I grabbed my camera and ran to the empty field side of the park. The wind blowing through my hair made me feel alive.

Liam.

I stopped running and turned around. He was nowhere to be seen. And during the moment when I had turned around, a figure ran past me. I recognized it as Liam, his red sweater was unmistakable.

I went into full speed and pulled my tongue out to annoy him. He just smirked. We grinned at each other.

I took his hand and ran to the perfect spot. His skin was soft and my smaller hand fits perfectly into his large one. It was like the last piece of a puzzle.

I shook those thoughts off as I released him and held my camera.

The sky was a mystery of colors. Red, pink, purple, orange, yellow, and brown all mixed together to create a picture perfect landscape. Just gazing at it brought me a sense of tranquility. The sun was melting into the sky. I basked in the warm glow that illuminated the place. The sun seemed to bring a sort of dense atmosphere that felt refreshing.

The night was pushing its way through. There was a strip of gray among the fiery colors of the sun. The sun was sinking into the sapphire ocean. The horizon was turning a darker gray. With every moment that went by there was a change in color of the sky. In comparison to the soft beauty of the sun, the night was beautiful in its own way. It was more mystifying than the sunset. The night had dissolved the sun and the sky was now a midnight blue.

I took a picture of every moment. Everything. I felt the same bubble of happiness and contentment in my heart again. I was meant to be here. Enjoying my life.

I sat on the grass and stopped taking pictures. I just stared at the sky.

What a beauty it was.

I wonder what it would be like to be a bird, I thought. It would signify complete freedom. I would have the ability to travel anywhere, without any weight on my shoulders. I wouldn't have to worry about what college I'd have to go to next year, or school, or anything else.

Someone tapped on my shoulder. Liam handed me his sketchbook. He had written: "Being a bird would be the best thing in the world."

I felt my cheeks get red. I'd spoken my thoughts out loud. He sat beside me and we both just contemplated the sky.

I remembered something. During the movie High School Musical, Gabriella had said: 'Do you remember in kindergarten, how you'd meet a kid and know nothing about them, then 10 seconds later you'd be playing like you were best friends, because you didn't have to be anyone but yourself?'

That was exactly how I felt. I knew, in my heart, that this moment with Liam would be the start of something new.

7

Wandering Souls

"I promise to stay, to see you at your worst and best and still love you. That's what friends are for."

Lena Rose Winter

A month later

"No, you're wrong, Liam," I answered confidently, crossing my arms around my chest. "The answer to this equation is 364!"

He just smiled with the same certainty I had.

We were sitting in Math class, working in teams. We'd grown close friends and I was on Cloud 9. We had so much in common. Same taste in music, art, food. The only subject we'd fight over was math. He thought he was smarter than me.

He was clearly enjoying this, as I was.

"I'll go ask the teacher, but if I'm right, you buy me an ice cream today. And if you're right, which is impossible, I'll buy you one. Deal?" I offered him my hand to shake. He agreed with a weird gleam in his eye.

I got up and made my way to the teacher's desk. Mrs. Burt was concentrating on some kind of work. I cleared my throat, which caused her to look up.

"Yes, Ms. Winter?" Her expression displayed at what point I'd annoyed her. I barely kept myself from rolling my eyes. Wasn't that her job, to help me?

"Excuse me, but I did question 5, yet my partner and I don't seem to agree on the answer. Would you kindly tell me what it is?" I asked, flashing my innocent face. She nodded and flipped through the pages of her corrected version.

"Ah, the answer is 464, Ms. Winter," she informed me. My face dropped, and my eyes went wide.

I walked in shame to Liam's table. "Youwereright," I mumbled, barely audible.

He smirked and put a hand behind his ear as if to say: What? Repeat that.

"I said, you were right!"

He grinned, and I pouted.

"You're mean."

He showed me his notebook, where he'd written: "It's not my fault I'm smart. You owe me ice cream."

I put my head down, mad at myself.

"Please smile?"

I ignored him. He sighed loudly. I heard his pencil scrape the paper again.

"Ready to die?"

It took me about 15 seconds to process what was happening. Before I knew it, my laugh resounded in the whole class. Liam's hands started moving around my stomach. Oh, he knew how ticklish I was.

"S-Stop p-please!" I gasped between giggles.

I didn't expect him to obey, because he continued even more. After what seemed like a lifetime of dying and laughing, he stopped.

I smiled. It was impossible to stay mad at him. He wiggled his eyebrows while grinning; he was happy he won.

I pulled my tongue out childishly.

A strict voice brought me back to reality. "Ms. Winter and Mr. Black. What do you two think you're doing?"

I turned around to see 27 pairs of wide eyes observing Liam and me, their mouths agape. I put on a serious face and answered: "Mrs. Burt, I'm sorry. Liam and I were just fooling around. It won't happen again."

I looked at Liam for help and he nodded feverishly. Mrs. Burt didn't seem convinced or forgiving.

"Oh, I'll make sure of that. Detention for both of you."

I heard snickers, but I just stared at Liam. Like me, his mouth was curved into a perfect "O."

"B-But Mrs. Burt, that's not fair!" I whined, shocked.

"Life's not fair. Go sit at your place, Ms. Winter, and I'll see you and your friend here at detention. And what are you all staring at? Back to work!"

Well, getting detention may have seemed horrible two months ago, but this time I would be with my friend.

This was going to be a very interesting afternoon.

***

The bell rang, startling me for a second.

I breathed a sigh of relief. Finally, school was over. Detention time was approaching. I still had fifteen minutes though. I put my stuff in my bag and walked to Liam's locker, 155. He was putting his books in his black bag. He looked so calm, concentrated, and peaceful.

I'll have to change that, then.

I tiptoed so I could come from behind him. I put my head on his right shoulder and said: "Hey there, peanut," in a grave, yet squeaky voice.

I don't know if he was just surprised or if he really got scared, but he must have jumped at least 5 feet into the air. I laughed, hard. Metaphorically speaking, I was laughing my ass off.

"Y-You...j-jumped...like a s-scared little bunny," I managed to say, between laughs.

After about five minutes of clutching my stomach to stop laughing and crying, I took a deep breath to calm myself. In, out. I took a look at Liam. He now had his bag lazily slung over his shoulder. His face was in a perfect poker face. He stared at me and then typed something on his phone. I came closer to him because I knew that whatever he was writing was meant for me.

"It's not even funny. You're immature and I am NOT a bunny! Do I have floppy ears to you? Or do I like carrots? Well the answer is no."

I struggled to keep a straight face. I bit my lip and looked at Liam through my eyelashes. We both knew what that gesture meant; I was sorry. He rolled his eyes and smiled. It was contagious.

"Now, how about going to detention? It's my first one." I linked my arm in his. "Let's go pay the price for being rebels."

We started walking in a funny way to where detention would be held. When we entered the room, Mrs. Burt glared at us.

"Sit down," she commanded. "Now, you rebels, I'm going to get a plate of doughnuts, stay here." I guessed the last sentence was directed to the whole group.

I obeyed and sat on the chair beside Liam's. Speaking of us 'rebels,' I was curious to know who was here too. I raked my eyes across the room. A buff, tough looking boy was sitting at the other end of the class, breaking his pencil. There were two girls sitting beside him, giggling about something.

"Looking for something hot? Over here, dumbass."

It was a voice I knew all too well.

Liam's head and mine turned toward the voice. My eyes narrowed at its owner. Jonah was staring right at me, slouched in his seat and his legs stretched out before him.

There was someone beside him. It was—Stacy?

She looked at me with an expression of hate and disgust. The wheels in my mind were turning. What was she doing here? Why is she looking at me like that? Our gazes locked.

"Want a picture?" she drawled at me. "I know I'm gorgeous, but I don't like filthy scum looking at me." Her voice was even squeakier than I remembered. How could I've ever been friends with her?

I sat back, speechless.

"Oh, stop drooling at us."

My eyes widened, and I looked at Liam. His expression mirrored mine, undoubtedly catching 'Us?'

"Don't worry, babe," Jonah told her. "She's just jealous. But I have you, and you're the whole package."

It was time to break my silence.

"Why would I be jealous?" I snapped, practically burning holes through him. "I dumped you."

Sadness, fury, and another emotion I couldn't place flashed in his eyes. He recomposed quickly by chuckling.

"Hon, I dumped you. I discovered girls who kill their own fathers are worthless and will always be unloved."

His words hit me like a slap in the face. I felt tears flood my eyes and I looked at Liam. His nostrils flared and he clenched his fists.

I stood up. "Shut up, Jonah."

"Why, is it because I'm right?"

Congratulations, Jonah. You have officially succeeded at being a complete asshole.

I took a step towards him. "No, you're far from right. In fact, you're the most ignorant person I know."

He laughed and stood up. "Would an ignorant person find out that your dad abused you?"

I gaped at him. "That's complete bullshit!"

"It's true," he shrugged.

I started walking towards him until I was close enough to jab a finger in his chest with every word I said. "Listen to me, Jonah. Don't you dare say one bad word about my dad. He is and always will be the most honorable man I know."

"You think you're so good, eh?" he chuckled. "But sleeping with the silent freak doesn't make you a better person," he blurted out.

I let out a small growl. "I wasn't done," I said, putting emphasis on every word.

"Don't you ever dare say anything bad about me, or the ones I love! For your information, my father was the noblest man on earth. The cement he walked on is a thousand times cleaner than you are." I didn't shout and my voice was calm, but the venom in it was enough to make him flinch again. "Grow up and get a life."

I walked out of the room, not caring about the fact that I was walking out of detention.

***

Liam Christopher Black

It was funny how sometimes, you had less than seconds to think about what to do. I had a choice: to follow her or to stay.

I stood up and ran after her.

She wasn't running, just walking fast. I caught up with her easily. I stopped her by grabbing her arm.

I felt the heat of her anger. Her muscles tensed. She turned to look at me, as if seeing me for the first time.

My heart ached when I saw the emotions in her eyes. They were infinite. One struck out: Pain. I realized just how much she'd been hurting. I nodded at her and hoped she understood what I meant. I sent her a mental message: He's not worth it.

Her bottom lip started to quiver and she gulped. She looked at me, and then shifted her gaze to my arms. I let her go, knowing her anger was now controlled.

As we walked through the halls, she kept her head down. Our legs just moved and moved. I didn't know where she was taking me. We were soon outside the school, standing on the freshly mown grass. I was on her side, confused.

What in the world was I supposed to do now? I am no expert with girls.

Suddenly, she put her arms around me. Tight. I hesitantly returned her embrace. She buried her face in my shoulder. She held on to me as if her life depended on it. I stroked her long, silky hair soothingly.

I waited for my shirt to get wet with her tears, but that never happened. I wondered why. A million thoughts were running through my head. But I was particularly focused on one. How could she have been punching a guy just a moment ago, looking fierce and invincible, yet now appearing so frail and breakable?

Lena was so strong.

We stayed like that for what seemed like a lifetime. Her heavy breathing blew against my shirt, giving me goose bumps.

At one point, she let go. Lena sat on the grass and crossed her legs. She put her head in her hands.

I sat in front of her and ducked my head. I removed her hands from her face, startling her. She looked at me, her expression so drained it struck my heart. I hated seeing her like this.

I mouthed, "Talk to me."

"You know, Liam, I hate myself so much." Her voice was raspy.

"I'm so vulnerable, so weak," she went on. "Ever since my dad died, my heart hurts. I've never been able to be truly happy. In primary school, everyone pitied me. When high school started, I moved. Nobody knew about the accident, no one knew what happened. People would come talk to me, and say, 'Oh Lena, you have a perfect life.' I'd just smile. No one knows how many times I'd cry myself to sleep, and dream about my accident." She stopped for a second.

"My dad died. I survived. Sometimes, no, I always wish I'd died with him. That would've been better. At least I wouldn't be feeling like this. I've been lying to myself. I've been lying to everyone, saying 'I'm fine.' Those words have been my best friends for as long as I can remember. I've already thought of ending it all, you know? But then I think of my mom and my dad. I know they wouldn't be proud of me. So I try to be happy, but no matter how hard I try, all I do is get more miserable.

"I'm so tired, Liam," she said, releasing a breath she was holding. Her eyes were glued to the ground, as if she was ashamed of herself. "I'm so tired of everything."

Her eyes were spilling tears, they seemed unstoppable.

"You know, my dream is to be a bird. They fly in the sky and seem so free. They're almost never alone." She finally looked up at me. "Would you like to be a bird with me, Liam?" she asked dryly.

I tried to restrain myself from reaching out and wiping her tears, but I failed. I wiped at the wet streaks on her cheeks. I grazed my fingers under her eyes, to keep more tears from falling. She sighed and closed her eyes.

I didn't bother thinking about why, but I had the urge to kiss her forehead.

I stared at her. Even in her unhappiness she was so beautiful to me.

She opened her eyes again.

"Thank you, Liam. You're the best thing that's ever happened to me in a while."

It took me five seconds to process her words. She'd said them so—meaningfully.

I nodded and mouthed, "You really are beautiful, you know."

She blushed and smiled. Lena put her head down, and started playing with the grass. I smiled in return, happy I was the cause for a little bit of joy.

"So," she said, "after this shitty day, how about going out for some ice cream?"

Mischievous Lena was back. Her eyes were glinting with excitement. I laughed. She looked like a little kid who was about to do something bad.

I wasn't about to skip school, though. I shook my head, making her smile turn upside down.

"Oh, please, please, please, Li, it'll be the first time and the last time."

I mouthed, "No way in hell."

She begged. "Please, pretty please with a cherry on top."

I stayed still.

Lena put on her puppy dog face.

I huffed in surrender. She stood up and jumped around. I copied her but I didn't jump around.

"Yay, but what do we do?" she asked.

I knew exactly what we were going to do. I took her hand and we started running towards my car. It was a 2005 Mercedes; it'd been passed down to me from my dad.

Confusion was written all over her delicate features. She stopped running and stomped her feet childishly.

"Tell me where we're going first or I'm not moving."

I raised my eyebrow, amused by her behavior.

I put my arms up in surrender and approached her.

In a split second, she was over my shoulder and hitting my back with her fist. That had the same effect an ant would have made when walking on a bear.

"Fine, fine. Now put me down."

I ignored her and put her in the front seat. I buckled the belt for her and walked over to sit in my seat. I started the car.

She stayed silent during the whole ride. I could tell she was a bit annoyed by not knowing where we were going. When I stopped the engine and she saw where we were, her old, bubbly self returned and she started laughing.

"Lily's Ice Cream parlor? Really?"

I shrugged.

I opened the door, ushering her into the parlor with a bow. She giggled melodically.

"Oh, let's sit there, beside the window!"

I pulled her chair for her and she sat down.

"So, you're awesome, bro. Ice cream is a girl's best friend." She winked playfully.

I typed on my phone and showed her the note: "Are you implying that I'm a girl?"

She smirked. "Well, you look like one."

I let out a laugh. "Seriously?"

"Nah, just kidding. You look like a boy."

Within minutes, a waitress came. It was Jodi, my mom's best friend. She was smiling kindly at me.

"Oh hello, darling! How are you and how is your grandma? Tell her that I said hello! Do you want the usual? And who is this beautiful young lady?" she blubbered on.

Lena and I shared a look. She was just as amused as I was.

I took out a pen from my pocket and wrote on a napkin, "I'll tell grandma you said hello. How are you? Yes, I would like a strawberry chocolate covered ice cream. This is Lena, she is a good friend of mine."

Jodi's eyes scrolled through the paper.

"I'm just fine, sweetie. Your order will be ready in a minute. Lena, darling, what would you like?"

My friend was scrolling through the menu and I could see her mouth watering.

"Um, I would like a caramel-covered cone of ice cream, please."

Jodi nodded her head, scribbling on a small notepad she held. "Five minutes, darlings."

She scampered off, leaving Lena and me alone.

"Caramel makes me sick." I showed her on my phone.

She let out a gasp. "You suck, then."

***

I stopped the car in front of her house. The weather was amazing, for the ending of October.

"Thank you, Liam," she said. "You're the best friend a girl could have." Her expression was displaying an emotion.

Happiness.

I nodded, smiling.

Before I could process what was happening, she pecked my cheek and got out of the car.

"Bye! Text me!" Lena waved as I restarted the engine.

I flashed her a small smile before driving away. I had one question in mind.

Why was my cheek burning?

8

Something about December

"I wonder if the snow loves the trees and fields, that it kisses them so gently? And then it covers them up snug, you know, with a white quilt; and perhaps it says 'Go to sleep, darlings, till the summer comes again.'"
~Lewis Carroll~
(Alice's Adventures in Wonderland & through the Looking-Glass)

Lena Rose Winter

You know those days where you feel like bouncing off the walls, when you just have a good feeling? That was how I felt.

"Liam, meet me in the park asap. x"

I pressed on *Send*, excitement flowing through me. I'd been planning this moment for days and today was *THE* day. I checked the weather and my suspicions had been right. Ah, Sundays were the best.

I put on my jacket and my mittens.

I walked to the park and immediately saw Liam pacing back and forth worriedly.

"What's wrong, Li?" I asked, intrigued.

"Are you okay?"

I furrowed my eyebrows. Just because I wanted to see him didn't mean I was sad or something.

"I'm fine, Liam! I only wanted to see you. Is that illegal now?"

He let out a breath and his shoulders relaxed.

"Race you to the field."

I felt a surge of adrenaline. The steady thump of my footsteps echoed in my ears and I felt a bead of sweat roll down my forehead, only to quickly evaporate. The only things stopping me from victory were my physical limits and my competition.

Before I knew it, I was the first one to reach the empty space.

"I won! Yeah! I won!" Happy dancing was one of my hobbies.

I looked at Liam, who had his arms crossed in annoyance, but he was slightly panting. I stuck my tongue out at him, a habit we both had, and advanced towards him. I cupped his face in my hands and said: "Poor little baby."

He shook my hands off and glared at me.

"Love you too."

He smiled at that, his eyes showing an emotion I couldn't identify. I turned away from his unreadable face to look up at the sky, watching as the clouds began taking over the clear, blue view.

Any time now.

"What did you want to show me?" Impatience flowed through his words.

I rolled my eyes and ushered for him to wait. I spread down on the grass and closed my eyes.

Peaceful.

I stayed there for a while, enjoying the moment and patiently waiting for my event to happen.

Then, *it* touched my cheek. I grinned and opened my eyes. Liam was lying beside me, eyes closed. I put pressure on his stomach.

"Liam, Liam!" I shouted. "Come on, it's time." His eyes fluttered open. For a second, I got lost in his eyes. They looked beautiful.

I stood up and spread my arms.

The first snowfall of the year.

Large flakes fell from heaven, as if the angels were having a pillow fight and the goose fell down to our humble home. Though beautiful, the snow was cold and sharp as it bit at our fingers and the wind kissed our cheeks. The snowflakes fell one by one, each in a different place. By now, they were grazing the grass. I just hoped the weather would be cold enough to make them stay.

I took my camera and captured the beauty of nature. Liam stood there, smiling.

Genuine smiles were plastered on our faces. "It's snowing, Li! That's what I wanted to show you!"

I went closer to him and out of nowhere, he picked me up and spun me around. All I could see were his blue eyes dancing with joy. His face was flushed with delight. I felt my heart skip a beat. His lips were red because of the weather. He put me down.

He tilted his head back and laughed heartily. It was a deep sound. *Mellow. Calming.*

I remembered reading somewhere before that mute people who lost their vocal cords couldn't laugh...I disregarded the thought and just let myself enjoy the moment.

Like a deep river, washing over a path of stones.

I joined him in his open delight.

We danced like mentally crazed freaks. It was like we were the only people in the world. It was all worth it because I was with him. It was at that moment that I realized that I would never handle losing him.

I wanted to stay here with him forever.

I suddenly remembered something. "Liam! I want to take pictures with you, I'm creating a scrapbook. I want you in it, because I care about you."

He nodded.

We took endless pictures together. From sticking our tongues out, to me watching him smile. Truthfully, I looked quite creepy.

"Last one!"

I gave him the camera, so he could capture the moment. I put my arms around his neck and planted a kiss on his cheek. It seemed like an appropriate thing to do.

We were friends, right? His skin became a little red, and he put his head down.

I was bewildered, was he *blushing?*

Can boys even blush?

"Aw," I cooed. "Lili is shy, just because his friend kissed his cheek."

That seemed to get him back. He chased after me, this time with full speed. Taken aback, I suddenly stopped moving.

But that didn't seem to stop him; he came at me and attacked me. Our weight was too much, we both lost balance. I ended up laying on him. I tried to wriggle out of this situation, but his grip on my waist only got stronger.

I giggled. He smiled.

His eyes were observing me. I looked into them and was swept away in the ocean of blue. I felt at home, looking into those eyes. It was remarkable how there were different shades of blue hidden in his eyes. I felt like I was in a different world.

His eyes flickered to something on my face, I wasn't sure what. All of a sudden, I was the one on the ground, and he was hovering over me, supporting his weight on his arms.

He started leaning in, his eyebrows furrowed and his expression looking more intense than ever. He was centimeters closer to my face. I felt his hot breath. I looked at his cherry red lips.

I closed my eyes, waiting for the moment they would be on mine.

"That's what makes you beautiful, oh, oh, that's what makes you beautiful."

My cell phone rang mercilessly. I stifled a groan. Liam quickly sat on the grass, scratching his neck.

I fumbled for my phone in my pockets. I felt my face get redder than hot pepper. My face was hot and my heart was beating uncontrollably fast.

I cleared my throat. "Hello?"

"Hello, darling." My mom's familiar voice rang on the phone. She sounded frantic.

"Uh, hey, Mom. What's up?"

"Well, I have a visitor over here. You need to come home."

Another voice came through the phone. "Margaret, why don't you just tell her that her sister's home?"

I paled.

9

Past Comes to Life

"Feed your faith and your doubts will starve to death."

Lena Rose Winter

"S-Sister?" I stuttered, my hands sweaty from their grip on my phone.

"Victoria!" The sound was blocked for a second. "Sorry, sweetie. There's a lot to talk about. Lena, come home, now," demanded my mother.

"Okay, mom." And with those words, I hung up.

I looked at Liam, who read my fear and shock. I shook my head tiredly and stood up.

"Sorry, Li, I've got to go," I said. "Family emergency."

He nodded understandingly.

I gave him a quick hug and ran to my house. The million questions popping into my mind gave me a headache.

I have a sister? How? Who was she? And if this isn't some kind of sick joke, why was she here now?

In front of my house, a flashy red car was parked. I took my time walking to the front door and hesitantly unlocked it. I could hear two people talking.

I entered the living room, only to see two women sitting face to face. One of them was my mom, the other one was a complete stranger to me. She had long, wavy, brown hair that cascaded to her waist. Her eyes were brown, chestnut-like. She had delicate features and high cheekbones. I had a feeling I'd seen her before.

When her gaze landed on mine, she immediately stood up and extended her hand to me. I hesitantly shook it.

"Who are you?" I asked, shifting my eyes between her and my mom, who looked like she was about to cry.

"I'm Victoria Winter, your sister." She talked with an English accent.

Her words hit me like a cold, hard slap in the face. I was astonished, surprised, and shocked. This was one of those moments where I really wanted a camera to pop up and my mom to laugh and say, "You got pranked!"

I shook my head. "I'm an only child."

Victoria's eyes flickered with fatigue. "No, Lena," she said. "I'm your half-sister."

I noticed the suitcases beside her.

"H-How?"

"I'm your half-sister. I'm older than you by approximately a year."

That didn't clear anything up.

"How?" I repeated.

Finally, my mom decided to answer. Her voice was throaty as she explained, "Your dad had a daughter with his ex-wife in Britain, before he married me."

My mouth went slack, falling slightly open. I felt all color drain from my face as I stared wide-eyed at—my sister.

I froze up to a point where I could hardly feel myself breathing, but when shock began to melt away, everything returned slowly. I let out a sudden sigh, and opened my mouth to speak. Then I snapped it shut.

I gulped. "Impossible," I said, my voice raspy and barely audible.

Victoria and Mom stayed very still, waiting for my reaction. Realization dawned on me and the situation was crystal clear in my head.

"Mom! He was married before you?" I stopped. "And he has a *daughter*?"

My mom shrunk down a little, and I could see a bubble of guilt forming itself around her demeanor.

"You knew?"

But the way she put her head down gave me the answer.

"How could you? How could you hide my own sister from me?"

Victoria advanced towards me and put her hand on my shoulder. I shook it off.

"She didn't know that I was going to come here," she explained calmly. "Everyone thought I'd live in England forever." That at least cleared up the fact that she had a thick, British accent.

"Why are you here *now*?" I struggled keeping my nerves collected.

"Well, my mom just died-"

I quickly said, "I'm so sorry for your loss." Regardless of how I felt at the moment, she'd just lost her mother. She must've been hurting.

"Thank you. Her will indicated for me to live with my father, but I just found out that-" She choked up.

I immediately put my arms around her in a tight hug. She *was* my sister. My dad's loss was hers too.

And worse, she was an orphan.

I felt my coat getting wet with her tears. I rubbed her back soothingly.

I kept muttering, "It's okay, everything's going to be okay."

Victoria pulled away and smiled through her tears.

"I now know why my mum used to say that Dad was kind. You inherited that from him, Lena."

Her words touched my heart. I gave her another hug. I already cared about her. I knew we would get along well. The shocked outrage I'd built up had disappeared, and I felt a sudden tranquility.

I turned to my mom. "She can stay here, right?"

"Yeah, but you two would have to share a room." My mom bit her lip. I shrugged, a smile forming on my face.

"Come on, Tori! I can call you that, right?"

Victoria chuckled and nodded.

"Yay! Now let's go, I'll show you my room." I took her hand, and excitedly hopped on the stairs.

"Well, it's perfect," Tori said, observing the room. "Where should I sleep?"

"I'm getting a job, so I'll try to save up the money for another bed. But for now, you sleep on the bed and I'll take my camping mattress."

The sleeping arrangements didn't please Tori. She wanted me to sleep on the bed. I'm stubborn, but so was she.

"Tori! I'm sleeping on the mattress, end of discussion."

She smiled shyly, and I was the one who felt like the adult.

My sister kicked her high heels off, and went to the bathroom to borrow some of my comfortable clothes. I didn't mind. I imitated her and then she sat on the bed with crossed legs.

She patted the empty place in front of her. "Come on, we have a lot to talk about. Are you really okay with all of this?" she asked.

I shrugged. "I guess it's a lot to take in, but I've always wanted a sister."

"Me too." She smiled. "Tell me everything about you. I want to catch up on everything I've missed in the last seventeen years."

We spent an hour or so talking about every single detail in our lives. I learned that her favorite color was red. She didn't like to read and she was a soccer fanatic. She liked to bake and she thought that Justin Bieber was overrated yet quite attractive. Apparently, her best friend, back in England, was in love with him and she forced Tori to go to one of his concerts.

"Can I tell you something?" I asked, shyly. She nodded feverishly. "I was about to get my first kiss today."

"Shut up!" Tori gasped. "Really?" she exclaimed, quite loudly.

"Yeah."

"Who is it? Is he cute?" she blabbered curiously.

I played with my sleeves. "He's my best friend," I said.

"Did he tell you he liked you, does he flirt with you?"

I laughed at the possibility of that happening. "He's mute."

Tori sucked in a sharp breath. "Wow."

"Yeah. He's the best."

"Aw, Lele's in love."

My mouth went agape. I took a pillow and hit her playfully with it.

"Don't call me that! And I don't love him! We're just friends, nothing more."

She raised her eyebrow, unconvinced. "Oh yeah? Why are you redder than a tomato right now, then?"

I hit her harder this time, making her laugh.

"Okay, okay, I'll close my trap. Do you have a picture of your—" She put imaginary quotations in the air. "—friend?"

"Yes, I do. Wait, let me look for my camera. We went to the park today."

"Aw," cooed Tori.

Where was the camera? I flipped through my scattered clothes, but it was nowhere.

"Where could I have put it?" I took a deep breath, trying to calm my frantic nerves.

"Retrace your steps, that helps," Tori offered.

"Well, I went to the park, took pictures with Liam. Then, the *incident* was about to happen. Mom called, I heard you, and I left in a hurry…" Suddenly, I felt lost.

Tori motioned with her hands impatiently, waiting for it to click in my head.

"OH! I left it in the park!" My eyes widened in fear. "Oh, no, no. It's the same camera Dad gave me eight years ago."

"Text Liam, you idiot." She pointed to her head, as if to say I was stupid. I opened my phone and looked through my unread messages. They were all from him.

"Hey, Lenaaaa the banana. Is everything okay at home? Text me when you see this. ☺ "

"Lenaaa, well, you forgot your camera here, so I took it with me. I'll guard it with my ninja skills, pinky promise. ;)"

"Lenaaaaa, you okay?"

"Why are you not answering meee?"

I smiled at the last one.

"Well, goodnight potatooo. Love youuu **mon amie special** *(my special friend)."*

Tori, who was noisily reading the messages over my shoulder, started mumbling, "Leliam? No, no. How about Leniam? Perfect."

And that was the beginning of a pillow fight.

10

Messy Friendships

Lena Rose Winter

I realized that making a new friend was the best choice I'd ever made. Tori was a gift sent from heaven, we were alike in so many ways and I already loved her. It felt nice to have a girl around.

"So, you're in my Literature and Calculus classes. We're locker buddies and lunch starts at 12, okay?" I said.

"OH-EM-GEE. I, like, officially love you," declared Tori in exaggeration, leaning against her locker, waiting for me. She was 18, but she hadn't finished high school in London, so Albany High was her school for senior year.

"OH-EM-GEE. I, like, totally love you more," I replied, winking at her as if I was a person with mental retardation. She giggled, weirdly.

Right now, though, my attention was directed towards the gum in my mouth.

Chew.

I shuddered. It had no more taste.

Chew.

Should I keep it?

Chew.

Disgusting.

Farewell, dear gum.

We had some good memories, but it's time to leave. I recalled an Adele song and it applied perfectly to the situation. *"Never mind, I'll find someone like you."*

I walked to the trash can, which was on the other side of the hall.

I heard Tori scream behind me. "Where are you going, weirdo?"

"Throwing my gum away, the hell does it look like I'm doing?" was my answer.

After spitting the chewed, tasteless piece of gum, I went back to my locker.

Oh, and how I wish I hadn't.

Jonah was leaning against Tori. She looked thrilled, while he had his *flirting* face on. Tori giggled at something he said.

I felt my breakfast churning in my stomach. This wasn't a sight I ever wanted to see. My face turned into a grimace and I tapped Jonah's shoulder, interrupting him from hitting on my sister. He turned around, his face masked in recognition and slight shock.

"Excuse me, Jonah," I said icily, "but hitting on my sister won't make you seem cool."

At the mention of the word 'sister,' he completely froze. Tori, on the other hand, hearing the word 'Jonah,' pushed him away with an incredible force. Her face was masked by complete revulsion. During Tori's first night at my house, I'd told her everything.

Everything.

Tori grimaced. "Ew."

She linked our arms and we walked away, our chins in the air. Now out of anyone's sight, hiding in the bathroom, we had to clutch our poor stomachs to stop the hysterical laughter coming out of us.

"D-Did you see his expression when I *ewed* him?" Tori managed to blurt out between laughs. My eyebrows furrowed together in confusion.

"Is '*ewed*' even a word?"

"Who cares?" She flipped her hair in a drama queen-like way. "But if you must ask: yes it is, in Victoria Grace Winter's dictionary."

I simply chuckled, *oh the joys of having a sister.* In the period of four days, we'd grown as close as best friends who knew each other since the age of five.

Speaking of best friends, where was Liam? He had missed three days of school, wasn't answering any of my texts, and I had even tried calling at his house, in case his Grandma was there.

I had had zilch communication with him in three days. It has been worrying me a lot, but I just hoped he was okay. It was weird how much I missed him in that small period of time.

"Hey, Tori, have you seen Liam?"

She looked at me as if I was a Martian. "I haven't met him yet."

I scurried out of the bathroom and practically sprinted to his locker.

There he was. I felt relief and worry wash over me in moments.

Something was wrong. He was standing there, an absent expression on his face. I could feel bad vibes emitting from him.

"Liam, where have you been?" I asked. "I've been worried sick about you." I peered at him closely. He didn't lift his gaze from the book he held in his hands.

"Liam?"

Still no response.

"Liiiaaaam?"

Nada.

I waved my hands under his nose to get his attention. Finally, his eyes flickered to me and he lifted his head up. I gasped. His blue eyes were a darker shade than they usually were. His lips were set in a thin line. His expression was cold and hard. I'd never seen him like that.

"Liam? Are you okay?" I asked hesitantly.

He swiftly closed his book and turned to walk away. He took long strides. I half-ran to be at his speed.

"Liam? Why are you ignoring me?"

He kept on walking.

Fed up with his attitude, I grabbed his arm, forcing him to stop. His lips pulled up in a disgusted smirk. I could sense his anger. His eyes went to my hand.

"No, I'm not letting go until you write me what's wrong."

He rolled his eyes and stayed very still. I groaned and let go of him long enough to take out a small notepad from my pocket. I kept that at all times with me; it was another source of communication I had with Liam.

I handed him the paper. He now held the special blue pen that he always kept in his right jacket pocket and he used it to roughly scribble something down before showing it to me.

"*Want to know what's wrong? You are. Leave me alone. Consider us, or whatever friendship we had, history.*"

I felt my bottom lip quiver, and he started to walk away. I ran after him and grabbed his arm again, but this time he resisted.

"No, please, Liam," I begged. "Why? What did I do? Just tell me."

He abruptly shook his arm off and turned in my direction. My hopes went slightly up. His expression softened for a second, then hardened again. His mouth moved, tracing three words.

"*Leave me alone.*"

Then he left me standing in the middle of the hallway, every step he made away from me, hurting me.

I felt tears well in my eyes. My heart was experiencing an emotion I'd only felt once. The day the nurses informed me of my father's death. Only this time it was more intense. I was feeling cold and lonely, like my heart and soul have been ripped out. There was an empty, cold feeling in my stomach, like butterflies, but more nervous than excited. My heart got ripped out of my chest without any warning. Being totally unprepared and having to deal with the outcome instantly hurt so much. I felt myself going numb and sad. My heart continued to sink as I came to the realization of what is reality.

No.

I refuse to go through this again.

I ran after him and grabbed his arm harshly. "Liam, I'm not letting you just leave like that."

"*Let go.*"

I stomped a foot angrily. "No, I'm not letting you go! Why are you acting like this?"

He just looked at me with hollowness in his eyes. I flinched. I let go.

Some moments make you realize just how much you care about someone. There are moments when you think: *I'd take a bullet for you.* And there are others when you realize that it all depends on a split-second decision.

I remembered an old quote, "*If you love something, let it go. If it comes back, it's yours. If not, it never was.*"

"Go," I said. "Just remember that I'll always be here for you."

He walked away.

11

Crestfallen

Lena Rose Winter

I walked towards Liam's house, my hands freezing from both the snow and my anxiety. There was a possibility of him kicking me out or not even answering the door. I was mortified coming to talk to him given the risks, but I simply *had* to tell him.

Last night I stayed awake until dawn, finishing my application for NYU. He had promised we would go get coffee together once we submitted them.

I was aware, of course, that we were currently far from being friends. But it seemed unthinkable for me to forget about that. I couldn't bear the thought of losing everything.

Best Case Scenario: he smiles at me, he admits that he sent his application too, and is just about to come see me. We go out for coffee and doughnuts or we can stay at his house and I can spend time with his more than lovely grandmother, Darla Black.

Worst Case Scenario: He doesn't open the door and hides from me.

My hopes deflated a little, but I forced myself to expect the worst yet hope for the best.

I knocked at the door three times, stomping my feet on the floor to get the snow off my boots.

No answer.

I knocked again and decided to leave if the door didn't open in ten seconds. They seemed to pass by too fast and I could feel the disappointment rushing in my head.

Suddenly, I heard a voice behind me. "Who you lookin' for?"

I turned to the voice and saw a woman in her thirties, leaning on the window with a scarf over her head.

"Liam Black and his grandma," I replied. "Do you know where they might be?"

She chuckled as if I were an ignorant child.

"They're at the hospital! Darla's sick."

I froze. "S-sick?"

The woman grimaced. "Yeah. It's bad, though. Last time I saw her, she was as pale as the snow you're stepping on right now." She stopped for a second, as if thinking. "Her little boy hasn't left her side in forever."

"Is it grave?" I asked.

The woman sighed. "Yeah. She has a few days, maybe two weeks left."

"Do you know which hospital?"

She nodded, "Sainte-Catherine's."

"Thank you," I said, before calling my mom. I gave her a quick resume of what I'd just found out. She came to pick me up in minutes and started driving me to the hospital.

It was a long, silent car ride. Sainte-Catherine's was about half an hour far from my house and forty-five minutes from Liam's.

Mom broke the comfortable silence. "Do you think she'll be okay?"

Darla Black was one of the kindest women I knew. When I went to study at Liam's house, she always made us hot chocolate and cookies and she made those horrible jokes that make you want to bang your head against a wall yet laugh at the same time.

Liam looked at her as if she were his home. She was the only family he had left, except for two estranged cousins who lived in Australia. She represented the only shelter he had from everything in the world. She was his grandmother, his mother, sister, and most importantly, friend.

"I don't know," I answered honestly.

If the loss of that amazing old woman could affect me, the feeling must be amplified a million times for Liam.

We got to the hospital a few minutes later and Mom decided to stay in the car. I promised to get her a coffee on my way back and rushed inside.

The hospital was quite elegant. It had wards arranged in a circular design, where the nurses' station was at the center of the ward with all the rooms visible to them. The walls and doors were made of glass and they had curtains that can be closed for a patient's privacy. I heard people moaning and calling for the nurses. The lights were dim. I heard beeps and monitors buzzing and an occasional intercom call.

"Excuse me?" I tapped on a nurse's shoulder. "Where's the reception?"

"Take a left, you'll find it there. As a matter of fact, I'm going there right now. Follow me."

I followed the nurse, who had fiery red hair stuffed into a net. The receiving desk was right where she said it would be. I walked to the receptionist and gave her a smile.

"Hello."

She didn't answer right away.

"Would you possibly know where a boy, Liam Black, would be? He's here, right now."

She finally looked up, her dark brown eyes piercing through me. "And who are you?" Her jaw chewed gum noisily and rapidly. I felt as if I was wasting every minute of her life that I was there.

"His best friend," I replied in less than a second. The nurse grimaced.

"Look, he's in the third floor. Room 561. Floor 3."

I went into the elevator and practically ran to Room 561. I stopped in my tracks only when I was already in front of the entrance.

Why was I even doing this? Liam still didn't want to be my friend.

Because he's suffering and you care about him.

I took my courage in two hands and knocked on the door three times. After a few seconds, the door opened, revealing a disheveled Liam. My heart softened at the sight in front of me.

His hair was completely messed up, there were tear streaks on his cheeks and his eyes were empty looking. They widened at the sight of me.

"I know I shouldn't have come here, but I wanted to see you, I wanted to tell you something." I stopped for a second, my eyes falling on the elderly woman sleeping in her bed, a million wires connected to her.

"Why didn't you tell me, you idiot?"

He looked at me with a blank stare, and I walked past him and sat on one of the chairs beside Darla Black. She was pale and tired. The soft risings of her chest and her faint heartbeat were the only signs of her still being alive.

"Hey, Darla," I said, tears forming in my eyes. "Can you believe your grandson? He didn't tell me that you were here." I chuckled dryly.

Someone tapped my shoulder and I turned to the familiar screen of Liam's phone.

"CHD (Coronary Heart Disease). She's been fine, but about two weeks ago, she got an attack. The doctors say that she doesn't have much time."

My heart fell. Even though Liam's neighbor had mostly informed me, I still couldn't believe that this was real, that this was happening.

"I'm sorry," traced his lips.

I replied, "No, I am."

And I hugged him.

He stiffened. I could feel him hesitate, but he reluctantly wrapped his arms around me as well.

We stayed that way for a long time, the seconds ticking by slowly, every moment taking its time to pass.

It was a silent confirmation of our friendship.

"Lena! Is that you, dear?" said a throaty voice. I jumped in the air, but smiled at the sight of Darla, now awake. Her blue eyes, which have the same shade as Liam's, held that same twinkle I'd seen so often when she was well. I went by her side, and so did Liam.

"Darla! Long time no see, eh?"

She chuckled and coughed at the same time, and Liam tensed.

"How's your life going?" she asked, as if she was just at home, knitting a winter sweater for Liam.

I shrugged. "Nothing special. I sent my college application last night, actually." I felt Liam's eyes on me. Darla's mouth dropped a little and she patted my hand.

"So did Liam, yesterday!" She chuckled softly. I was alarmed and I clutched her hand in fear.

"You okay?"

She waved her hand over her face and nodded. "Never better."

Liam reached out and held her hand as well, placing it over mine. I tried to ignore the shocks that slightly jolted my body. Darla's eyes went to our hands and she chuckled, as if sharing an old joke with herself.

"Do you have any new jokes?" I asked.

Her eyes lit up, and the wrinkles on her face seemed to fade from the joy. "What did the green grape say to the purple grape?"

I stayed silent.

"Breathe, idiot. Breathe!" And she broke into laughter. We laughed heartily with her, but remained cautious.

I had to admit though, hearing Liam laugh made me feel somewhat better. And it felt like old times, when Darla would sit on her old, oak rocking chair and tell us jokes, as her face glowed with tranquility.

She blinked several times and her presence was deflated every time she blinked. She finally closed her eyes, and soft snores were heard. She'd fallen asleep again.

I looked down to our hands, which hadn't left Darla's. Liam typed something on his phone with his free hand and showed me.

"You came for the coffee, didn't you?"

I simply replied with, "You promised."

"The hospital's cafe has the best coffee around."

I smiled. "Let's go then. Mom wants a coffee too; I'll give her one and then tell her to go home. You'll drive me home anyway."

I turned to him, and his eyes were burning into me.

They could say every word his lips and tongue couldn't. They were the way he expressed himself and I found it bizarre yet normal that I could read them so easily.

Today, there was fear laced with relief.

I nodded. "I'm glad we're friends again too, idiot."

12

Love Jitters

Lena Rose Winter

I laid my head against the cold, hard metal of my locker. I felt my eyes close, as I melted into Ed Sheeran's raspy voice in *Give Me Love*. It felt as if I was in a different world. I felt peaceful, considering that it was lunch time and I still had an hour ahead of me.

I had eaten, then extricated myself from Liam's company with the excuse that I had some "homework" to do. Frankly, I just wanted a little time to myself.

"Oi, why are you sitting in front of your locker being all depressed?" said a voice that could only belong to Victoria. I opened my eyes to see her sitting beside me. Her face softened when she saw my expression. I took off one earphone, to hear her better.

"What's wrong, babe?"

I smiled a little. I always loved it when she called me "babe" and it was cute, unlike the way Jonah used to say it.

"Well..." I trailed off, not knowing exactly how to explain anything.

"Can I guess?"

"Sure," I shrugged, highly doubting she knew what was on my mind.

"You really want Liam to ask you to the dance, but he's not doing anything," said Tori, stroking her invisible beard.

My eyes widened. How could she do that? I hadn't mentioned anything to anyone.

She grinned mischievously and then held one finger up. "Wait, I'm not done. You're in love with Liam, but you don't want to confess anything," she finished in a singsong voice. I snuck a peek at her, frowning when I saw her eyebrows wiggling suggestively.

"I do not like him."

Tori raised an eyebrow. "And you're worried about his grandma and you want to take his mind off things."

I didn't answer because it seemed as if this was the only piece of indisputable truth she'd said so far.

Tori's expression only got worse. Then, she poked me. She perfectly poked my belly button.

Coincidence? I think not. I ignored her, replacing both of my earphones in place.

Poke.

I squirmed a little.

Poke, belly button poke.

I let out a small squeak and tried to find refuge in the music.

"No, I just want to hold you.
Give a little time to me, to burn this out,
We'll play hide and seek, to turn this around..."

Tori started fully tickling me. She giggled as she achieved a series of shrieks out of me. My legs started kicking the air and I felt as if I was being tortured.

In no time at all, she had almost finished me. "Hide and seek, my arse."

I felt my smile turn upside down.

No one gets away with insulting Edward Christopher Sheeran.

"Hey! He's beautiful and perfect, okay! You ruined my mood," I exclaimed, retrieving my iPod from her hands.

"Your mood wouldn't be ruined if you asked Liam to the dance."

I re-crossed my arms. "No, I most certainly will not ask him to the dance."

"You know you want to."

"I do," I sighed. "But a girl's got to have some pride."

Tori groaned in frustration. "Come on."

"No."

"If you don't, I'll tell—" She paused, a dramatic look only a maniac could muster appearing on her face, "—Jonah that you've always loved him."

That made me gasp. "You wouldn't."

She smirked. "Oh, I most certainly would."

"Fine," I surrendered.

Tori got up in a flash and started jumping up and down—also known as *Winter Happy Dancing.*

"But how should I…ask?" I stuttered, whispering the last part. Tori put her hands on my shoulder and looked at me with dead serious eyes.

"You just say it, okay, Lena?"

Receiving no change in my facial expression, she shook me frantically.

"Lena! I'm going to go tell him to come here and you just do it, okay? Where would he be?"

"Library," was my automatic answer.

"He'll be here in a jiffy."

Jiffy?

Breathe, Lena. Breathe, I commanded myself.

"Okay," I managed to say, just before Tori stormed off, reminding me of a lightning bolt.

What if he says no?

You'll be strong.

He wouldn't hate me, right?

No, Lena. He'd never hate you.

How do *you* know? You're just me.

I know a lot more than you do about everything.

Oh yeah? Like what?

You like Liam, more than as a friend.

Oh, me. Always lying to me. I *don't* like him!

Yes, you do.

It's my mistake anyway, who has a conversation with themselves?

You.

During all this time, I was searching the hallways for *his* red sneakers.

He walked towards me, looking worried. In his arms, there were several, heavy looking books. I recognized *The Host*.

That's your typical Liam.

"*What's wrong?*" he mouthed, running a hand through his perfectly tousled, soft chestnut hair.

"N-Nothing, I-I..." The floor was suddenly the most interesting thing to look at.

Pride, regain yourself, Lena.

I felt myself get stronger, a surge of adrenaline coursing through my body. I lifted my head up, directly looking through Liam's beautiful, deep, ocean blue eyes. I melted. I fiddled with my arms.

"I-It's just, you know!" I grunted. "Would you stop that?"

Liam raised his eyebrow questioningly.

"Stop being all you, when you know exactly what I want to say," I blabbered, my hands getting strangely sweaty.

I sighed loudly, waving my hands around. "Ah, I'm just going to say this. Don't find me weird or stupid, okay?"

"Never."

"Willyougowithmetothedance?" I said, barely coherent. "Justasfriends, ofcourse, likeduh."

I put my head down, letting the heavy silence settle in. *I should've never said anything.* Being a coward, I couldn't even look at Liam.

He was going to say no.

I took a chance and lifted my head a little, only to meet adorably confused eyes. He furrowed his eyebrows.

Darn it, he didn't understand me.

"Well, I just...will you go to the dance with me, as friends of course?" I asked, never taking my gaze off him this time.

His eyes went wide and his mouth was agape.

I shouldn't have.

I felt my bottom lip slightly quiver, thinking I had just ruined everything. My eyes met the ground again.

Soft hands held my chin and slowly lifted my head up.

Liam was smiling.

His eyes were shining with happiness. Cheeks, faintly tainted with a fair color reminding me of a rose, merely blooming. Loose strands of smooth brown hair perfectly framed his face. The blue eyes brought out his striking natural beauty and I couldn't help but stare. His thick light eyebrows showed contentment, but amused at the same time. My eyes unconsciously flickered to the lips. Red, was all I could think. He licked his lips, making them even more of a strawberry color.

I liked strawberries.

I bit my lip. *Expect the worst.*

Liam blinked. My nervousness made my muscles tense.

Don't get your hopes up, I reminded myself.

His lips moved, making my heart race faster. I sighed in relief and then realized what was happening.

I felt my mouth curve into a smile, which immediately transformed into a huge grin.

"Yes."

That was the one word I would've died to hear his voice say, but his mouth tracing it was good enough. It was better than that, it was extraordinary.

I don't know if it was something about his smiling expression or the way his mouth curved around that word, but it took me all the restraint and will in the world not to break into a happy dance right there.

13

Girl Days

"A best friend isn't just someone who's always there for you. It's someone who understands you a bit more than you understand yourself."

Lena Rose Winter

The dance was on a Friday and everyone had school. The girls complained, but the boys couldn't care less. Well, obviously, they didn't have to prepare for perfect hair and makeup that took hours to master.

The thing was, I didn't have anything to wear. I was horrified. All I had was a dress that was now two sizes too small, worn on Valentine's Day, *three years ago.*

I wiped the sleep out of my eye, taking the Cheerios box and shaking some into my bowl. My mom was still asleep, which was really strange. Ever since Tori came into our lives, she'd always been going out in the afternoon and coming back after midnight. Frankly, curiosity was killing me, but I decided to give her time.

She'll probably tell me at one point in my life.

Ha, as if. I was determined to have a talk with her, but after the dance.

Tori was eyeing me suspiciously. She looked as if she'd forgotten something.

"What are you wearing to the dance, Lena?" asked my sister, as she poured milk on her cereal.

I shrugged innocently. "Noshing." I accidentally spit a bit of milk on Tori. She gave me a death glare, then took a napkin and wiped my spit off her shirt.

"First, do you have *any* manners? It's extremely rude to speak while eating. Now, finish munching the bloody food and give me a real answer."

I smiled. Taking my precious time, I chewed and chewed and then swallowed.

"Finally, now, do you have a dress or not?"

"Nope."

Tori froze for a second it took her time to process my answer.

"Earth to Tori," I said, waving my hand in her face.

Then, she gasped loudly.

"Lena Rose Winter!" she yelled, making me jump in the air. "How in bloody hell do you consider yourself going to the dance? In your penguin pajamas?"

I held my hands up in surrender. "Calm down, woman. I'll figure something out."

"What do you mean? Americans, these days. Are you sure you're a girl? Honestly, all I see in movies are women always freaking out about how they have to look perfect."

I rolled my eyes, slightly annoyed. "Shut up."

Hurt flashed in her eyes, then she recomposed herself quite quickly.

"I'm sorry, I didn't mean it like that!" I sighed, feeling guilt washing over me. Tori stuck her tongue out.

I grabbed my bag, heading for the door.

"Come on, we're going to be late for school. I'll figure something out later."

A hand clutched my arm. I turned to face Tori, who had a mischievous glint in her eyes.

Uh-oh, not good.

"No, missy. You ain't going anywhere. We're going shopping."

My eyes widened. "Tori. We have school. I'm not skipping it just because of a stupid dress."

She raised her eyebrows, as if daring me to challenge her.

"Oh, don't look at me that way," I exclaimed, cowering a bit. That did nothing but intensify her glare.

"Stop it, Tori."

She smirked, knowing I was about to crack.

"Stop smirking, for God's sake!"

My she-devil sister smiled fully.

"Yeah, yeah we're going shopping. Wipe that grin off your face."

We headed for her bright red car and Tori started the engine.

"Mission Dance: Find Lena a Suitable Outfit. Mission F.L.A.S.O. begins now," shouted Tori, as the car moved in the direction of Riverside Mall.

***

My older sister and I scanned the display glass in different stores. I was extremely bored and tired, while Tori resembled a child who'd eaten too much candy. Her chocolate brown hair bounced on her shoulders from all the jumping around.

"Step one: Find a dress," said Tori in a robotic voice. She added, "Still failing, so far."

She grabbed my hand and practically ran into a random store, the name of which I didn't catch. Once inside, I was astonished. It was the fanciest store I've ever been in.

The walls were painted a creamy, elegant white and in some parts, there were rosy vines. A huge chandelier lit up the store, making it look as if a thousand candles were hanging just beneath the ceiling. Cozy-looking, chic cushions were almost everywhere. Beside each one, there was a cup of tea. But that wasn't what made my mouth go dry.

The dresses were the reason. They were in every place I laid my eyes on. A hundred shades of every single color in the world.

"Hello, dear," a kindly voice said, interrupting my dreamy bewilderment. I turned to face a sophisticated looking, middle-aged saleswoman. Her hair was held neatly by a clip, her face had the perfect amount of makeup on it, and her clothes looked more expensive than the contents of my entire closet put together. I had to frown, looking down at my puffy black jacket, red jeans, and ratty sneakers.

I took that moment to close my mouth, fearing that I'd embarrassed myself even more.

"Hello, Susie!" Tori, my lifesaver, replied on my behalf. "This is my sister, Lena. We're looking for a dress, she has a dance to attend."

I shot her a grateful smile and she winked at me.

Susie nodded her head and motioned gracefully toward a rack of different dresses.

"These are all probably your size. Which ones would you like to try on?"

I cleared my throat and gave Tori a glare. How was I supposed to know which one was *The One*?

My sister grabbed about 10 dresses and handed them to me.

"Oh, I don't think we'll need your help anymore, Susie. I think I can deal with my little bear," said Tori, addressing herself to the saleswoman.

I felt my eyes widen. I was seriously scared, yet amused at the same time.

Tori could be a cute koala, but she can equally be a mean, mama bear.

"Go try them on," ordered Tori.

I did a salute, then muttered "Yes, ma'am," as I headed for a dressing room.

I took a random dress from Tori's selection, then tried it on. I frowned. It was a tube, floor-length, bright green dress. There was absolutely nothing special about it, save for a few jewels lining the hem to make it look less plain.

I opened the curtain, prepared to face Tori's opinion.

Her face scrunched up in a grimace and with the hand that didn't hold a cup of tea, she motioned for me to turn around. I obeyed.

"No, no, no! You look like a vegetable I would never eat! Lena, you look like a celery!"

I stuck my tongue out childishly, then went back to the dressing room. I sighed.

And so it went on for at least two hours. Me, trying on every single dress Tori had picked out and she, finding an undesirable quirk in every single one. She seemed to have a thing against fruits and vegetables.

Apple, orange, banana, cucumber, tomato…the list goes on and on.

SOS, I texted Liam quickly, *Tori took me shopping.*

I was absolutely exhausted. I just wanted to go home. But there was a part of me that really hoped to find a nice, presentable dress. After all, I didn't want Liam to regret saying yes.

Suck it up, woman, was his merciless reply. I could see him laughing at me.

I was fed up with these dresses. They were all beautiful, but I made them look *plain.* I looked down at the one I was currently wearing. It was a short, puffy pale orange dress with diamonds everywhere. I liked it, but I wasn't sure Tori would.

"Tori!" I called out. "I look like a peach, I don't want to come out!"

"Get out here, dummy!"

I grunted, but did as she asked.

"Tada!" I exclaimed dully as I stepped out.

I was greeted by the same grimace. "You were right about the peach part."

Surprising me, she sighed, exasperated. "Argh, why are there no *It* dresses!"

I looked at her, realizing for the first time how tired she was. Yeah, sure, she'd been annoying during the day, but she really cared about me.

"If I may, I think I have the perfect dress for you, Ms. Winter," said Susie, who'd been silently standing there all along.

"Please, help me," I pleaded, still in my peach dress.

Susie disappeared for a couple of minutes, then came back with a white box.

"Try it on, what are you waiting for?" I saw curiosity and excitement written all over Tori's expression. I took the box and sprinted into the dressing room.

I opened the huge white box and inside, laid a perfectly folded midnight blue gown. I drew it out of its box and shook it out, and only then did it reveal its true glory.

Breathlessly, I took in the beauty of it. The way the subtly sequined fabric flowed was elegant. If a dress could illustrate perfection, this would be it. I was itching to try it on. Suddenly, I felt excited. I tried to picture it: me at the dance, wearing this amazing thing of beauty, and blushing at Liam's surprised expression. I could already see the twinkle in his beautiful, blue eyes. This dress was the most faultless, wonderful thing I've ever seen.

I slipped it on and to my surprise, it fit me flawlessly. I faced the mirror.

Who was the stranger standing there? Her long hair fell almost down to her waist, and her chestnut eyes seemed to be glittering. Her skin seemed to be glowing.

And it hit me.

That girl was me.

The dress molded to my torso beautifully, complimenting my shape. The gown drifted slightly from my legs and ended at a brush past my toes. It was the color of a beautiful midnight blue, a shade darker than Liam's eyes. Its strapless style highlighted my collarbone and made it look wrapped in smooth, alluring, skin. There were subtle ruffles on the hem of the dress, making me feel like a princess. In this dress, I wasn't *"just"* Lena, I was a beautiful girl.

I felt like something was missing. I looked in the box and saw my answer. A gorgeous pair of heels the same color as the dress was lying there. I searched for the size. I felt myself gasp. It was a size 6. *I* was a size 6. How could this be possible?

I'd have to ask Susie.

I put them on and marveled at their comfort.

"Lena! I'm dying over here!" yelled an overly excited Tori. I could hear her impatient feet stomping around.

I smiled a little, then opened the curtain. Susie grinned knowingly and Tori took in a sharp breath.

"Y-You. Look. Bloody. Fit," muttered Tori while encircling me, her eyes full of wonder.

"Thank you so much, Susie," I told my new lifesaver. She nodded. "How is it possible that everything fits me perfectly?" I asked, intrigued.

"Well, dear," answered Susie. "We have a new member in the staff and she'd been working on this masterpiece, day and night."

"Who?" I asked, her answer only making me more confused.

As soon as the words left my mouth, it clicked in my head. I felt shock and gratitude all over me. Susie smiled and nodded, confirming my unspoken revelation.

"I knew all that hard work would've never gone to waste. I was designing that dress for a special occasion, and there you are, looking so beautiful."

I turned toward the voice and saw the face of 'the new staff member' shine with pride. I felt my eyes prickle with tears.

I ran into her arms and muttered, "Thank you, thank you, thank you."

My mother cupped my face in her hands and smiled.

Being herself, Tori wrapped her arms around both of us. We laughed, and I felt my face get wet with tears.

"Family love! Oh my god, Lena! You're not supposed to cry!" complained Tori. "We still have 6 hours before the dance. How about we go to Starbucks and act all family-cute over there?"

I looked back and forth at Tori and my amazing mother.

It's been a long time since I last felt like a little bear, sheltered and protected by the most extraordinary people in the world.

14

Feeling like Love

"You can't blame gravity for falling in love."
~Albert Einstein~

Lena Rose Winter

"Bloody hell, time passes by!" exclaimed Tori while examining me. "We have three hours to get you ready."

"Yes. We have three hours to make her look like a princess," agreed Mom. "*Liam*'s princess," she added, making a blush rise on my cheeks.

"Oh, come on! I just need a little makeup, my hair down, and my dress on!" I protested. "That doesn't take three freaking hours!"

"Tut, tut. You're pretty, but we need to make you look like the most beautiful girl at the dance," shushed my mother.

I huffed and crossed my arms together.

Are you confused? Let me clear that up. I was sitting on a chair, back directed towards a big mirror. My dear mother and sister were examining every inch of my face. They insisted on making my final look a surprise—to *me*. Apparently, I had no right to look at my reflection until the very end of their work.

"We'll start with makeup," declared Tori, taking her kit. My mom agreed.

I sighed. This was going to be the longest three hours of my life.

***

After two hours and forty-five minutes of pampering, Tori and Mom smirked with pride.

"So? How do I look?" I asked nervously. Tori smiled. *Oh come on! Just reassure me, for God's sake!*

"Stand up, and take a look at our marvelous work," ordered Mom. I stood up, and finally turned to face the mirror.

There stood a brunette with an indescribable beauty. Her hair was a rich shade of chestnut brown. It flowed in waves to adorn her glowing, olive skin. Her eyes, framed by long lashes and eyeliner, were popping out in a bright, chestnut color. I saw a gleam of excitement and bewilderment in them. Her cheeks were tainted by a dark color of red. Her full lips made the stranger look mature, as they were curved into a smile. That wasn't all. The dress she was wearing fit her like a second skin, but in an elegant way.

"W-Who is this?" I managed to say, and strangely enough, the lips in the mirror reflected my action.

Tori and Mom smiled, and my sister put a hand on my shoulder.

"You," revealed Tori, nodding in my direction.

I felt myself slowly recover from the shock I was in and my eyes widened.

The alien in the mirror was me. Me?

Yes, me, idiot.

Shut up, me.

Well, we look beautiful and I don't feel like fighting with me right now.

I looked like a princess and I felt like one.

I grinned, then gave my family a bone-crushing hug. I was Mama Bear right now. A very happy one.

"L-Lena, I need to b-breathe," stuttered Mom. I immediately let go and broadly smiled at them.

Their smiles widened. "You two are officially my favorite people in the whole world," I declared.

"Tut, tut. We know we're great, but everyone knows Mr. Prince Charming is on top of your list," teased Tori, winking at me.

I felt my face get hot, but I was determined to defend myself.

"Who are you talking about?" I asked, eyebrows raising. Tori chuckled.

"Oh, I think you know exactly who I'm talking about."

I sent my mom a look, signaling for her to help me out.

"Hush, Tori, don't embarrass her," said Mom, slapping Tori's shoulder lightly. I thanked her with my eyes.

"But, I have to admit. You two are perfect together," shrugged my mother, making me take back the gratefulness I felt.

My mouth fell open and I glared at her. Tori grinned, feeling successful.

"Liam and Lena sitting in a tree, K-I-S-S-I-N-G. First comes love, then comes marriage, then comes a Leniam baby, in a baby carriage," sang Tori, dancing a little while she was at it.

A poking war began. My revenge commenced by directly poking my finger on her belly button. Tori shrieked.

As soon as I started, Tori's cries, giggles and screams filled the room.

"Girls!" yelled Mom, breaking us apart.

I stuck my tongue out at Tori.

She blew a raspberry tongue at me.

"Grow up! Now, it's 6 o'clock and Liam should be here any minute, so behave yourselves," reminded my mom.

Oh.

My.

God.

He's coming.

He might be on his way, he might even be in front of the doorstep.

Mom went downstairs, leaving me with Tori. She eyed me with a playful look. Frankly, she looked quite comic, wearing her Tweety pajamas.

"Oh, stop it! I'm just really nervous okay!" I cried out.

She commanded, "Lena, breathe."

I let the air flow deeply through my lungs, and indeed, I felt more relaxed. I opened my eyes, which I'd closed, then faced Tori.

She smiled, as if she knew something I didn't. "Bear, why do I feel like this?" I whined.

"Now, the answer to this question is really simple. But I'll leave it to you. Figure it out," said Tori, just as the bell rang.

Deep breaths.

He's here.

"Go, your prince wants you," urged Tori, nodding towards the door. I frantically grasped her arm, refusing to let go.

She shook off my grip and pushed me away. I put on a coat, as it was freezing outside.

What if I pretended that I was really sick? Liam's really kind, he wouldn't mind.

"LENA ROSE WINTER, GET DOWN HERE, LIAM HAS ARRIVED," shouted my mom loud enough for the whole neighborhood to hear.

Damn it.

I blew Tori a kiss as she whispered, "Good luck."

My heels made a "click" noise on the stairs. My legs were shaking, my palms were sweating, and I felt slightly dizzy. As the staircase was on the side of the door, I'd probably see Liam right away. My eyes were glued down on the stairs as I made my way down. I was afraid I'd fall.

As I stepped on the landing, I finally looked up.

Oh, how I wished I hadn't.

His hair was messy, yet perfectly falling in his eyes. The blue gems danced and twinkled in amusement, happiness, and shock. He was dressed in a black tuxedo and a white shirt perfectly tucked into his pants. His hands held a bouquet of a dozen roses.

I felt woozy, just looking at him. His mouth fell when he saw me and he gaped for about 10 seconds. When I was done checking him out, my eyes met his. Liam cleared his throat and smiled at me. It was contagious.

"*Utterly beautiful*," he mouthed to himself, I think. I bit my lip and felt a blush rise on my cheeks. I'd momentarily forgotten my mom was still standing here. She eyed us with joy and mischievousness.

"Liam, bring her back by 11. Have fun, kids." Mom winked and left us alone.

I looked at Liam through my eyelashes and saw him intently staring at me. He took the notepad and pen he always kept in his left pocket, then scribbled something down and showed it to me.

"I always believed that angels didn't exist on Earth, but you proved me wrong. You look quite perfect, as always."

Maybe it was how cheesy that line seemed, or how nervous I was, but I started uncontrollably laughing and giggling.

Liam looked at me as if I were a Martian.

"Don't look at me like that! You know why I was laughing, this line is just so cheesy!" I exclaimed, still laughing my butt off.

Surprisingly, his shoulders slumped and his expression fell. His eyes read, "I really meant that." Guilt washed over me and I immediately put my arms around him.

"I'm so so so sorry, Liam! I didn't think, I-just-" I blabbered, to be cut off by Liam's hands lifting my chin up. His expression softened and his eyes took my breath away. I could feel his hot breath.

"It's okay," moved his full, red lips.

I nodded, speechless. The way he was looking at me made me melt like ice cream exposed to 500-degree weather. If it wasn't for his hand firmly, but softly, holding my waist, I was pretty sure my wobbly legs would abandon me.

Liam released his grip and opened the door. He slightly bowed down and offered his arm to me.

He asked, lips tracing the words, *"Shall we?"*

I felt a surge of adrenaline pulse through my veins. I shot him a small smile and nodded.

"We shall," I replied, taking his arm.

There was a fine layer of snow outside. And with fine, I meant huge. Little snowflakes fell, twinkling in the moonlight. Sure, it was only 6, but the sun went down early in winter, here.

We headed for his black Mercedes. He opened the passenger door in a gentlemanly way.

My cheeks already hurt so much from smiling.

***

Liam and I stepped into the gym, which had gotten a very successful makeover. There were huge snowflakes *"floating"* in the air. The floor had been covered by fake snow and the air just twinkled.

Apparently, we'd been the last to arrive, because everyone turned to look at us. Gasps could be heard. Girls shot Liam and me a jealous glare and boys groaned. I was still clutching the bouquet with my right hand and on Liam's arm with the other.

Tired of their stares, I yelled, "Nothing to look at here! Back to your onions." They did exactly as demanded. I was almost certain that everyone had heard about my little fights with Jonah.

Liam smirked. We headed for a spot where there were two chairs. We sat down and I could still feel Liam looking at me with that smirk of his.

"Oh, would you stop it! It's really annoying," I said, blankly staring at the dance floor. He shook his head, chuckling. His laugh made me laugh too.

Why was I thinking this way about Liam?

Simple.

Stupid mind, please shut up.

Oh, okay. But just so you know, I know exactly why you feel like this.

Tell me why, then.

You'll figure it out on your own.

I mentally groaned. Why was everyone speaking in puzzles today?

Liam turned to me, confusion written all over his features.

"Oh, you don't want to know."

"I do," moved his lips.

I felt myself panic. I couldn't just tell him that I was feeling strange things towards him! I had to make up an excuse. If I wasn't sure of what I was feeling for him, I was certain that telling him would be the worst option.

"Excuse me, I have to go to the little ladies' room," I mumbled, standing up.

Little ladies' room? *Really,* me? Really?

I went to the bathroom and locked myself in a stall. I had to regain my coolness. Oh, who was I kidding! I had no coolness to regain.

Hahaha, you're an idiot.

Shut it, you. It's all your fault. If you didn't act so dumb, I wouldn't be here fake-peeing.

Mentally fighting with me was really annoying.

I got out, then went to the spot Liam was supposed to be in. He wasn't there.

What if he ditched me? Was I too clumsy and dumb for him?

Stop being paranoid.

Someone tapped on my shoulder. I turned to face Liam, holding two cups of punch. I sighed in relief. Of course. He was too nice to actually do any of the horrible things that popped into my imagination. I smiled and took the drink from his hand. We each took small sips.

Liam's face scrunched up. I mirrored his action. The punch was absolutely horrible.

"Come on, let's dance," I exclaimed, suddenly feeling hyper. I placed our drinks on a nearby table and took his hand. Just as we arrived on the dance floor, *Don't Stop the Party* by Pitbull stopped. A slow song came on. I gasped.

"It's *Kiss Me!*" I jumped excitedly. Liam looked at me with a cute, crooked smile.

Wait. He had to ask me to dance. But considering that he couldn't exactly talk, I had to be the one to ask.

"May I have this dance, my handsome peanut?"

He grinned and swiftly took my waist, holding me extremely close. My breath caught in my throat.

"I thought you'd never ask." His mouth traced the words just as a small, adorable smile formed on his face.

I placed my hand on his shoulder and we swayed to the music. I constantly looked at my feet, hoping I wouldn't step on him. I was a horrid dancer.

"I'm really sorry, I'm just a really terrible dancer and I could step on your feet. I don't want to embarrass myself," I blabbered, still looking at my feet.

This felt very awkward, though. The snow increased my fear, it spread everywhere. Liam's feet reflected mine, his chuckles making me feel extremely self-conscious.

Liam lifted my head up, his eyes reading through me. I instantly relaxed but tensed at the same time. The smile wiped off his face, and he was intensely looking at me.

Was there something on my face?

I itched to touch my face, but I was unable to look away ever since Liam's eyes met mine. It felt as if Liam and I were in another world, where we were the only ones on the dance floor.

I admired his boyish features. He was just—unique. In every way possible. He was certainly the most beautiful guy I'd ever met. The most perfect one. His eyebrows furrowed and his gaze went from my eyes to something lower on my face.

My nose? Why would he be looking at my nose?

Liam was leaning closer and closer to my face. He gave a small, quirky smile, the one he knew that I had loved for a long time ago; it gave me the feeling as if he knew something that I didn't. Caressing my cheek, he lifted my chin, our noses almost touching. I could feel the warmth of his breath brushing the top of my lip.

Oh. He was *definitely* not staring at my nose. My heart's pace quickened.

Just as the last piece of the jigsaw was about to complete the puzzle of my feelings for him, I felt a cold, sticky liquid poured down my back. I gasped. The space between Liam and I was now bigger than I would've wanted it to be. Tears formed in my eyes, as the coldness gave me goose bumps.

"Oops?" exclaimed a squeaky female voice I instantly recognized. I turned, only to see the girl I despised most in the world, holding a now-empty cup of punch.

15

He is All I Need

Lena Rose Winter

My first *friend* in this school. The screechy mouse who was dating an asshole with a huge ego, but not as humongous as hers. I took in her appearance, with a disgusted smirk on my face. She was wearing a glittering long red dress that reached the floor.

Her hair was pulled to the side, falling on her right shoulder in cascading waves. With about a ton of make up on her face, she resembled the ugliest creature I'd ever seen in my whole life.

I was not a hypocrite. I didn't see the *gorgeous* girl everyone saw. I saw a frail wannabe seeking attention.

She looked like the last horcrux in *Harry Potter and The Deathly Hallows*, weak but feeding on others to gain strength. I saw through that prideful smirk. I knew Jonah was a bad influence on her. But Stacy didn't.

Stacy Hennings.

She crossed the line. It was now or never.

I heard gasps in the gym; every eye was once again glued on my enemy and me. Anger bubbled in me, my nostrils flared and my face got hot. I clenched my fist and looked at her.

"Oops? That's all you can find to say? Why did you do that, Hennings?" I asked, raising an eyebrow. My fury was *not* going to get out of control this time.

My eyes flickered to her hands, still holding the empty glass, clutching it for life. They were slightly shaking. This ought to be easy.

"Well? Cat got your tongue?" I smirked, crossing my arms together.

"You're a bitch," she stated, shrugging her shoulders. I felt my eyebrows go higher on my forehead.

Suddenly, a staggering Jonah appeared and slid his arm around her shoulder. He was positively drunk because his eyes were half closed and his hand held a bottle of beer.

"Heeeeey, caatfiight! Gooooo prettyyyy…" slurred Jonah, barely comprehensible. My eyes met Liam's, whose face was covered with shock, anger, and anxiousness.

"*I got this,*" I mouthed, in hopes of reassuring him. Well, I failed. He had a reason to be worried, though. Last time I talked to Jonah, my fist connected with his face.

"Nice boyfriend you got here, Hennings."

Stacy shot me a death glare, before turning to Jonah.

"For your information, my man is a hundred times better than the Silent Freak here," she declared, placing a sloppy kiss on Jonah's cheek. I didn't have time to think about the fact that she'd insulted Liam, because, to everyone's surprise, Jonah shook her off, then wiped her *kiss.*

"Ew! I got uglyyyy cooties," he exclaimed, still wiping his cheek. My mouth fell open. So did Stacy's.

"Jonah, what do you mean by ugly?" gasped Stacy, eyeing her boyfriend. He pointed at her and grimaced.

"*Youuu're* ugly, dumdum."

I bit my lip from laughing. He was acting like a little kid.

This was priceless, but not as much as Stacy's expression. She recomposed from her bewilderment by wrapping her arms around his waist.

By now, the entire gym had gone wild. Everyone was hooting for Jonah.

"GUYS, GUYS. He's just drunk. He-he doesn't know what he's saying," stuttered 'Ugly.' Jonah shook her off for a second time. He took a deep breath, looking quite like a little kid confessing something.

"Yes, I'm drunk. And you're ugly. But yesterday and tomorrow I was and will be sober. And you'll still be ugly. If there's anyone pretty here, it's Elena. She's *really* pretty," said Jonah.

Pure awe was written on each student's face. Including mine. Even though he'd said my name wrong, the finger pointing in my direction confirmed his statement. Although I added a little smirk.

I took Liam's hand and advanced towards her frozen expression. She looked like a fish, her mouth forming a perfect *O*.

I patted her back, feeling pity. "I'll repeat again, just for you, Stacy. *Nice boyfriend you've got here."*

She whimpered, sounding like a lost puppy.

All of a sudden, I remembered why I was here.

The sticky substance on my back.

I let go of Liam's extremely soft, warm hand and eyed the room for the item I needed.

Liam handed me exactly what I was looking for, with a knowing smile.

I approached Stacy, who was still frozen. Jonah had left her to hang out with random people. I tapped her shoulder, making her face me.

"What do you want from me, you monster!" she screeched.

I smiled a little, then poured the liquid I had in my hands on her hair. I was pretty sure Stacy's scream could be heard from China. I shrugged nonchalantly.

"Oops?" This time, the word came out of my mouth. I walked away.

"You're nothing but a little bitch. By the way, the Silent Freak is ugly, fat and disgusting. I know what you two have in common."

I stopped in my tracks. My eyes met Liam's; he was pleading me: *Don't do anything stupid.*

The pain that flickered in his sad eyes made me even madder. In a flash, I was in front of her again.

Her lips pulled up, evilly, knowing she'd won. "Excuse you, what did you just say?" I asked, my level of patience reaching its end.

"I *said,* you, Lena Winter, are a bitch. And the Silent Freak is the ugliest, most repulsive human I'd ever seen. That explains you getting along with him so well."

That was when my palm collided with her face.

"Listen right here, Stacy Hennings. If anyone's a *bitch* here, it's *you.* Liam Christopher Black is my best friend and the most amazing guy in the *entire* world. Insult him again, you'll have to cross me," I said calmly, while she was still clutching her now red cheek.

For the last time, and without turning back, I took Liam's hand and walked out the gym.

***

Liam had been giving me looks ever since the incident at the gym. He was eyeing me with a judging look in his eyes, then shook his head. We were walking through the halls, heading for my locker. I hoped I'd find *anything* to wear. Frankly, the sticky substance on my back made my mood horrible.

"Liam! Stop looking at me like that!" I exclaimed, having had enough. He raised an eyebrow, then continued to stare at the cold, hard floor.

Fine, be like that.

I opened my locker, rummaging through it, wishing I'd be lucky enough to find an old shirt and sweatpants or something. Liam leaned against the locker beside me, observing me. I didn't take my eyes off the mess I call my locker.

"I mean, honestly, she ruined my dress and insulted me—" I half-yelled, talking to myself.

"—and she insulted *you.* She could've done anything else but *that!* You're my best friend, and a person I really care about, a-as a friend of course. No one gets away with—"

I was cut off by a peck on my cheek. I stopped, then turned to face him.

"*Thank you,*" he mouthed, smiling at me. For a moment, I was so mesmerized by the way he'd smiled, that I just wanted to stay like this forever.

I shook my head to get a reality check.

"Liaaam, what am I going to wear now?" I whined, sounding like a little baby. He grinned, then typed something on his phone.

"Stay like this, you still look beautiful."

I blushed, and looked at him through my eyelashes.

"Really?" I asked, biting my lip. He nodded, still smiling at me. I took my coat out and wrapped it around myself, my skin suddenly feeling a lot colder.

"What shall we do now, peanut?" I asked.

A twinkle appeared in his eye. Before I could even process what was happening, Liam was running and carrying me at the same time.

"LIAM CHRISTOPHER BLACK! PUT ME DOWN, NOW." But my pleas did nothing. I closed my eyes, and got comfortable.

Might as well get something out of it, right?

When I felt a cold breeze on my face, I opened my eyes. Liam gently set me on the ground, widely grinning. I took in our surroundings.

We were standing on the snow covered grass, outside the school. Crisp, white, shining covering that transformed the landscape, making it a magical land full of wonder and undiscovered mysteries. The snow did not glide, but rather it created random patterns within the air. As it settled, it dissolved slowly into the snow already placed there by the last sprinkling. Everything looked breathtakingly beautiful, including the angel standing in front of me.

I felt confusion flood over me, though.

"Liam, why are we here?"

He smiled even more, a hidden secret appearing more mysterious than ever. He held one finger up, signaling for me to wait. He turned, his back to me as he did something on his phone.

I focused on the weather, and shivered. I was freezing. Goosebumps were present all over my arms. My teeth were chattering.

Liam finally turned to face me, then music was blasting from his phone. He took out a handkerchief from his pocket, laid it on the snow and put his phone on it.

I immediately recognized the song.

"Settle down with me, cover me up, cuddle me in…"

"Liam! Will you please tell me what's going on? I'm dying over here," I said. I felt warmer. He placed his hand on my waist and my hand on his shoulder.

"You owe me a dance," moved his mouth, as he shrugged. My breath caught in my throat. I gulped what was left of my saliva, as my mouth went completely dry. I took deep breaths to steady my heart which, as usual, was beating inhumanely.

This time, I didn't concentrate on dancing. My attention was fully directed towards the guy holding me.

And all of a sudden, nothing in the world mattered. The way he was looking at me was making me melt. As if my insides were being mashed. I finally understood the riddles. I figured everything out. From the sweaty palms, to my heart racing when I see him. From admiring his blue eyes, to having dreams about him.

I felt this way about Liam because I loved him.

"I'm falling for your eyes, but they don't know me yet. And with this feeling I'll forget, I'm in love now," sang Edward Christopher Sheeran, who shared his middle name with Liam's.

I don't know what came over me at that moment: was it the way his eyes were reading my soul or the way he was absent-mindedly smiling at me, making his eyes sparkle?

"Liam, can I tell you something?"

He nodded, curiosity shining on his face now. I let go of him, so we weren't dancing anymore. The song had been over for more than five minutes now.

I plopped myself on the grass; he mirrored my actions. I pulled on the grass, slightly easing my nervousness.

"Promise me that no matter what happens, we stay friends after I say what I need to confess, deal?" I said, butterflies exploding in my stomach. His eyebrows furrowed now, with worry. I looked at him in the eyes. It was almost like he glowed.

"Liam, I lo-" I was cut off by a ringtone.

Maybe that was a sign, I shouldn't say anything.

"You need me, but I don't need you, you need me, nah I don't need you."

Liam jumped and grabbed his phone. When he saw the caller's I.D, his face flushed and he gave me the phone, his hand shaking with worry and concern. He reminded me of a little scared child. I immediately pressed the green answer button. That's how it worked; when someone was calling him, he had to give the phone to the nearest person beside him. I put it on speaker.

"Hello?"

"Hello, I'm guessing this is a friend of Liam's," greeted a manly voice, slightly trembling.

Liam was observing my every move. "Yes, what's wrong?"

"This is Doctor Morrison, it's about his grandmother."

Liam tensed.

"Yes? What's wrong with her?" I asked, worried myself. There was a long pause.

"Well, her heartbeat's slowing and she's barely breathing-" trailed off Dr. Morrison. Liam clenched his fists.

"Spit it out, Doc," I exclaimed, troubled. There was a long, tired sigh on the phone.

"He has to come as soon as possible. His grandmother only has about an hour or two left before-"

My breath hitched in my throat, just as Liam gasped.

"Just tell him that he has to come... it's time to say goodbye," finished the doctor, before muttering something about having work to do and hanging up.

I had to run to catch up with a very worried and angry Liam sprinting towards his car.

"Take me with you," I demanded, huffing, now standing in front of his black automobile. He ignored me and I took that as a yes. I buckled my seat belt on, just as Liam started the engine. He drove.

What terrified me wasn't the fact that he was fuming. It was that behind that cover, I saw a little boy, afraid of losing *everyone* he loved.

16

Thanatophobia

Liam Christopher Black

I felt like I could explode at any moment. My mind was filled with a million questions, but only one was standing out: Why me? *I couldn't lose her.* I just couldn't.

Grandma was and will always be the only person in the entire world who understands me better than anyone. She simply couldn't leave me. I wouldn't allow it.

I couldn't stand the thought of arriving at home and not seeing her smiling face asking me how my day went. If she left me, I would be alone. I was not counting Lena of course.

But she was *Lena.* Ever so unique and so freaking beautiful.

Back to your dying grandmother, Liam.

I had to control myself from completely destroying the gas pedal. I had to get to the hospital as soon as possible. I took deep breaths to calm myself down when the lights turned red. I avoided looking at the brunette observing me from her seat.

After what seemed like a lifetime, I pulled up to the entrance. Taking the keys, I closed the car door and forgot there was a girl with me. Now, all I cared about was being with Grandma.

"Son! Son! No running in the halls!" called a nurse whose name I vaguely remembered: *Cindy.* I paid no attention to her.

Without looking back, I ran and ran through what seemed like a million halls, a never-ending maze. I knew the way to her room by heart. After all, I came here everyday after school. The intensive care ward.

My most hated place.

I halted to stop in front of her door. I couldn't get in. I couldn't see her die before my eyes. But I *had* to.

She was the most important person in my life. My hand shaking, I turned the knob. Instantly, I regretted doing so.

"Grandma! Where are you? Please don't-" came out a voice that resembled mine.

She wasn't there. The bed was empty. And I wanted a hole to dig itself up in the ground and swallow me.

My knees gave out and I fell to the floor. Soon enough, every part of me was shaking. Tears came out of my eyes, without stopping. I was too late.

It's my fault. I should've—no, I could've—I don't know, damn it!

Out of nowhere, a hand rested on my shoulder. I turned to see Dr. Morrison looking at me with concern and pity in his eyes.

"Where is she?" I whispered, barely audible. Doc sadly shook his head, his face looking exhausted.

Voila. There goes the last crumble of hope inside me.

"Son, she's not...We just transferred her to another room, she requested that. She's in her old room. Mrs. Black said she wanted to see you," he softly explained. I shot up, my legs carrying me to room 561.

For the second time today, I hesitated. No, I wouldn't waste time.

Every second, every moment had to be spent with her. She couldn't leave without saying goodbye.

I turned the doorknob, hoping she'd be there. Through my tears, I managed a small, fake smile so she'd see that I was all right.

There she was, lying on the bed, a million wires connected to every part of her body. Trembling like a leaf, as white as a sheet, her cracked lips managed a small smile when she saw me. She looked a hundred years old, every wrinkle on her face visible. Somehow, I didn't see the old, wrinkled lady everyone saw. Darla Black was the most beautiful woman in the world. Her face glowed.

In a flash, I was sitting by her side. Holding her hand as gently as I can, I cried. Her eyebrows furrowed when she saw my tears fall on her hand. She let go, then wiped my cheek with her hand just like every time I cried in the past. That soft, motherly face that would comfort me. I couldn't. How could I live without her?

"L-Liam, my little boy," she whispered, her voice cracking. I stayed silent. I didn't care if in the movies people in a similar situation would hush the dying down because speaking was bad for them. I wanted to remember her voice.

"It's me," I muttered. She patted my hand, before holding it again. I felt like the little 10-year-old boy she'd take care of. The same boy who'd lost his mother, his father, and Serena, his sister.

Her ever so blue, gleaming eyes were smiling at me. "Don't cry, Liam. Everything's going to be all right." She was reading me. I'd inherited my eyes from her. I felt my eyes betray me and they fell mercilessly.

"H-how can you be so sure? You're going to leave me! You're everything I have left," I exclaimed, crying harder. A small, sad smile appeared on her face and I wondered if angels really existed.

"Knock, knock!" she murmured, cheekily winking at me. I let out a chuckle. She was famous for those.

Grandma was one of those special people who immediately enter your heart, without you having time to process what was happening.

"Who's there?" I'd decided to play along.

"I am!" She hoarsely laughed, I joined along. It was difficult to imagine or think that no one would be there anymore to tell those horribly lame, yet strangely funny jokes.

"I'm fine, I'm fine." I didn't know if she was talking to me or to herself. After deep breaths, she looked almost better.

"How's Lena?" she asked, as if we were sitting on the couch, chatting about our day. *Oh, I wish.* Strangely, a blush rose to my cheeks. I lowered my gaze to our hands.

Grandma stared at me with a secret smile. "Fine. You saw her yesterday anyway, Grandma. Say…want to know a secret?"

She nodded. I had a feeling she knew what I was about to say.

"I think I might possibly be in love with her," I confessed. Her smile widened, and her grip tightened.

"Why do you say that?" she questioned, just trying to tease me. This was hard.

"I-I don't exactly know. I think...Honestly, I have absolutely no idea. Well, I do love the way her eyes sparkle when she's happy, the way her hair bounces over her shoulder when she's *'happy dancing.'*" I found myself smiling.

"She has this way of making the simplest of things special, you know? I adore the way her nose twitches when she's sleeping. Her laugh is contagious, it's music to my ears. Seeing her smile makes my day, it's like she stole my heart. In some way, you know? I love it when she sings, even though it's horrible. And when I show her a new song, she pretends to know it so she won't look dumb. I love it when she blushes, especially when I'm the reason. If I continue talking, I think I would never stop, because—I would write a book about her.

"You see, she's like a star. No, she's like a million stars. They are all connected to form the biggest constellation in the sky."

I found myself fully grinning.

"You're sappy." My grandmother genuinely smiled at me. "Does she know?" Grandma asked, her face suddenly serious. I put my head down, ashamed. That seemed enough.

"Liam Christopher Black, promise me you'll tell her, okay? She deserves to know. She also deserves to hear your beautiful voice."

That brought the tears back.

"I promise," I managed to blurt out hoarsely.

Her frail hand lifted my chin up.

"You know what?" she quoted me from earlier.

"What?"

"I think she might possibly be in love with you too," she whispered, winking at me. I smiled.

"How do you know?"

"Oh, I'm sure. She looks at you the same way I looked at George." Her eyes watered, making my eyes verse their emotions out. George Black was my grandfather. He died when I was five.

"I love you, Grandma."

"I love you more, Liam."

We stayed like that, in silence for a couple of minutes. Suddenly, she squeezed my hand. I looked at her. Her skin looked paler, if that was possible. In some way, she looked calm.

"Liam?"

"Yeah?"

"Promise me I'll get buried beside George. I want us to be close. We were never apart, but I want to be beside him, please. I love you, Liam," she pleaded. Fear spread through me.

"I promise."

Darla Black smiled for the last time and closed her eyes.

Her face was frozen, yet peaceful. She looked happy. She looked younger than I've ever seen her. The wrinkles were just a few, here and there. Her gray hair was spread around her head, on the pillow. Her features were impossibly soft. Her long eyelashes were glued to her bottom lid.

But what was most fascinating was that her lips were pulled up in an innocent, delicate smile. I shook my head. Angels would always be angels. Darla Martha Black would always stay in my heart, forever and always.

That's when the beeps went off. Before the nurses could come, I gently placed my lips on her forehead.

"Sleep tight, my angel," I said, before kissing her forehead again. I placed her hand on her chest, before turning and opening the door.

I snuck a last peek at her. I smiled, even though my face was wet with fresh tears.

"I love you, Grandma, I always will. I promise to do everything you said," I whispered, closing the door. I sighed, making the tears fall harder.

"Do you promise to tell me that you can speak, Mr. Black?" exclaimed a very emotional Lena Rose Winter, her hand on her hips, looking the opposite of frightening with tears streaming down her face. Her lips were pulled up in a smile.

I gasped. "I'm really sorry—" I started, before being cut off. Like lightning, she was an inch close to me in less than a second. She held my face with her hands. Tears streamed down her face, a melancholic smile on her beautiful face.

She chuckled a little. "I forgive you, because your angelic grandmother was right." I was confused.

"Yeah, she was right. Because one, your voice is the most amazing and beautiful thing I've ever heard in my life—" stopped Lena, intently gazing at me. I waited, because I was pretty sure there was a number two. I held my breath.

"And?"

I felt my heartbeat quicken and all breath knocked out of my body when she said:

"Because I might possibly be in love with you, too."

She paused for a second, and I can feel time stopping. Everything was still. We were the only people in the world.

"You're not just a star, you're my whole damn sky, you idiot."

It was at that moment that she kissed me. And all I could wonder was how sadness and hope could possibly form love.

17

Wherever You Are

Lena Rose Winter

    Loss was something I was used to my entire life. In fact, it all started when my hamster Gibby died when I was about three years old. Although, every time I lost someone dear to me, it was like salt being added to a fresh wound. Your whole body feels numb and fresh memories crush their heavy weight on a newly broken heart.

    Watching someone lose a loved one is entirely different though. You can see the person crumbling like a dry pastry before your eyes. You can do nothing but stare at them. You itch to comfort them, to convince them that everything was going to be all right. It was easier said than done. You are aware that they are suffering and you want to take all that sadness away from them.

    I currently stood a few feet away from a casket that contained my best friend's deceased grandmother.

I clutched Liam's hand with every piece of power I had. His hand seemed lifeless, yet I never let go.

Mom and Tori were behind me, their heads bowed down in respect. Tori's eyes never left the snow. Liam's neighbor stood by his side, her cheeks wet with tears. A few other people I couldn't recognize stared at the casket with a couple of betraying tears falling.

"Lena, it's your turn," Tori nudged me. I noticed that the priest present with us had been done with his prayers. It was time for me to say the poem Liam had written this morning.

I stepped forward, reluctantly letting go of Liam's hand. I cleared my throat and got the small piece of paper out of my jacket. I held it in the same hand as the white and blue roses.

"Well, uhm, to me, Darla Black was one of the kindest women I'd ever met. She is a happy, caring, and generous soul. She took care of everyone in her life and they will forever be grateful for that."

I looked at Liam over my shoulder; his eyes were glued to the casket.

"This is a poem by Victoria L. Payne that Liam wanted me to read."

"In my Rose Garden of memories
I see you standing there
An angel in disguise
who taught me how to care
I long to hear your voice
for real not in my dreams,"

I paused for a second, letting a tear splatter on the paper.

"I am missing you so much these days
how empty my world seems
People say time heals all wounds
that someday the pain will subside
But Grandma I can tell you
I think they must have lied
The emptiness I am feeling now
is strong and I am weak
These days go by without you
so dreary and so bleak

In my Rose Garden of memories
I know you'll always be
for though you're gone
from this mortal world
in my heart you'll always be"

There was a sudden silence as a cold breeze blew over us, making me feel as if Darla had heard me and she saw how much we loved her.

My legs shook as I walked closer to the casket, my steps making tracks on the snow. I put the flowers on top of the coffin and whispered, "I'll try to take care of him like you did."

I walked to Liam and put my hand in his again. Despite the freezing weather, his hand couldn't possibly be warmer. I refrained from talking to him this whole morning. He avoided my eyes.

The priest and a man beside him looked at us with pity. "It's time for the burial," the man said. I stiffened.

He was giving us a choice on whether to stay and watch, or leave. The burial would take a longer time, since there was snow. The caretakers of the cemetery took care of cleaning the places of snow, but it didn't stop nature from crying frozen tears in places where dead bodies lay.

For the first time that entire morning, I spoke to him, "Liam?"

He nodded.

"I'll stay too."

He squeezed my hand and our eyes met. He pleaded for me to go—he wanted to go through this alone. In a way, I understood. A part of me wanted to stay with him and another comprehended that this was something he wanted to see alone.

"Okay. I'll go."

He nodded in gratitude.

Liam's neighbor shook his hand and there was a mutual understanding between them. The few others—a middle-aged woman and two men—did the same with him. They were gone by now.

Mom blinked at me and headed towards the car. Tori patted his shoulder and walked away. It was a matter of seconds before I had to leave as well.

I positioned myself face to face with him. He looked down at me with a passiveness that made my blood get cooler in my veins.

I wrapped my arms around his waist, catching him off guard. He never responded, he just put his head down to my shoulder for a few moments.

"Come over when it's all over, all right?"

He didn't answer. He hadn't talked to me again since Friday night and it was slightly disappointing. I didn't expect him to talk again, but a small part of me hoped he would.

I put my hands on his shoulders and looked straight into his eyes. They were an empty blue, as if the ocean in them had lost life. There were no waves.

"Everything's going to be okay, I promise."

I half-heartedly believed my own words. I heard them over the years so many times, I couldn't understand if they were true or just lies that are supposed to make you feel better.

But for now, it was all I had to help.

***

12:01

I wondered how easy life would be if we could all transform into animals whenever we wanted. And that spirit was the one that revealed your true form to others.

I wished to be a bird; a dove, precisely. They were simple, tiny, sneaky, and innocent-looking.

The doorbell broke off my concentration and I jumped off my bed in seconds. Tori was soundly sleeping, mumbling something about different kinds of tea. I crept into my mother's room and she was bundled in her covers, soft snores signaling just at what point she was exhausted.

I slowly went down the stairs, took a freshly washed pot from the kitchen and held it in my hand as I looked in the peephole. It was dark, yet the person's head was down. They were slightly swaying.

He raised his arm to bang on the door and I let out a small shriek. I recognized him within seconds, dropped the pot on the ground, and hesitantly opened the door.

"...Liam?"

He looked at me with a crazy gleam in his eyes. The smell of alcohol seemed to have been sprayed on him. His clothes were messy and they were the same he'd worn this morning.

"Liam," I repeated, instantly steadying him. I had to breathe through my mouth to avoid the reek of alcohol.

He gave me a little hysterical laugh. "Lena," he said in the same tone. I was momentarily stunned that he was talking. I led him to a small chair beside the door, but he refused to sit.

"Please sit, Liam."

He shook his head. "No, you're not my mom."

I tried to push down his shoulders to make him sit.

"In fact, my mom can't even tell me what to do, because she's dead!" He chuckled dryly. I tensed and stared at him.

"Neither can my dad…say anything…because his body is underground! He's dead!" His tone rose.

I put my hand on his arm. "Liam, pl—"

He abruptly took his arm away from me.

"And they say that siblings will always be here for you, eh? Mine, where is she, huh? She's DEAD, too! How old was she, Lena? FIVE YEARS OLD!" He was shouting by now.

I stayed frozen.

"And Grandma, she used to tell me what to do." He paused, taking ragged breaths. "But now she can't, you know why, Lena?"

I didn't answer.

"You know why? Do you?"

I shook my head, feeling that it was the right thing to do.

He put his hands on my shoulder and looked at me in the eye.

"She's DEAD TOO!"

I wasn't used to Liam talking just yet, much less to him yelling. I decided to stay calm and silent, just to let him get everything out.

"And why?" he whispered, walking around the living room. His steps made stains on the carpet.

He turned to me and pointed at himself. "Me. It's all my fucking fault! I'm letting them die, Lena! For god's sake, I'm losing everyone around me! I'm an orphan!" he shouted.

Every fiber of me was shaking.

"It's not your fault," I said. "It never was."

He scoffed. "My family died because of my god damned birthday present! I was a selfish brat who couldn't wait for an airplane for his tenth birthday! They got killed in that car crash! It was *my* fault! And then, Grandma came to live with me! And maybe she wouldn't have gotten sick, and maybe she wouldn't have fucking died, Lena!"

He swung his fist into the closest thing to him, which was the old lamp Mom had always refused to get rid of. He grimaced at the blood on his knuckles and looked up at me.

The anger was gone and it was replaced by a look of heartbreak.

"They're all gone," he mumbled, falling to his knees. In a flash, I was by his side.

"None of this was your fault, I promise. It wasn't your fault that a drunk driver crashed into their car. It wasn't yours. It wasn't your fault that your grandma got sick," I kept on repeating.

He let out a sob and covered his face with his hands. "They're all gone," he kept on saying.

My heart broke at the sight of him. I put my arms around him, feeling our bodies vibrate as he cried. We remained like that for a long time. I held a broken soul and watched as he got out of the shell he hid behind.

A small trash can was placed in front of me and I realized that Tori and Mom were awake. Mom leaned against the wall and looked at us with a broken expression.

Tori gave me the trash can and nodded. As if by telepathy, Liam grabbed the trash can and started retching. I breathed through my mouth and Tori turned away.

I rubbed his back as he got every drop of alcohol out of his system. He coughed repeatedly and I grabbed a tissue box. I handed him about five of them and watched as he wiped his mouth.

Mom handed me a bottle of water and he cleaned the puke in his mouth out with it.

I helped him get up and I put him on the red couch I loved to read on. He blinked at me several times. I took his hand.

"It isn't your fault, Liam," I said.

"It is," he replied, his voice barely audible. His cheeks were wet from the tears that were still falling.

I shook my head fervently. "It isn't. Your mom, your dad, Serena, and Grandma Darla are looking down on you right now, guarding you. They will always be in your heart. They wouldn't want to see you like this."

"But they're not here."

"They are." I pressed my palm on the place where his heart should be. "They're right here."

He closed his eyes and opened them with difficulty. "…will you leave me?"

"Never."

He took a deep breath and fell asleep. I turned to my mom and sibling. They looked at me with sadness and pity.

Mom scrunched her nose. "I never really liked that lamp, anyway."

18

Something About December

Lena Rose Winter

Christmas was a time of the year I absolutely adored. The fun was in decorating the tree and making cookies. And of course, my family tradition that broke the rules, sleeping all day and staying up on Christmas Eve, trying to catch Santa and playing games.

Happily enough, we completely forgot about decorating the tree. It was the 21st, the first day after Christmas break. Tori and I went out to buy a medium-sized tree and we rushed home after school.

We started decorating it with little figures: doves, reindeers, elves and a mini fat Santa Claus. We put on traditional music and sang along.

To sum it all up, I felt jolly.

Placing the red ball on one of the tree's branches, I sang my heart out. *"I ought to say no, no, no."*

"Mind if I move in closer?" Tori sang in a fake, deep voice. She came next to me and wiggled her eyebrows at me.

I continued, smiling. *"At least I'm gonna say that I tried."*

Tori furrowed her eyebrows and gave me a pedophilic smile. *"What's the sense in hurting my pride?"*

"I really can't stay." I faked a tear of sadness.

"Ah, baby it's cold outside," we sang together in falsetto.

We burst into laughter and I realized how grateful I was for Tori's entrance in my life. She's the best friend I never had and luckily enough, she's my sister. It felt good to have another teenager with me.

I glanced at the family clock, ticking, *7:40 p.m.* Out of the blue, a question randomly haunted my mind.

"Tori?"

"Yeah?" she answered, eyes glued to adjusting some of the colorful balls.

"Have you ever fallen in love?"

My question took her aback; she turned to face me and froze. Slowly, her cheeks turned a crimson color and she fidgeted with the cookie in her hands.

"Well, there was someone-" she started, but then almost immediately stopped. She lifted her head to face me, her caramel brown eyes brimming with tears.

"Who?" I asked, hoping to get an answer. "Tori? Talk to me."

Her bottom lip quivered and I was terrified, because I've never seen her so sad, so…vulnerable. She shook her head.

"Victoria, speak, please," I begged. She cleared her throat, then vaguely looked at me, as if in another world.

"His name was Daniel; we completed one another. He made me bloody happy and I think I did the same. We met on the first day of...I think you call it preschool...He offered me an apple and I accepted, thinking of it as a friendship offering.

"He was the most beautiful boy I'd ever seen. I have utterly and completely fallen for him. He soon turned into the bad boy of the school, but when we were together, he was the same Daniel I always knew. He made me feel special, beautiful—hell, I felt *wanted.* Until, one day, I-" Her voice was dry, and hoarse. She was hurt and broken, how could I not see that?

I stayed silent, awaiting the continuation. Out of nowhere, fire glazed in her eyes, like a flame that had been recently lightened.

"H-He cheated on me. I found him snogging a freshman in the girls' locker room. I remember that day because I'd just finished football practice and couldn't wait to see him...

***

Victoria Grace Winter

I dried my sweat with a towel, entering the girls' locker room. I was ready to win the match that would lead our team to Regionals. Coach Blogs has faith in me, as do all the other girls. I just hope my mum doesn't mind me being so late, after all, practice finishes at 5 and it's 7 now.

I heard someone panting and stopped in my tracks. No one's supposed to be here, I was pretty sure that I was the last one around.

"Sydney, babe! Are you still here?" I cried out, thinking my best friend might still be here.

No answer.

I walked a little, then regretted it.

There he was.

He had his hands on her waist and she was clutching his hair. He was aggressively making out with her, almost snogging her face off. I recognized her as the freshman that had just joined the team. That was the moment when I understood exactly what heartbreak and anger was. I remembered my English teacher's words, defining fury.

"An emotion so strong, so visible, yet to those who choose to see only what they want to, see only the flash of fire in your eyes, feel only a burn in the deepest depth of your souls, hear only the drop of one tear as it passes past your cheek, these signs catch those who care and they look only into your eyes with the power of ice, calm your soul with just one touch and dry the tear with just one word."

At that moment, I wanted to explode like a time bomb that has no hope of being stopped. But I also wanted to shout until my throat runs dry and mostly, I wanted to cry. I wanted to cry like I've never ever cried before, like I didn't know how to do anything else. My biggest wish was to punch him, but that would prove that I cared.

"Daniel," I breathed, clenching my fists to calm down. He broke off, then his eyes were the size of tennis balls.

"Tori, I-I, this is not what it looks like."

The freshman, Dina, fixed her hair and clothes, her cheeks flushing.

"This is exactly what it looks like, Daniel."

That's when I spat on him and walked away.

***

Lena Rose Winter

When she finished, her cheeks were hot with tears and her features fallen. Her eyes were puffy, because she wouldn't stop sniffling during the whole thing.

Instinctively, I wrapped my arms around her in a tight hug. I stroked her hair, as my shoulder became wet with tears.

"It's his loss," I said, handing her tissues. She blew her nose and smiled.

"Yes, after all, I *am* the great Tori Bear."

We giggled, but she was unaware of the plan forming in my mind. We swayed to the songs and continued decorating the tree while talking about anything BUT her love life, which included the topic of me and Liam.

Click.

Click.

Click.

I heard heels stomping on the stairs, making me turn. My own mother was standing there at the bottom of the steps, wearing a long elegant black gown. Her hair was down in curls and makeup defined her cheeks and eyes.

She was classy and beautiful.

Tori let out a gasp.

"Mother, where are you going dressed like this?"

Just as I blurt that out, the doorbell rang. Tori was the one who moved first and rushed over to open the door which made her trip over the box of garlands.

I followed Tori and saw a man in a fancy suit smiling like an idiot by the door.

An eyebrow rose. "Who are you?"

"Roger. I'm here for Margaret." His words hit me like a cold bucket of water on a December night. I plastered a fake smile on my face.

"Excuse me for a moment, *Mr.-Roger-who-is-here-for-Margaret-aka-my-mom.*" I closed the door. I advanced towards my mom, who shrugged.

"Mother, you have five minutes to explain."

Beads of sweat formed on her forehead.

"Well, I-I, he's my date."

This was the second time I got splashed with icy cold water in December.

"Your date?" Tori was by my side now, equally shocked. There were tear streaks on her cheeks, but she definitely was back to her old self.

I was bewildered.

"Yes, my date," Mom replied, confident now.

"What about Dad? Huh? Did you completely forget about him, Margaret?" Those words came out of Tori's mouth, who was wearing a furious expression on her face.

My mom's face softened. "I would never forget about him, but I need to move on. It's been seven years and Roger's really nice."

"MOM! WHAT'S WRONG WITH YOU?" I shouted, resisting the urge to shake her shoulders. But then I remembered that she was my mother.

"Lena, don't you dare speak to me like that," she calmly answered.

"Why didn't you tell me, at least tell me!" I exclaimed, waving my hands around.

"Tell you what?" Her reply was so infuriating, I think I could've exploded right there. I stroked an invisible beard with my hand, taking deep breaths.

"Oh, I don't know. Maybe that you're cheating on Dad!" The words left my mouth without any thought. Mom's nostrils flared and her face turned red, the same way they would when she's really mad.

"I'M NOT CHEATING ON YOUR FATHER, HE'S DEAD. DEAD, LENA. HE CEASES TO EXIST, I NEED TO GET MY LIFE BACK."

"I THINK THIS IS WHY I'VE ALWAYS PREFERRED DAD. HE AND I WOULDN'T BE HAVING THIS CONVERSATION."

I froze. The words again left my mouth without any thought. I obviously hurt her. In less than a second, her palm collided with my cheek. Tori sucked in a breath.

"Okay, have fun." I shrugged, opening the door for her. I hoped that Roger wouldn't still be here, but *nooo*, he stood there, smiling with pride. It took me all the will in the world not to punch him right there.

I could see the guilt in Mom's eyes. Without saying anything, she hastily left, slamming the door behind her. After a few seconds of pure silence, I grabbed my coat and put my boots on.

"Where are you going?" asked Tori, biting her lip.

"I need fresh air."

She slid her coat on and put on her brown Uggs. She checked her pockets, making sure the keys were in there. She nodded upon hearing the familiar jingling.

"Take me with you." She stopped to look at the tree.

She locked the door and we headed for Liam's house.

I crossed my fingers, hoping that he'd be there. I wanted to talk to him, tell him everything. As always, I knew he'd listen. Over the week, we'd gotten a lot closer. I figured that seeing him would make me feel better anyway.

Right?

19

What Now?

"It's too cold for you here, and now, so let me hold both your hands in the holes of my sweater."

Lena Rose Winter

The cold breeze blew through my hair, as I watched the snow-covered pavement. Tori's and my footsteps crunched in the snow, our pace slow. I had a million thoughts throbbing in my head. I couldn't concentrate, my mind was almost hazy. A thousand questions popped up and infuriatingly, I couldn't find the answer to any of them. A single one stood out, almost like a glowing bird flying through a thick fog.

How could I be such a monster to my own mother?

Strangely enough, I wasn't crying. I only felt confusion, sadness, and utter guilt. The pain throbbing in my chest and the weight on my shoulders were enough to make me feel like hell. I deserved that. At that moment, all the memories flooded back: Dad, Mom, and I, reunited as a big, happy family. All of the birthdays we celebrated together, playing hide and seek, and making each other smile. As childish as that sounds, I missed my daddy.

I was just a little girl who lost her way.

You're wrong. You're not the only one suffering.

I knew that.

All this time, I was concentrating on how I was feeling. Although, I knew Mom was hurting. There were nights when she'd be sure I was sleeping, she'd cry in her room at night. I peeked through the keyhole once and what I saw broke my heart: she was clutching her marriage picture and crying. She'd mumble, "Come back, I miss you."

Those nights were the ones I'd go to sleep with tears on my cheeks.

I never bothered to ask if she was okay and when I did, she'd reply, "I'm fine, just tired."

I'd always mentally agree with her. No, not because of fatigue.

I was simply tired.

Just tired, that's all.

Tired of never being good enough, tired of trying and not getting credit, tired of getting put down, tired of people calling me names, tired of backstabbers, tired of crying, tired of insecurities, tired of being unconfident, tired of being tired.

Still selfish.

I agreed with myself, as weird as that sounds. I should've been compassionate towards Mom. Putting myself in her shoes might've been a good idea.

Imagine having to raise a child, alone. Losing your only love and losing a piece of your soul at the same time.

In a way, Mom needed her own savior, her own Liam. Liam saved me from a dark hole I was trapped in for a long time. He's my Superman. Maybe Roger was Margaret Winter's Batman. What about *Tori*'s hero?

"Tori?" I suddenly asked, feeling déjà-vu.

"Yeah?"

"Did it hurt?"

Her face scrunched up in confusion. She looked quite adorable, almost like a little girl.

"What do you mean?"

"When you saw Daniel with her." I hesitated, fearing that I hurt her. She turned and kicked the snow while walking.

Her hands twitched. "Seeing them together was like having a million arrows clashing through the armor that surrounded my heart. My heart broke like a vase shattering on the floor."

I felt a pang in my chest, because she'd used the same metaphor my dad used to describe heart break.

"I'm really sorry, Victoria," I said gently. The wind blew through tendrils of her hair, as she pursed her lips.

"I loved him," she whispered and something about her voice shook as she said those words.

"Are you sure?" I tucked a strand of my wild hair behind my ear.

"No, I'm not. I don't think I'll ever be able to let go."

At that moment, it was to my complete wonder, as my nineteen-year-old sister resembled a tiny girl, who lost her teddy bear.

"Your superhero will come; I'll make sure of it," I mentally promised.

A comfortable silence set in, as we both had busy thoughts. Her, about Daniel; I, about her.

How could a beautiful, angelic person like Tori have so much pain bottled up inside?

Everything was possible. Right now, I had to distract Tori from a horrible demon; her own memories.

"Was I being a bitch to Mom?" I blurted out.

There was a long, pregnant silence. I feared her answer. Even if I knew that Tori would always support me, the truth had to be told. And I wanted to hear it from someone I trusted, someone who would never lie to me.

"Maybe."

I let out a long sigh. "I know."

"I'm sorry, babe." Tori squeezed my shoulder soothingly.

"I'm fine."

It was her turn to say, "I know."

An alarm siren suddenly rang in my head, panic flooding all over me.

Oh, no.

"Tori?" I said, urgently. I tugged on the ends of my jacket nervously.

"Yes?"

"I think we're lost," I admitted shyly.

"Are you serious?" she exclaimed, stopping me and holding my shoulders. Her eyes widened and her mouth was wide open, forming a perfect *O*.

"Yes."

Tori clutched her stomach and started laughing. Her giggles were very contagious, so I joined along. After about five minutes of laughing our bums off, I steadied myself. The light in her eyes returned, and I mentally cheered.

"In what way, exactly, do you find this funny?" I demanded, smiling.

Tori grinned like a Cheshire cat. "Because I knew, I realized that a long time ago."

Her answer took me by surprise.

"You little peanut!"

She smiled and childishly winked at me. My shoulders slumped as I remembered our dilemma.

"But how are we getting back?" I whined. Tori waved her cell phone at me.

"You know how I've been looking at my phone a lot?"

I enthusiastically nodded, resembling a puppy. I've always taken a liking to puppies.

"Well...Your smart, amazing sister was using a GPS this whole time," she declared, her chin up high. I jumped on her to engulf her in a huge hug.

"Anyway, where are we supposed to go now?" I asked, staring at her. In a way, I was grateful.

That girl was like a puzzle that completes me. If it wasn't for her, I would've never enjoyed the perks of having a best friend, knowing how it feels like to have someone behind your back, always there to support you and be by your side.

Her dark eyebrows furrowed in deep thought and then she eyed me with a confused look etched on her features.

"Well, we're on Maple Avenue, so we should turn left and the house would be there! I guess we weren't that lost after all!"

My heart's pace quickened, as I ran a hand through my hair, in hopes of detangling it. I took a peek at my clothing and felt a grimace form on my face. My old, gray sweatpants managed to look presentable, but my baggy, pink, t-shirt made me similar to a homeless teenager.

Liam doesn't mind.

I smiled a little and nodded. He would be the last person in the world to judge me. I ran a hand through my hair, hoping to tame its nest but failed miserably.

Our footsteps softly crunched on the snow, as my heart's pace quickened. Normally, I wouldn't be in this state after not seeing a person for a week, but this was Liam. He was different, so unique in every single way. His eyes sparkle mischievously whenever he's planning something, or the way his features are defined, perfectly and indescribably making me drool, interiorly of course. The most extraordinary thing about him is the pair of blue eyes he had. They read me, almost like an open book.

After the incident a week ago, he chose to lie low at school. He never talked to me more than a few sentences, but it was enough. There was a mutual feeling of comprehension between us. He held my hand from time to time and I knew he was still suffering over having an empty house.

"Lena?" questioned Tori, waving her hand in front of my face. I realized that I spaced out, blankly staring at the snow.

"Huh, sorry."

"Is that Liam's house?"

She nudged my shoulder, pointing to a small, modest house.

Looking at the house hit me hard in the chest, because I could smell the cookies Darla used to make. There were so many memories in that house, and it was hard to imagine that one of its guardians were gone.

I gave Tori the address a long time ago, so she can know where to contact me if I'm late, which never happened.

I noticed a blue, impressive Jeep parked beside Liam's car.

Whose car was this? I thought, trying to recall any of the neighbors' car colors. Maybe one of them had come to check up on Liam.

I nodded in confirmation, as my palms became suddenly sweaty. Tori took my hand and ran towards Liam's abode. I struggled to keep up with her; after all, I'd never exactly been the sporty one in the family. My sister, on the other hand, was a soccer freak.

She knocked on the door three times, not even slightly, breathing out of the ordinary.

While I was panting. I wasn't sure if it was because I was tired, or because I was about to see Liam.

No answer.

Tori's eyes were fiery now, underneath the slightly frozen eyelashes. She tried again, this time a bit harshly.

Still no answer.

My sister was flaming with anger now.

Her palms and fists violently pounded on the door, as her face was red.

"LIAM, OPEN THE DOOR, OR SO HELP ME I'LL-"

She was cut off by the door opening. I expected to meet a drowsy, sleepy Liam, but instead, I was greeted by a slightly lighter shade of Liam's eyes.

Tori and I sucked in a breath at the same time. I gulped.

The guy standing in front of us was a bombshell. His dark golden hair was tousled, as if perfectly messed up to look this way. A few tendrils fell into his beautiful, striking eyes.

Oh, his eyes.

They reminded me of a Caribbean ocean on a perfectly sunny day. Something about him was familiar. Full, beautiful lips, just yearning to be kissed, playfully smirked at Tori and me.

He had a mischievous look that often was present in bad boys. He was quite well built, his white plain shirt showed his toned abs. Baggy sweat pants showed that he was comfortable and I felt like an intruder.

What if this was the wrong house?

"Liam, Lena, *Liam,"* I desperately reminded myself.

I opened my mouth to say something, but my throat was completely dry.

"Ey, Liam, you never told me you had such beautiful lady friends," his defined jaw line moved and I realized he was shouting. Captivating voice, too. A dazzling smile never left his lips. A strong accent dripped in his words.

"Australian," I thought.

Wait, what? Did he just say Liam?

Liam himself appeared at the doorway, scratching the back of his neck nervously and tiredly. He looked handsome and somewhat a younger version of the magnificent stranger.

"These are Lena and Tori, my friends," said Liam, his lips barely moving. Tori's expression was still agape and I nudged her. She recovered and blinked several times.

The stranger chuckled and then offered us his hand.

I shook his hand, as electricity buzzed.

"Oh, so this is the famous Lena?"

I felt weak at the knees. I stayed silent, as if any word would even come out of my mouth.

He did the same to Tori, who appeared dumbfounded, star struck. Her eyes twinkled in a way I'd never seen before.

"Hello, I'm Adam Damien Black, Liam's cousin."

I think that's when he winked at me.

20

Estranged Blood

"I'm not the comeback girl, the awkward girl, the hipster girl, or the popular girl. I don't want a label unless it's your *girl."*

Liam Christopher Black

It took me a few seconds to process what exactly was happening. My messy state didn't deprive me from seeing Lena literally devouring him with her eyes. I felt my blood boil. That idiot even had the nerve to wink at her!

Liam, man the fuck up, she told you she loved you. Have some confidence in yourself for her sake, you egghead.

I mentally agreed with my mind, if that made any sense. It suddenly clicked in my mind, how Tori was acting so normal about me talking?

Lena told her, duh.

Ah, sometimes I hated my sassy side.

Trust me, the feeling's mutual.

"Hey, Lena?"

My voice seemed to snap her back to reality and I saw that sparkle in her eyes. I felt my heart beat a little faster.

"Yeah?"

I shot her a small, sheepish smile. Her eyes met mine and all confidence lost was found. Those chestnut orbs shared my secrets, they were like a beautiful garden full of roses.

"Hi."

She giggled and shared a look with Tori. Although I knew that I made her feel happy and that was enough for me. Her cheeks flushed with an adorable shade of rose, but I figured that shyness wasn't the main reason for them.

Before I could ask the ladies to come in, to warm up from this freezing weather, someone pinched my cheeks.

"Aw, well isn't this adowable! Wittle Wiam has a girlfriend!" Annabelle exclaimed loudly, just as I gasped in pain. She wrapped her arms around me, almost choking me to death. She looked like a koala hugging a unicorn.

I rubbed my cheeks in frustration and embarrassment. Lena coughed.

Meeting her eyes, I let out a small gasp, this time in bewilderment. The amount of shock in her expression was like a pang in my chest. I realized what her thoughts wandered by; why would a *girl* be at my house?

For a split second, I looked at Belle. Her long, sandy hair was almost pin straight, falling down her waist. Her wide blue eyes seem frozen in that *puppy dog face*. Her pink lips were pulled into a wide grin. Her skin glowed. She had an incredible beauty; that was undeniable. Her petite frame added to her fairy-like features. It was hard to believe that she was related to Adam in any way.

Belle let go of me and smiled broadly in Lena's direction, offering her hand for a shake.

"Hello there, I'm Annabelle Black. Adam's twin sis and Liam's cousin! Call me Belle," her cheery and Australian tone rang in our ears. Lena's features immediately softened and her confused expression now flooded with kindness and friendliness.

"Ah, these boys! Never the gentleman type. Come in, girls, you must be freezing! The weather here is bloody horrible." Belle ushered the Winter girls to come in, as Adam and I both received a smack on the head.

"Oi! That hurt!" cried out Adam.

I glared at my cousin's back, hoping to burn a hole in her hair. I took a glance at Adam, but he was too busy drooling over Tori.

We all awkwardly sat on the couch, the Blacks next to each other and the Winters by each other's side. We almost resembled those clans in *Twilight*.

The tension thickened and you could almost cut through it with a knife. Thankfully, Tori broke the unwanted silence.

"So, Adam and Belle, what brings you guys to America?"

Two heads snapped up and smiled at each other sadly. Belle eyed me.

"Well, it's that, ever since Grandma died, we figured that no one could take care of Liam-"

"I'm eighteen, not a kid!" I protested; the way she talked about me made me feel like a baby.

"-and since Adam and I are 20, it would look less fishy than Liam staying here alone. Mum's upstairs, sleeping. Jet lag is shit."

I earned a glare from Belle.

"Well, that's awesome. We do need some friends around here," said Tori with a secret smile, her eyes glued on Adam. Lena and I shared a look and agreed to set these two up.

"What about a truth or dare game?" Adam suddenly blurted out, a familiar glint of mischief in his eyes. Belle grinned and then stood up.

"I'll go get the hot chocolate and marshmallows," she exclaimed, heading to the kitchen. Adam stood up as well and ushered for the girls to go in the basement. I followed and was once again proud of having decorated that part of the house.

The electric fireplace had a certain antique look about it. The hardwood floor was the perfect type to slide and dance on with your favorite socks. There were three creamy colored love seats, although they resembled a pet bed, but in a bigger size. The lighting was soothing, giving the room that final homely, comfortable touch. I smiled with pride.

Lena and Tori's eyes widened and they turned to look at me, their eyes asking: "Did you do this?" I felt a small blush rise in my cheeks and shyly nodded.

They plopped themselves on one of the love seats and talked in hushed voices. Meanwhile, Adam sat on the opposite one and I raced back to the kitchen to see what was taking Belle so long.

I found her humming *"I Got a Feeling,"* while putting marshmallows in five mugs filled with hot chocolate.

I leaned against the counter, a million thoughts running in my head. Silence seemed to be quite comforting at the moment.

"Oh hey, Liam," she acknowledged me. "You really like her, don't you?" asked Belle softly, smiling.

I nodded.

"Are you two together yet?"

How I wish.

I shook my head.

Belle nodded, as if expecting this answer. She placed the mugs on a tray, then bored her eyes into mine.

"You never know how much time you have." Her steps echoed in my ears.

"Liam, get your bum here! We're about to start!" Adam's booming voice pulled me away from my thoughts.

I ran to the basement and my heart beat quickened when I saw Lena sitting alone on one of the love seats. Tori was beside Adam and Belle chose to be alone. Lena patted the space next to her and I sat there. We weren't *that* close, each one on the opposite sides of the love seat.

"Liam, truth or dare?" asked Belle, smirking amusingly. Her brother copied her.

Smirking + Belle or Adam + Truth or Dare = Uh, oh.

"Um, truth," I answered almost immediately. Their truth questions could be bearable, but the dares were absolutely frightening.

When I was nine, I visited them in Australia. Truth or Dare was played. I was foolish enough to say **dare** and that caused their neighbor to slap me for asking her if *"her muffin was buttered and if she wanted anyone to butter it for her."*

"Okay, can you remember the very first time you fell in love and with whom?"

The hot chocolate in my hands was suddenly very interesting.

"Yes, I remember my first love." I hoped that this answer would satisfy Belle's question.

"*Who* did you fall in love with, Liam?" asked my cousin, a certain impatience and amusement in her tone. I could feel Lena's eyes burning in me.

"Lena."

The room was so silent, a pin could drop. Lena wrapped her arms around me and there they stayed.

"Aw," cooed Belle, Tori and Adam at the same time.

The awkwardness was broken and the game continued. No one chose dare, we all feared one another. The questions were funky and funny.

We'd all discovered weird facts about each other: Adam had his first kiss at five, Tori had an obsession with bears, Lena's most embarrassing moment was when she wet her pants when the teacher asked her to sing a song in kindergarten, Adam had a fetish for girls who like noodles and Lena's first crush was some kid named Parker in kindergarten.

"Tori, truth or dare?" asked Belle, the devil of all. Tori's eyes lightened with mischief.

"Dare."

Oh god.

We all held our breaths until Belle blurted out the demand or dare.

"Kiss the hottest guy in this room."

Tori's eyes immediately flickered and lingered on Adam. He smiled, perfectly portraying the "bad boy who gets all girls" image.

I could see Lena intensely eyeing both of them. She looked concentrated and worried. Her eyebrows were furrowed and she looked absolutely adorable.

Victoria leaned in, slowly anticipating the moment. Adam's eyes were glued on her lips. The chemistry between them was literally glowing.

Just as their lips were about to collide, "Can't Hold Us" blasted from Adam's phone. Flustered and frustrated, he looked at the caller and his face darkened. Tori fumbled to keep her breathing steady, I could see. Belle's expression darkened the same way Adam's did. She seemed to read her brother with ease.

"Hello?" Adam answered, appearing a bit nervous. "Um, hey babe."

Tori raised her eyebrow at the nickname.

"Oh, nothing special, just hanging with Liam."

"I miss you more, Kylie." Although, the words seemed to get caught in his throat. "Listen, um, I've got to go, love. I-I love you too."

The phone call ended, leaving everyone confused, anxious or afraid to say one word.

"Who was that?" Tori tried to ask that without displaying her obvious curiosity. Adam preferred to stay silent for a couple of seconds, then he and his sister talked at the same time.

"That's Kylie."

"His girlfriend."

Belle earned a death glare from Adam. Tori's face fell, sadness clouding in her eyes.

"What time is it, Liam?" asked Lena, fury making her voice tremble. I took a peek at my watch.

"11:00."

"Tori and I need to get back, Mom's going to kill us!" she exclaimed, and I was uncertain if she just wanted an excuse to leave or if her words were truthful.

"Absolutely not, you two aren't walking back home. The snowstorm outside will turn you into human ice cubes. Sleep over. We don't mind, right, Liam?" Adam said in a strict voice. I nodded in agreement.

Tori didn't seem to like this. "No," she disagreed.

"Yes."

"No."

"Yes."

"Absolutely not."

"Yes."

"Yes."

"No."

Tori smirked in success as Adam groaned. She got up, brushed invisible wrinkles off her outfit and looked at Lena expectantly.

"Come on, let's go."

Adam grabbed her wrist, making her swiftly direct her eyes to him.

"Stay," he said, a pleading expression in his eyes.

"No." Tori's expression softened a little.

"Please stay," Adam begged.

Tori gave up and eyed Lena. "Do you want to stay?"

Please, stay here.

Lena shyly nodded her head, burying her face in my chest. I just hoped she couldn't hear how loud my heart was beating. Tori sighed and called Mrs. Winter, informing her that they're sleeping here.

"Well, she's grounding both of us for Christmas and the week after that, but it's okay." She shrugged. Adam fist-pumped in success.

"Belle, hand me the covers to your right, will you?" asked Lena. She took the covers and set them on us.

Adam made himself comfortable on one of the love seats. Tori raised an eyebrow sassily.

"What do you think you're doing?" she demanded, both hands on her hips.

"Sleeping, duh?"

"Go sleep in your rooms, boys."

After a lot of fighting and begging, us boys grumbled our way to the room we shared.

I slipped into bed, the lights still on. I heard Adam do the same as we both had busy minds. Me, thinking about Lena. Him, thinking about the other Winter girl.

"Adam?"

"Yeah?"

"We're going to sneak back there, right?"

"Absolutely."

After an hour or two, Adam got up and ushered for me to follow him. I happily obliged. We had to be careful, because the wood would creak at any touch. Tiptoeing was the ideal choice.

The basement might've as well been the coziest-looking place. The creaking of the fire was the only sound heard. Belle was snuggling and slightly snoring in the love seat. Tori was curled up in a ball, peace reigning over her. The person who made my breath catch in my throat was Lena.

Eyelids closed against the dim light of the room and her breathing deep and relaxed, all the muscles in her face and body were totally at peace, like a baby in its first throes of slumber. She twitched her nose, just like the time she slept on my shoulder at the park when we first met. Innocence showed onher sleeping face, the peaceful and serene dreams blocking out the dangers of the outside. Her soft breathing, making the world seemingly standing still.

I slowly lay beside her and pulled the covers on us. I wrapped my arms around her and I felt complete. She fit exactly in my arms.

"Beautiful," I whispered in her ear.

I immediately froze when her thick eyelashes fluttered to reveal sleepy chestnut brown eyes.

"Hey there," her voice sounded angel-like, her sleepy state coaxing it. She snuggled up closer to me.

"Hey, beautiful."

Pink lips pulled up in a small smile and I saw adoration in her eyes. I closed my own eyes, resting my chin over her head, but sleep seemed to be impossible.

"Liam?"

"Hm?"

"What are we?"

Her question caught me by surprise. I opened my eyes and looked at her. Her expression displayed curiosity. Her olive skin was struck by the light and she resembled a Disney princess. The question: *Was I the prince?*

"I don't know."

I felt her head nod a little.

"Liam?"

"Yeah, Lena?"

"Why do you love me?"

"The answer to that would be as long as a Stephenie Meyer typical novel. But you know what? What have I got to lose? I love how you light up at the sight of ice cream. You care about everything, even the little things. Your eyes always display the emotion you're feeling and I love that about you.

"Your kindness couldn't be measured and you're the sweetest person I've ever known. You're beautiful. I love how you criticize your quirks because you don't see how unique and gorgeous they make you. You read through me like a book and you know exactly what I feel. You know how to make me happy and how to cheer me up. I love how you prefer spending the day in sweats and a baggy shirt than skinny jeans and a fancy shirt.

"Everything you do just shines and you're adorable in every single way. You're sensible and when you cry, I just want to wipe your tears away because you're worth it. You-"

I was cut off by a drowsy Lena kissing me softly. She broke off the kiss and smiled at me. A small chuckle escaped her mouth.

"Shut up, Liam. I love you too."

Soon enough the only movement was the slow rising and falling of her chest, each intake of air, showing the depth of her oblivion. She was totally at peace, at rest. I was truly happy.

My eyes flickered to Adam and Tori and I smiled.

He chose to sleep on the opposite side of the love seat and she was on the other one. He didn't want to get in the way of Tori's wrath if they wake up in each other's arms. Although, their hands slightly touched one another. They both had small unconscious smiles on their faces. They reminded me of Tonks and Lupin, when they died only slightly brushing each other's hand.

Of course, Tori and Adam weren't dead.

Everything was perfect, just perfect.

I closed my eyes and fell into the deepest sleep I'd ever had in a long time. I knew that my heart felt peaceful and truly happy for the first time in years.

21

You are Wanted

"The moment you start being in love with what you're doing, and thinking it's beautiful or rich, then you're in danger."
~Miuccia Prada~

Lena Rose Winter

The warmth of Liam made me feel like I was a small baby being cradled in a beautiful human's arms. Safety reigned over me and I couldn't feel more comfortable. I fit perfectly in his arms. I couldn't dare open an eye because I just wanted to cherish this moment. Even though this felt like heaven, there was a slight, tiny problem.

I needed to pee.

The urge of my bladder obviously couldn't wait and I cursed myself for not taking a trip to the bathroom before. *But a woman has to do what has to be done, am I right?*

So, I gently took Liam's arms and placed them by his sides. His calm, peaceful demeanor suddenly grew duller. I regretted doing what I'd done, but I had to pee. I didn't think Liam would like it very much if he woke up the next morning with a wet girl in his arms.

I bet he'd like that very much.

Shut up, dirty-minded me.

A small smile appeared on my face as I saw Adam literally resting his chin on Tori's head. Weird, because last time I saw them, they were barely grazing each other's hands.

I had a feeling that even though Adam had a girlfriend, Tori was the one for him. They were exactly the same.

Sometimes I wonder why I'm so dumb.

Will you shut your pie-hole please?

Meanwhile, Annabelle Black was cuddling up with one of the pillows. I bit my lip from laughing because she looked so innocent. My instincts told me that if I tried to snatch that small pillow away from her, she'd ninja attack me and Jackie Chan would be jealous.

Honestly, I already loved Belle. She was a new addition to my life, as was Adam, but she had this aura about her that was so kind, yet badass. She seemed like the kind of the girl who'd gladly listen to your problems and would be up to prank Barack Obama.

As I had to pass by Bella's love seat to go upstairs, I patted her head, making her snuggle closer to her pillow. Suddenly, I saw something that made me freeze in my tracks.

Tear streaks.

Her cheeks were damp, puffy, and completely red. Her lips were slightly trembling and I figured she was having a bad dream.

"No, daddy, don't leave, please!" she murmured repeatedly, tears falling from her closed eyelids. Just as I made a mental note to investigate this later, her murmur changed, shocking me.

"Leo, please. I love you; don't let me go, please." The way she'd said this contained so much pain, it hurt me.

Ah, I should've known. There was *always* a certain boy involved in every girl's story.

I pulled up the covers on her more and decided to let her be with her nightmare. I wished I could do anything about it, but dreams, especially horrible nightmares, are impossible to deal with.

Crossing my arms helped redeem the warmth. I slowly tiptoed my way back upstairs. Now, the dilemma was: Where was the bathroom?

I traveled my way around the house, almost jumping up and down. I had to piss. It was crucial at this point of my life.

Crossing my fingers and hoping to die, I reluctantly turned the doorknob of a random room. At the sight of an oven, a refrigerator and a dishwasher, I came to a realization that I was in the kitchen. Although I peeked a little, I couldn't see the source of the voice suddenly startling me.

"Belle? Is that you, honey?" asked a motherly voice sounding American. I fully opened the door only to meet a pair of bewildered blue eyes. The stranger took an antique vase from the small dining table and held it up, prepared to break my skull with it.

"Who are you?" she demanded with a fiery glint in her eyes that I recognized in Belle's orbs. I held my hands up like a deer caught in headlights.

"I'm Lena Rose Winter, Liam's girlfr-I mean friend. My older sister and I are slumbering in the basement because the weather outside is freezing and we could get hypothermia."

Face palm. What a great first impression on this woman.

Surprisingly, the woman, a complete stranger who seemed abnormally familiar, started laughing. And she wouldn't stop. She placed the vase on the table and clutched her stomach, laughing. I chuckled nervously, not knowing what to do.

After about five minutes of her laughing her bum off and me standing there, being awkward, the lady regained her composure.

Sort of.

She was biting her lip, forcing her laughter to die down.

"Excuse me, I'm being terribly impolite! It's just that you're so cute and I've never met someone so downright awkward. I already love you though. I'm Catherine Black, Liam's aunt and the twins' mother."

I shook her offered hand, smiling. *I should've known!* The resemblance was simply uncanny. Belle's sandy hair pulled in a messy ponytail and Adam's striking eyes and cheekbones. For an adult, she was simply beautiful.

"Um, may I ask you an embarrassing question?" I questioned shyly, after she'd finished talking about how Liam had never said *we* had guests.

"Sure, sweetie. Is it about how to ask Liam out? Because just the way you stuttered saying his name shows how in love you are with him."

My eyes widened and my eyebrows rose. What kind of question was that?

My cheeks flamed because Catherine Black had asked that question so bluntly, as if she'd known me all my life. "Uh, um, uh, no. Actually, I-I, where's your bathroom, Mrs. Black?"

"Oh, sweetie, call me Catherine. The bathroom is opposite Liam's room. Third door after the kitchen, on the right," she said, winking at me. I liked this woman already. I knew for a fact that if she and my mom met, they'd instantly become friends.

"Thank you, Mrs. Bla- I mean Catherine." I flashed her one last smile and headed for heaven—the bathroom.

Counting the third door, I found a room with a lousy LIAM written in permanent marker. I smiled a little, imagining a tiny Liam writing this on his door. But what was truly funny was imagining his older face as he miserably tried to remove it.

Ah, that boy.

I rushed into the bathroom and satisfied my needs, loudly sighing. The soft beige ceramic was elegant. I was done quickly and washed my hands. Unfortunately, I looked in the mirror. Let me just say, zombies would be jealous of me right now. My hair was everywhere, my eyes were puffy and my complexion was dull and tired. I smiled, though, thinking about the last words I heard before going to sleep.

Liam's words were like the whisper of an angel. This was the longest he'd ever spoken to me since the drunken night. I unconsciously touched my lips and my heart fluttered remembering our kiss. That boy just made me weak and happy.

A little mischief was in my thoughts, so I entered Liam's room. I hoped he wouldn't mind, though. No one said anything about him finding out, *right?*

On the contrary of what a typical teenager's room would seem like, Liam's was impeccably organized.

Two beds were made, the pillows neatly placed. His desk was clean, not a speck of dust on it. His laptop was closed and there were a couple of books lying lazily on the desk. I grazed my fingers over them, scanning the titles: *The Host, The Notebook* and *The Fault in Our Stars*. I smiled, because these were his favorite books and it wasn't going to be his first time reading them.

What caught my attention was his sketchpad, the same one he had when I met him at the park. My hands itched to look through it, but that would be intruding his privacy. Curiosity won over me and opened the first page. I slightly gasped at what I saw.

A family happily enjoying a picnic. Strawberries, sandwiches, along with several other food elements were on the checkered blanket. The father was laughing, his features soft and smooth. The mother was braiding her daughter's hair, to look the same as hers. She had an absent smile on her face, as if she was the happiest person in the world. The little girl had long hair. Her expression displayed pure innocence and happiness. The last character in the picture was a young boy, 10 years old or so, he was smiling while looking at his parents with a loving expression. My heart broke as I recognized the features.

The boy was Liam.

At the bottom of the page, Liam quoted Melanie Stryder, the main character from **The Host**. *You never know how much time you'll have,* was scribbled in a perfect handwriting.

I turned the pages, most of them portraying the little girl, the father, the mother, and sometimes it was a family drawing. Some were tear-stained. He always puts quotes instead of signing his name. Some were of him or his grandmother.

I fell upon the first drawing of me, a girl with curls, hiding her face between her knees. My heart ached at this one, because he had put a small heart. The next ones were mostly of me. One of me smiling widely, another of us cuddling, one of us dancing, the one that made me laugh was the one where we made snow angels.

The last one literally tore my heart apart. Grandma Black was sitting on a couch, knitting. Her expression was relaxed and peaceful. She smiled happily, the familiar wrinkles around her eyes showing. He portrayed every detail so perfectly, I wanted to break down.

This page was completely dry and slightly crumpled, the way paper reacted with water. Not water, **tears**.

This is how he wanted to remember her.

I felt myself tracing the quote he'd written.

"Oh heart, if one should say to you that the soul perishes like the body, answer that the flower withers, but the seed remains." Kahlil Gibran

Out of nowhere, a pair of arms wrapped themselves around me. Just as I was about to scream, a hand clasped itself upon my mouth. I turned to see Liam. He was smiling with grief, his eyes tearful. He didn't even look slightly offended that I'd invaded his privacy.

His eyes were glued on the drawing. "Isn't she lovely?" he murmured.

"Liam?" I asked, slightly nervous and heavy hearted.

"Yeah?" He averted his eyes to me, blinking rapidly. He didn't want me to see him cry.

I did the unexpected; I placed my lips on his. He tasted like tears and hot chocolate. The kiss wasn't rough; it was just gentle, sweet, and passionate. He was in such pain, I could literally feel it. An explosion of total peace and serenity overwhelmed us both. The true meaning of life, love, and utter relief of having each other, hoping this night would never end. Knowing that for both of us, this was the perfect chance to prove our melancholic love, so strong, so deep, and yet so sad to never want to let go, to the sadness of life.

He finally broke off the kiss, and bored his eyes into mine. His pupils dilated and his blue orbs were gleaming with fresh tears.

So, I did what I had to do.

I took him in my arms and let him cry there. My shirt got wet as he sobbed, letting everything out. I tightened my grip on him, knowing that doing that always made me feel better when I was crying.

Because before my eyes, I did not see a man. There stood a broken boy who'd lost his father, mother, sister, and grandmother. In the process, almost losing himself.

Was he worth it?

Was he worth saving?

Was he worth loving?

Absolutely.

Here I was, holding the most beautiful human in the world, who was emptying his heavy heart of gold.

22

Mi Madre

"All that I am, or hope to be, I owe to my angel mother."
~Abraham Lincoln~

Lena Rose Winter

Guilt was like a Pac-Man—it ate up every piece of emotion inside of you until you apologized to the person you caused pain to. The longer you deny feeling bad about what you did, the longer you overthink every single word you said.

"Mom?" I said, sitting beside her on the couch. We had two hours before the dinner and there was a relaxed moment in the house.

She looked up from her tea and looked at me. There was a dull look in her hazel eyes.

"I wanted to talk to you," I said. She nodded.

I sighed, and clutched the cup of green tea in my hands tighter. "I'm sorry." She didn't answer, so I kept on talking. "I was being selfish and bratty."

She rose her eyebrows at that, as if it was an understatement.

"I know you have to start seeing others now. I just never imagined you without Dad." I paused for a second, the sound of that name on my lips making me shiver. "I want to see you happy. I over exaggerated this whole thing and I'm really sorry about it."

"I need you to be okay with all this," she said.

I nodded fervently. "I am. I want to see you happy and since Dad wants to see you happy too, you should really call that Roger guy again."

She ushered for me to come closer and I put myself into a one-armed embrace.

I immediately felt like a kid again. It was bizarre to feel like this, but Mom's hugs always made me feel better about whatever was happening at the moment. She was safety for me.

"I love you, mom."

She chuckled softly. "I know."

I let out a small, mocking gasp.

"No I love you too? What is this, a one-sided love?"

She laughed, and mumbled, "Yeah, yeah. Love you too."

"That's better," I said.

"Speaking of apologies and making amends, guess who called me today?"

I furrowed my eyebrows together. "Who?"

"Stacy Hennings."

I let out a laugh.

"What did she want?"

Mom smiled at my reaction. "She wants to come over today and apologize."

I grimaced. "And what did you say, Mother?"

"She'll be here in about ten minutes."

I gasped. "Mom! I don't want to see her!"

"Too bad, you two need to have a clean slate."

I groaned. "You seriously want us to be friends again? After everything she did?"

"Of course not." Mom shook her head and took a sip of her tea calmly. "I just don't want you to have any enemies or whatever at school."

She was right, she knew it, and she made sure I knew it too. "Fine," I grumbled.

Mom stood up to put the empty cup into the kitchen. "I wasn't asking for permission." She winked.

A few minutes later, the doorbell rang and I had to drag myself over to open it. Stacy stood there, dressed in simple clothes. She had a blank look on her face. I nodded.

"Stacy."

She gave me a small, hesitant smile. "Can I come in?"

"No," I said. "I'm sorry."

Her smile fell, but she nodded in understanding. "I wanted to apologize."

"For what?" I let out an unladylike snort. "Insulting me repeatedly, or spilling drinks down my back, or insulting people I care about?"

"Everything," she said. "I'm sorry for everything."

I shrugged. "I don't know if I can believe you."

"Please, do. Every second of every day these days, I keep on thinking about how horrible I was with you. I am disgusted with myself, and I swear, I am sincere." Tears shone in her eyes, but head held high, she refused to let them fall. "Please, forgive me."

I sighed, feeling a bit of pity for her, "Fine." Her face lit up.

"But this doesn't mean that we're friends," I said, remembering Mom's words, "just that we have a clean slate."

She eagerly nodded. "Thank you." A few stray golden hairs betrayed her messy bun and she put them back in place with a leather gloved hand. She extended the same hand to me.

I shook it and gave her a semi-passable smile. A honk interrupted the moment and she widened her eyes.

"Mom's being cranky." She chuckled. "I better go."

I gave her a small nod, feeling a small weight get off my chest.

"Thank you, again," she said. I didn't answer.

She walked away and I closed the door.

"Mom, come out! I know you were spying!" I called out, laughing as Mom appeared from behind the couch, a look of shame on her face.

I shook my head at her. "You're too old for spying on people, Mother!"

Her eyes got wide and she looked at me with shock and disbelief. "Did you just call me old?" I shrugged, grinning in amusement. "Young lady, you are officially forbidden from saying the word old at home."

It was my turn to wink at her. "I wasn't asking for permission to say it."

23

Princess to the Rescue

"Should you fight for someone who may not even want you to fight for them? Or may not even give you the chance to."
~Anonymous~

Liam Christopher Black

"Liam! Come on, we're going to be late! Stop checking yourself out, that's Lena's job," said Adam, popping his head in the room. I chuckled and grabbed my favorite watch.

That boy was the best cousin in the world, even though he could easily get on my nerves. He was a prankster, but a good guy at heart. And I found out that he liked Tori but he had to deal with Kylie first. He wanted to think properly, to prevent doing any rash actions.

My thoughts drifted away a little and I hoped tonight would go well. Catherine and Mrs. Winter met this morning and instantly became the other version of SpongeBob and Patrick.

Catherine insisted on inviting everyone on a night out, at one of the most chic restaurants in town: *Rio Bello's*. Lena kissed my cheek and her mom was raging at her because she wouldn't let go of my hug.

Ah, that girl.

I raced downstairs and found Catherine stuffing a lipstick, a pair of tissues, and her cell phone into her red purse. She looked great, wearing a knee length red dress. She smiled upon seeing me and cupped my face with her hands.

"Your parents would be so proud of you!"

My smile slightly faltered and I nodded softly. Catherine seemed oblivious to my reaction and called Belle down. Adam was already in the car, as he was the one driving us.

Belle was stunning, wearing a white skirt, a black shirt with BAD written across it and a blue leather jacket. It was very...Belle. I ruffled her hair playfully, and she stuck her tongue out at me.

Catherine locked the door as everyone got in Adam's 2013 Ford. His family was quite rich. Actually, his dad was, but he was a forbidden subject everywhere. He abandoned Catherine upon finding out about her pregnancy. Adam and Belle despised him, but Belle has always loved him because he came to visit her when she was younger. Adam always kicked him out of the house; he hated how he hurt his mom.

The car ride was silent. Everyone had something on their mind. Adam thought about Tori, Belle was thinking about her nightmares—which she refused to talk about although Adam knew everything—Catherine's thoughts were a mystery to me, while my mind was circling around how I was lucky to have Lena. I just hoped that I'd never lose her.

Adam turned the radio on, just as *Thrift Shop*'s familiar chorus was on. Catherine groaned, as all the youngsters smiled.

"I'M GONNA POP SOME TAGS ONLY GOT TWENTY DOLLARS IN MY POCKET. I-I-I'M HUNTIN', LOOKING FOR A COME UP, THIS IS FUCKING AWESOME."

"Adam Damien Black, keep your bloody eyes on the road. I don't want to die!"

Her son jumped at the urgent tone of her voice and kept his gaze straight ahead. Annabelle, sitting beside me, wouldn't leave me alone.

"Lena and Liam sitting in a tree, K-I-S-S-I-N-G, first comes love; then comes marriage, then comes a-*oomph.*"

I put my hand on her mouth to shut her up.

I hoped bribing was going to work. "I'll buy you dessert."

Belle went into business mode and raised her eyebrow. She ushered for me to "go on."

"Extra large double chocolate sundae with huge Oreo pieces on it."

My cousin's eyes widened and she suddenly threw her arms around me to literally take all breath out of me.

"YOU ARE THE BEST COUSIN IN THE WHOLE WIDE WORLD, LIAMPOOPOO."

I raised an eyebrow.

"Liampoopoo?" I demanded. That nickname was quite childish. Annabelle shrugged and turned back to her side, listening to music. I could hear Pierce the Veil blasting from her earphones.

After that incident, I supported my head on the window, admiring the full moon out. I had a bad feeling, though. A nagging in my chest, but I shook that away. Tonight had to be absolutely perfect, because maybe, just maybe, it would be my chance to ask Lena to be my official girlfriend.

A couple of minutes later, Adam stopped the car and said, "We're here."

I admired the restaurant. It had a homey glow to it and that makes it special, because not all restaurants can produce that. We took our places on a huge table, waiting for the Winters to arrive. I sipped on a glass of water, boredom reigning over me. Annabelle munched on a bread roll while Adam was texting with complete concentration. Kylie, possibly.

Catherine had the phone to her ear, talking to Mrs. Winter.

"Okay, okay. Bye," concluded Catherine, nodding towards us. I took that as a sign that they were here. I kept my eyes glued on the door, tapping my foot on the floor in slight impatience. Suddenly, Lena opened the door, giggling towards Tori. All breath got caught in my throat.

Her hair was messily styled and her eyes were defined with dark purple eye shadow. A blue dress with different abnormal forms made her figure look absolutely stunning. Her long, defined legs seemed endless, kept cozy in black leggings. Our eyes met and she smiled and my heart fluttered.

Man up, Liam. You sound like a love-crazed teenager.

Adam wore the same expression as me, his eyes glued on Tori. She looked quite gorgeous, wearing a long-sleeved knee length dress, of which the top was absolutely black and the bottom was striped in black and white. They shared a look and Tori blushed.

Annabelle rolled her eyes, but smiled at us. There was a glint in her eye showing a little jealousy or envy, but she was very hard to read. Her walls were higher than the Great Wall of

China. I'd learned to understand that she hated love, because it had hurt her before.

No one knew the details, except Adam, who'd wake up in the middle of the night to comfort her from haunting nightmares.

I stood up and pulled the chair beside me, winking at Lena. She shook her head and chuckled a little. By now, all of us were seated. Catherine opposite Mrs. Winter, Annabelle and Victoria on one side, opposite Adam, and finally, Lena and I seated beside Adam.

"So, how's life, you love birds?" asked Catherine, smiling mischievously at Lena and me. Lena blushed, and spontaneously laid her hand on mine underneath the table. Apparently, she chose to be silent, while everyone was expecting an answer from me.

Lena squeezed my hand, encouraging me. "Fine, everything's just fine," I stammered, not quite used to talking in public. I smiled absent-mindedly.

"Adam and Annabelle, since you're continuing your University classes here, what section are you guys in?" asked Mrs. Winter kindly, taking a sip of cold, icy water.

"Well, I've been offered a soccer scholarship here, at NYU," said Adam, appearing proud. Tori's eyes widened in shock and quickly recomposed herself. Lena stifled a laugh. I turned to her, slightly confused.

"He's the man of her dreams," whispered Lena in my ear. I nodded in understanding.

"And I'm studying law," stated Annabelle, coughing to cover her laugh and nudging Tori to snap out of her daze. Adam simply smirked.

"Who's hungry? I know I am!" exclaimed Catherine, a small smile on her face as well. Mrs. Winter winked at Tori and the ambiance in the room was suddenly very comfortable and nice.

We all felt like we belonged. We each took a menu and scanned it. After a couple of seconds and having decided what our meals would be, Mrs. Winter was just about to call a waiter over but she was a little too late.

Just as if he had overheard us, a tall waiter came to us, smiling. Although, he did flash Lena, Tori, and Annabelle a secret smile that made me tense. Lena looked at me in confusion and rubbed her thumb in my palm soothingly.

"What will be your orders?"

"Two lasagnas and ham potato soups, please," said Lena.

"Three Sicilian spaghettis with meatballs," ordered Catherine, speaking for Adam, Mrs. Winter, and herself.

"Okay, perfect. And what will the beautiful lady have?" asked the idiotic waiter, winking at Victoria. Her face reddened and Adam's eyes flashed with anger. He took her hand from across the table and held it tightly in his hands as he put on a forced smile.

"My lady will have Ricotta and Spinach Tortellini with Italian meatballs."

We were all debating on being surprised by his attitude and calling her his *"lady"* or by her expression.

The waiter whose name tag reads "Julian" stiffened. But he looked at Lena and Belle and almost immediately regained a self-pompous smirk.

"Very well then, your orders will be done soon. It's my break though, so if you two lovely ladies pass me your numbers, it would be perfect," finished a soon-to-be-dead Julian with a wink at Belle and Lena. The girl beside me froze, then turned her gaze to our entwined fingers uncomfortably.

I opened my mouth to say something, but Adam beat me to it.

"If I had a dog that looked like you, I'd shave its arse and make it walk backwards. So, jerk, get the fuck out of here before I make you regret ever working here."

"Wait until Leo meets you, he'd beat the heck out of you, stupid Aussie."

Adam shot him a death glare; if looks could kill, that waiter's flesh would be slowly roasted on a barbecue. Julian's eyes darkened, then, without another word, he left. An awkward silence set upon the table. Victoria snatched her hand from Adam's and went to the bathroom, while Lena was very silent and Annabelle was expressionless. The mothers had disapproving looks on their faces. Strangely enough, Catherine and Adam were eyeing Belle carefully.

Wait. Leo, Leo, why does that name seem so familiar?

Then, out of the blue, Belle's eyes watered and she got up in a flash to the bathroom. Adam was about to get up, but Lena stopped him.

"I've got it."

She rushed behind Belle, leaving Adam, Catherine, Mrs. Black and I in a weird moment. Catherine and Adam seemed to be having a silent conversation with their eyes. Adam was raging, while his mom was sad. Finally, after about a couple of minutes, I was sick of being left out.

"What on Earth are you people talking about? It's very impolite to leave people out of a conversation, you know."

Mrs. Winter nodded in agreement with me. Adam turned to me.

"Do you remember Leo? Belle's *Leo*?"

Oh, that *Leo.*

I remembered Annabelle vaguely talking to me about her new boyfriend, Leo, by Skype. I'd usually just nod and smile, or chat, because at that time, the only person I talked to was Grandma. She told me about how he made her happy and during the video chat, a boy with dark brown hair hugged her from the back.

I smiled a little at how happy they looked and that was the first and last time I'd seen Leo. It was also the only time I'd ever seen Belle so happy. That was about a year ago.

I nodded feverishly.

"Well, h-he abu- I mean did terrible stuff to her when they were together. He also cheated on her and wasn't afraid to admit it. He was an exchange student, as you may know, and he was from here, so she got reminded of him. She has nightmares about him all the time." It was the first time I see Adam stutter.

Shock and anger pounded in my veins.

"I hate him and everything he's done, but there's still a part in her that loves him," he explained and then turned to Catherine. Her eyes were cloudy with tears and sadness.

I put myself in their shoes for a second and felt indescribably guilt.

Imagine knowing that someone you love is hurt, but helping them is impossible, because you don't know what to say.

Even though Adam didn't say the word completely, I knew that Leo abused her.

Mrs. Winter pulled out a tissue and handed it to Catherine, who was hiding her face in her hands. After all, the apple doesn't fall far from the tree; Belle and her mom both despised displaying their emotions.

"Here are your orders," said a voice that seemed strangely familiar. I looked up and saw the devil himself, handing out our plates in no respective order.

Apparently, he hadn't directly looked at our faces so he couldn't see Adam's surprised, bewildered expression. My cousin was boiling with anger.

"What the fuck are you doing here?" asked Adam, his face as red as a cherry. Catherine was looking at the waiter standing in front of us with surprise. The guy turned to look at Adam. His face flashed into different emotions in only a couple of seconds; shock, anger, and cockiness.

He smirked at Adam. "Hey, Adam. What a nice way of treating me," drawled sarcastically the waiter, acting as if the ground owed him something. I sensed a bubble of annoyance forming in me.

"Leo." Adam's eyes were shooting fire. If only looks could kill. My cousin stood up, now face to face with *the* Leo himself.

"You know, that glare isn't getting you anywhere. Oh, who is this? Is that your pitiful cousin who's too much of a *wittwe* baby to speak? Lucas?" I didn't know if it was the way he spoke or the way he'd insulted me in a baby voice, but in a flash, I stood up as well, so I was beside Adam.

"For your information, it's Liam. You're. A. Fucking. Asshole. See? I *can* speak."

He raised his eyebrows, debating if he would answer or stay silent.

"Whatever. Anyway, where's your pathetic excuse of a-" His words were cut off by a red-eyed Annabelle.

"Leo," she whispered, barely audible. Tears threatened to fall again as Victoria and Lena each stood by her side, eyes wider than Dobby's. Leo raked his eyes on the three girls.

"Hey, baby, come back to me." Leo opened his arms wide, getting closer to Annabelle. Adam took his collar and harshly pulled him back.

"I don't think so, pretty boy. Dirt is a hundred times cleaner and better than you and I don't like scum getting close to my sister."

Leo shook him off and smirked again. He looked at Lena with a lustful look in his eyes.

"What about this pretty girl right here, huh? I bet no one is with her," he said, advancing towards Lena. He placed his arm around her and frankly, she looked scared to death.

Before I knew what I was doing, I stormed to him, and my fist connected with his face. About five waiters were immediately on Leo's side shooting me glares, including Julian. The whole restaurant had gone completely silent, anticipating every move. Belle's ex-boyfriend looked at me for a second with absolute fury, his broken nose oozing blood.

"She's mine; keep your dirty hands off her."

Leo cracked his neck and advanced towards me. He was towering over me, he was quite tall. But I kept my eyes locked on his, feeling no fear at all. He raised his fist, and after a second, all I could feel was blood trickling down my lips.

"You know what, never mind. I don't like sluts and your wattle girlfriend, pathetic little Belle, and that skimpy little whore with them are—"

Adam crashed his balled fists into Leo's face with no mercy. He wouldn't stop. He punched Leo more than a child could count.

"Don't. Insult. Them."

That was when it all began.

Julian was the only waiter who came closer to me and slammed his fists into my stomach. The pain was bearable, but the more he punched, the more the power in his scrawny arms got stronger. I kneed him in the groin and then pushed him away, making him stumble to the ground, groaning. Adrenaline was pumping in my veins. It was the first time in a long time since I've felt like this, my fighting lessons fresh in my mind.

I turned to Adam and his opponent. Leo had Adam in a tight headlock. A really tight one. Every breath of air seemed to escape from Adam's body, his face was turning purple. If he stayed like this for a couple more seconds, he could faint or possibly die.

Leo was whispering words in Adam's ear that seemed to make Adam furious. He tried to struggle, but it was nearly impossible. Every last drop of power had drained from him.

So, I elbowed Leo as hard as I could on his back. Taken by surprise, he let go of Adam and it was our opportunity to get him. Adam kicked his knees, so he crumpled back on the ground. I punched Leo repetitively. With every blow, blood spattered on the ground. My hands were surely bruised because they ached.

After about a couple of minutes of just punching him, I got up. Sure he was unconscious. The first thing I saw was Lena. Tears freely streamed down her face and her face was flashing with so many emotions I simply couldn't place. Her eyes displayed hurt and fear, but it wasn't for me; it was **from** me. Her trembling lips showed anxiety and her shaking hands showed fear for me this time. A pang hit my chest.

She'd never seen me fight before.

Victoria was in the same position, but her eyes were on Adam, who was wiping blood off his face with the tip of his sleeve. Catherine and Mrs. Winter were shocked.

But what really hit me was Belle. She was on the ground, fully shaking and sobbing. A complete breakdown tore her apart. I've never seen her so vulnerable and weak. Annabelle has always been strong and not afraid of anything.

The next seconds were a complete blur to me. It seemed like everything was in slow motion.

"NO!" screamed Lena in alert.

Lena was running to me at full speed, but it was certain that she wasn't about to hug me. The terror in her eyes alarmed my senses. Before I could ask what was wrong, she passed me and her back was literally brushing mine. What was she doing? I swiftly turned, only to see Lena standing on the tip of her heels.

Leo was holding two bottles of full champagne above my head, or Lena's in fact. Before I could realize what was going on, those two bottles came crashing on Lena's head. I fell to the ground beside Lena.

Her head was oozing a huge quantity of blood and her eyes were squeezed shut. Her features were etched with pain but she was unconscious. Tears sprung to my own eyes, as I took her in my arms. I began walking rapidly towards the door; a pool of blood was wetting my shirt. But I didn't care.

"Where are you going?" exclaimed a voice I couldn't recognize. I didn't even stop as I answered:

"To the hospital. There's no way in fucking hell that I'm losing her."

24

Don't let Me Go

"I am awake most nights because I am afraid someone else will leave me, and I won't be awake to stop them."

Liam Christopher Black

"OPEN THE DOOR, PLEASE. TELL ME IF SHE'S OKAY. PLEASE, JUST OPEN THE DOOR, I WANT TO SEE HER!"

I pounded my already bruised fists with all the power that I could muster on the ED doors, which were locked. The emergency department was the place Lena was in right now. My heart shattered with worry. The quantity of blood oozing from her head wasn't a good sign. As soon as the hospital had seen her in my arms, she'd been taken in a flash on an ambulance cot. The way her skin had lost any color in it, becoming completely pale and the loss of any body heat in her, scared me to death. My thoughts were scattered everywhere in my head, making it impossible to concentrate on anything. A million thoughts were running a marathon in my head and kept pushing each other to get to the finish line. I couldn't think of anything else but *Lena*.

I can't lose her, screamed my subconscious.

"PLEASE, I'M BEGGING YOU! GOD, DAMN IT! PLEASE!"

It's been two whole hours; a hundred and twenty minutes of absolute hell. The nurses wouldn't let me in. After a while, they got sick of my persistence, so they just locked the door and kept me out. I kept on pounding on the doors separating Lena from me, my anxiety giving me adrenaline. I knew that the old, mute Liam would've sat in a corner and cried, but this was before Lena came into my life. I couldn't give up on her; I wasn't going to just let her get away from me.

After one last pound at the door, I figured the possibility of them opening the door was improbable. I dragged myself onto the nearest chair, and placing my elbows on my legs, I buried my head in my hands. Closing my eyes helped the massive headache knocking on every corner in my mind. I took a deep breath; the fresh air circulating in my lungs relaxed me a little.

A hand was placed on my shoulder, startling me. I lift my head to see Adam, pity seeping from his eyes, of which one was black. Actually, we both had one eye that had purple completely surrounding it. Adam had bruises around his neck and a broken arm, whilst I only had bruises in several parts of my body: face, stomach, chest. I hadn't taken a look but my aching body told me so.

He sat down on the chair beside me and looked at me with a sad expression. "Mate, it'll be all right," said my cousin, patting my shoulder. I shook my head, and turned to him.

"No, you don't understand. I've lost every single person that I ever cared about. I can't lose her, I just can't." My voice was trembling with fury and slight desperation.

"I know," mumbled Adam, lying his head on the wall behind him. His tired expression showed that he was thinking about a lot of things.

I knew I wasn't the only one who'd lost people in his life. My cousin's father had a big impact on Adam, because he'd ingrained hatred in him. Ever since at a young age, Adam would fight his dad, or kick him out of the house. And well, he'd just lost his grandmother too. Although, she wasn't as close to my cousins as she was to me.

She was and will always be *my everything*; she was my mother, sister, friend, and grandmother who'd console me whenever I was down. She understood me and knew how to help. I felt like Atlas, the Greek Titan who supposedly held the whole world on his shoulders. Grandma would take some of that weight off me, but it never completely left.

But even *she* was gone.

I was somehow mad, sad, and *desperado* at the same time. Mad, because of how unfair the universe could be. Sad, because I could've saved Lena by being more careful, or, oh, I don't know, being smart enough to turn in time and take those bottles on my head. The feeling of desperation was because she was my only hope. I just couldn't bear the thought of losing her, losing anyone else. I'm utterly and absolutely sick and tired of it. Call me selfish or whatever, but I think I deserve to have someone.

"Liam, it'll be fine. She's not going to…you know," said Adam, breaking our little moment of silence. I nodded, hoping he was right.

"I can't lose her," I whispered so low I doubted Adam had heard, every drop of energy draining from me. The fight, Lena, everything just made me so tired.

"You won't. Now come on, let's go check on the ladies."

I looked up at his standing figure, my eyebrows slightly furrowed. I'd completely forgotten about them.

"Where are they?" I asked, my voice coming out raspy.

"With Belle. The doctors saw her state and deducted that she was having an anxiety attack. They gave her medication and she's staying in a room for a couple of hours, so she can calm down." Even though Adam's tone was calm and collected, his expression was begging me to go with him. He wanted to see his sister and was frantically worried about her. I stood up, but then immediately remembered something.

"Does the doctor know that we'll be over there, in case you know, he needs to tell-"

"Liam, calm down. He knows. Now, let's go. I'm worried sick about that little annoying sister of mine," he said, mumbling the last part. I mustered a small smile and followed him.

The impeccably clean hospital halls seemed endless, the smell of medicine and chlorine familiar to my nose. My eyes noticed a few familiar faces and I nodded politely in their direction. The glass walls displayed sick patients with their relatives or loved ones. Of course, the occasional moaning and call for nurses was present. I knew this hospital so well and I wish I hadn't. The reason was that I came here during Grandma's sickness.

Although, my eye caught something that made me freeze. Adam stopped and looked at me impatiently. I nodded in the direction of whom I was looking at and his expression instantly softened. A little girl, not older than six or seven years old, was sitting on a chair, with no one by her side. Her face was crestfallen and her shoulders slumped. Her long, blonde hair was loosely framing her face. She had her arms crossed and directed her face at the ground. I was almost certain that she was crying.

I took small steps in her direction and squatted in front of her. She lifted her head and my eyes met hers. They were pale blue and the redness in them meant that I was right. Her red cheeks were wet and puffy.

"Hey there," I said, seeing the hesitation in her eyes. She ignored me and turned away. "Well, I know about the don't-speak-to-strangers rule, but I'm not a mean person. I want to be your friend."

That caught her attention; she faced me with hopeful eyes.

"Really?" she asked, slightly nervous.

I nodded eagerly. "I would really, really like to be your friend."

"I'm Ellie, and what's your name? I've got to know your name to be your friend. I mean, I can't call you my No-Name friend."

A small smile appeared on my face. "I'm Liam."

Her face lit up and her little hand patted the seat next to her. I sat next to her, and she fully turned to me.

"So, tell me what's wrong," I said, wiping the tears on her cheek with my hand.

Suddenly, she attacked me in the biggest hug someone her age could possibly give. Her frail arms held my waist tightly and I felt my shirt getting wet. So, I put my arms around her petite body as well. I stroked her golden hair, as her tears came rushing faster. After a few moments of staying like this, she pulled herself away from the hug and sniffled a little. I waited for an answer to my question, as I knew by her expression that she was ready to talk.

"My daddy's really sad and my mommy won't talk to me."

"Why?" I questioned softly.

"Well, it's because my mommy was in this white bed and then there was a lot of beeping and it hurt my ears. Daddy starts crying and I called mommy to make him happy, b-but she wouldn't answer me. And then I asked Daddy, why she wasn't answering me and he said that she was gone. But she was right there! But she won't answer me, why won't she answer me, Lee-yum?"

Tears sprung into my eyes straight away and her sad face broke my heart. I took her in my arms and held her tightly, as she sobbed again. I knew exactly how she felt, although I was older than her when I lost my parents. This little angel would have to grow up without a mom and come to a realization at one point, that the reason her mom wasn't answering her was because she was dead. She was too young to face this.

She pulled away and held my face in her hands. She tipped her head slightly to the right, as if she was confused.

"Lee-yum, why are you crying?"

I suddenly realized that I was fully crying as well. I sniffled and wiped my tear-streaked cheeks with the back of my hand. Ellie wiped my other cheek. I smiled and put her on my lap.

"I'm just scared to lose someone I love very much," I said, looking at Ellie. Her eyes widened and she patted my cheek.

"Don't worry, love is always stronger than anything," she spoke with such certainty and confidence, hope was growing on me.

"Um, Liam?"

I averted my eyes to see Adam, who awkwardly stood there, looking a bit sorry for interrupting my little moment. He scratched the back of his head and ushered at me that we had to go.

"Ellie, I'll be right back, okay?"

She furiously shook her head, hopped off my lap and stood in front of me with crossed arms. She stomped one foot on the ground stubbornly.

"I go wherever you go, Lee-yum."

"No, you've got to go see your daddy. Do you know where he is?"

She pouted her lips and put on a professional pleading face that could crack anyone.

"Yes, I do, but I'm not telling you. You have to take me with you."

I didn't know Ellie *that* long, but I knew she was determined to go with me. But, that was wrong. I huffed and rubbed my invisible beard, watching her hopeful expression.

Out of nowhere, I scooped her up in my arms, hearing her sweet, melodious giggles fill my ear.

"Fine, if you won't tell me, then I'LL TICKLE YOU UNTILL YOU SPILL!" My hands poked her belly as she squirmed and squealed. I held her tightly with one arm, as she was tiny, and my grip was firm enough to assure that she wouldn't fall.

"LEE-YUM, PWEEASE STOP!"

I immediately froze and looked at her with utter seriousness. "Are you going to tell me?" I asked, raising one eyebrow. She nodded obediently, a smile present on her face.

"Room 412."

I gently put her down and took her hand in mine. I looked up to Adam, who was quite amused by this situation.

"I'll meet you over there. What's her room number?"

"586."

"All right, see you later."

Adam left, leaving me alone with Ellie. She was grinning.

"Let's go now, shall we?" I ruffled her hair. And we walked towards the hall where rooms starting with 4 were.

The small walk was anything but silent. Ellie talked about her preferred food, her hobbies, how her mom always reads her a story before she went to sleep; her favorite was Cinderella. She was a little bundle of joy, someone whom it was impossible not to smile upon seeing. I knew she would grow up to be a successful and happy person, I just hoped life wouldn't bring her down. I also wished that she would cope with her mom's absence, through time.

400,402,404, I mentally counted.

"I also have a sister, she's really pretty."

"Really? What's her name?"

"Scarlett, but I call her Scar. It's easier."

408, 410, 412...Here we go.

I stood in front of the open door, my body becoming suddenly tense. My eyes scanned the room and saw a man, probably in his fifties, sobbing uncontrollably beside the bed which contained a covered body. His body shook with every breath he took. On the corner, a girl with long hair sat on a chair, her face in her hands, her shoulders were somewhat quivering. I noticed that she was crying.

"Scar!" cried out Ellie, running towards the girl. "Scar" looked up and engulfed her sister in an embrace.

"Where were you? I was s-so worried!" Her voice was shaky, but her condition was more stable than her dad's.

"I went outside, and met my new friend Lee-yum." She pointed at me. Scar averted her gaze to me, and stood up, advancing towards me. Her eyes couldn't meet mine, somehow. She offered her hand to shake.

I took her hand and nodded. "Thank you so much for bringing her back. I'm Scarlett."

"I'm Liam, and you're welcome."

My voice seemed to wake something in her, because she immediately locked her teary eyes with mine. Their pale ocean blue color was mesmerizing. But they weren't the beautiful chestnut brown Lena's were.

"Well, I've got to go."

I squatted to be in Ellie's level and hugged her closely. She offered me her pinky finger, as I furrowed my eyebrows in confusion.

"Do you promise to stay my friend?"

"I promise." I locked my pinky with hers.

I stood up and scribbled my number on one of the smaller papers I always had with me. I handed it to Scarlett, whose eyes were open wide. It suddenly clicked into my head.

"Um, it's not what you think. This is if Ellie needs anything, or if you need a babysitter, I'm here. I-I have a girlfriend anyway."

Scarlett chuckled dryly, then took the paper and put in her pocket.

"Don't worry about it; I see that look in your eyes."

I smiled, and waved one last time to Ellie, then walked away. Although, I stopped almost immediately in my tracks, remembering something.

I turned back and looked at Scarlett.

"I'm really sorry for your loss."

She nodded, fresh tears already falling from her eyes.

And this time, I walked in the direction of room 586, hoping that I wouldn't get any bad news. This world deserved a little happiness.

After a couple of minutes, I finally reached the room. The door was open, so I immediately went in. The first thing I saw was Annabelle, peacefully sleeping on the bed situated in the middle of the room. Catherine was by her side, completely expressionless. Mrs. Winter was sitting on a chair, silently weeping. Adam and Tori were sitting on the other side, my cousin hugging Tori as she cried. I knew for a fact that they weren't crying about Annabelle.

"What is it?"

The room stayed silent, apart from the weeping and hiccuping. A pin could drop. Frustration made me nervous.

"Did the doctor come?"

I took their silence as a yes. I suddenly felt weak and all I could hear was my heart pounding at an incredible speed.

"What did he say?" I whispered, barely audible.

No answer.

"Tell me, please! I need to know she's not dead. She's not gone, right? Please tell me she's not," I pleaded, looking at Adam, knowing that he would be able to tell me. He shook his head as a no and I sighed in relief. But the expressions everyone wore still worried me.

"Adam, tell me."

He cleared his throat and then stood up so he could be facing me. I saw the hesitation in his eyes and braced myself for his next words.

"Well, as the bottles were full, and the glass hit her cranium with huge power, which affected her brain, that caused head trauma. That led to…" He trailed off, his gaze now glued to the ground.

The temperature in the room had suddenly dropped a hundred degrees. "Just come out with it."

Adam's eyes met mine, and seeing the pity and sadness in them, I prepared myself for the worst.

"Lena's in a coma."

25

Hold You

"The worst day of loving someone is the day you lose them."
~Elena Gilbert~

Liam Christopher Black

I finished my History test, certain of getting at least a 90%. I'd studied my butt off last night and information about Renaissance was still fresh in my mind. Mrs. Brown shot me a small smile as I handed her my exam. I nodded in response; smiling was an impossible thing to do these days. Holding my new leather jacket in one hand, I opened the door to leave. Unlike most teachers, Mrs. Brown was kind enough to let the students go as soon as they finished their test. But of course, this wasn't a midterm evaluation; these were before the Christmas vacation. Opening my report card last week, I'd received no surprise. I was still a straight A student. That was one of the things that hadn't changed.

Heading towards my locker, I earned some stares, but that was nothing new. The only thing that may have differed was that a few girls sent me flirty stares, which I replied to with a stony hard glare. I stuffed the books I would need in my bag and slammed my locker. I put my jacket on and went out of the school.

Frankly, this place felt unwelcoming and all I could do was stay silent to the not-so-secret whispers, that hadn't stopped ever since Christmas break. Although, the only thing that kept me here was learning. I was determined to finish my year with high scores, and I wanted to get a scholarship in any university. I wasn't really sure about who I wanted to be yet. As nerdy as this sounded, I also loved learning and studying.

I patted my pockets, checking to see if my keys and cell phone were there.

The final bell rang, signaling the end of a Friday school day, its noise fading in the background. I could almost see the rushing students, laughing and chatting with one another, not possessing a care in the world. I started the car's engine and headed towards Sainte-Catherine's hospital.

Where else would I go anyway?

Home was dull and empty. Catherine was constantly at work, Adam and Belle spent their days at University. The homely spirit in the house had been broken. Ever since that damned day at the restaurant, Annabelle had gone through a severe case of depression.

I would see her crying in her room almost every day. She also had nightmares, every night. She would wake up screaming and crying. As I never went to sleep, I would sometimes make her a cup of hot chocolate and sit with her in a comfortable silence. It always made her feel better and made me feel better.

She talked and I sat there, letting her words sink in. Through those moments, we learned to form a strong bond of friendship. I'd never thought to see the rebel Annabelle Black in such state, but the impossible happens.

As for Adam, my cousin broke up with his girlfriend a few days after the incident happened. He figured if he couldn't go to Australia, the best thing to do was to do it on a video chat. He refused to be an asshole and break it off through text, or email. He and Victoria had been growing a lot closer lately and he confessed that he would ask her out when the time was right. At the time, I nodded and turned my night light off and just laid my head on my pillow. We both knew that I wasn't sleeping.

When I tried to, the nightmares would wake me up. Only one, actually. It repeated itself and it got worse every time I was tired and foolish enough to drift off. Plus, I never slept any more than three or four hours.

My heart felt heavy as I locked the car and looked up at the building *she* was in. I hated it with all my heart and soul. I despised that hospital. It brought me every ounce of sadness a person could ever get. Here, at the age of ten, I found out that my family was dead. About two months and a week ago, my grandmother died here. Now, *she* was in a coma in the same damned hospital.

I walked through the halls, only stopping a couple of times to nod in appreciation to a few faces I knew. My mind was only in one room, *173*. Trudy had just gotten out of the room, clutching her clipboard. She gently shut the door and finally noticed me. She walked towards me, as my mouth moved to trace the familiar words I mouthed, every time I came here.

"Is she better?"

"I'm sorry, son, there's no progress," said the old nurse, slightly shaking her head in pity. She patted my shoulder and walked away, probably to check on another patient. Dread washed over me. What had I expected anyway? My shoulders slumped, and I went into *her* room. I found my chair by her side and sat there.

Her hair was gently placed around her on the pillow, laying beneath her head in such a soft way; I couldn't stop myself from grazing it. Her long eyelashes framed her eyes, which were tightly shut. Unlike any patient I'd ever seen, she had no circles beneath her eyes. Her features were serene and her mouth was slightly parted in a relaxed way. The tube in her nose was still there, enabling her to breath. She looked so peaceful; I would've thought that she was just sleeping.

Just sleeping, for two whole months?

I had this hope of just waking up, to see her by my side. To know that this was all just a dream.

But it wasn't.

I placed my lips on hers, then pulled back and cleared my throat. I wrapped her hand with mine and took a deep breath.

"Hey, Lena," I whispered, barely audible.

My voice was hoarse. Well, it would be a surprise if it wasn't, because I hadn't spoken during the whole day. I just couldn't force any words out of me, I had no reason to. After all, I'd started speaking to people again because of her. And it would make me so happy to see her eyes proudly smiling at me. How she'd squeeze my hand when I hesitated to talk. And that was just the night of the restaurant.

"How are you today? You feelin' better?"

I just tried every time, hoping with all my heart and soul to get an answer. I sighed heavily, the usual disappointment making my heart ache.

"So, today, we had a test about Renaissance. I aced it and it was really funny seeing others sweating like pathetic pigs because of how hard the test were to them. I also have a social studies project to do, about who I'd like to be in the future. I've been thinking, and I-I want to be a cancer researcher or whatever the name is. I want to help and find a cure for that horrible sickness. A cure that will no longer force little children to lose their parents; or women and men to lose their children."

I waited for a couple of seconds, hoping to get any answer.

Anything.

"And, um, well, you'll be happy to know that Adam's planning on asking Tori out. They really like each other and I can see it. But, you know, I'm ashamed of something. When he told me that, I got really jealous. Because, well, uh… He had that same excitement I had, when I wanted to ask you to be my official girlfriend. But you're asleep now, so I'll just ask you when you wake up."

If any other boy was in my position, I was pretty sure the atmosphere would've gotten awkward, although, I felt really comfortable. I knew that Lena was somehow listening, but she didn't mind.

Are you even sure she's listening?

"I know you're pretty tired of hearing this every day, but I just wanted to say that I-I really miss you. Please, come back. Please, just do. I miss you so much."

By now, my voice was breaking, because tears had collected in my eyes.

"I mean, it's so *hard* to live with this every day. The guilt. Knowing that I should've taken that hit, not you. I should be in that bed right now, but you are. I should've done something. I should've knocked Leo unconscious so he couldn't have hit you. I-I should've told my parents that I didn't want anything for my birthday. I should've stopped them from going out that night.

"You know what I wanted?" I chuckled dryly, the tears now freely falling on my face. I didn't feel any shame of doing so, because she was *Lena.* She didn't mind.

"I wanted an airplane, you know, the kind that's remotely controlled. I wanted to see it fly.

"But I...never did. I lost my parents and little sister a week before my birthday. And now, here you are."

An angry bubble was forming in me. So many thoughts ran through my head and I had to let them out.

"You can't leave me, Lena. You can't, okay? You're going to fight this and wake up. You're going to wake up, all right? I miss you so damn much and you have no idea how much everything hurts. I want to hear your voice. I want you to smile, or laugh because I'm tickling you. I want us to sit in the library, with two identical books in hand, doing competitions on who'll finish it first. I want you to *come back* to me."

"Please," I mumbled, kissing her head.

A little hand wiped the tears freshly falling on my face. I lifted my head, startled to see a little angel.

"Lee-yum. Don't cry, pwease?" Ellie's frail voice said, patting my cheek affectionately. I raised my eyebrow upon seeing her here and she pointed to the door. I saw Annabelle, casually leaning against the door. She had a small smile on her face, something rare to see these days. I looked at her questioningly and she nodded towards Ellie.

"It's Friday, remember? Scar asked me to get Ellie because she had to go to work early today. Her boss called and asked her to work an earlier shift. So, I drove Ellie here, knowing that you're always here."

I nodded gratefully. I babysat the seven-year old girl, because Scar had to work on Monday and Friday. On the weekends their dad wasn't at work, so Ellie spent time with him. Sometimes, I brought her here. She seemed to be the only other person that didn't mind seeing me at my weakest. She grew to love Lena, even.

"It's good to see you talking, even though it wasn't for anyone else but Lena."

And with those words, Belle turned on her heel and left. I turned to Ellie and gave her a tight hug. I took her in my arms and set her on my lap. She reached over and gave Lena a kiss on the cheek. I smiled a little.

"Hi Lena. It's me again, Ellie."

Ellie waited for a moment, as if expecting an answer. Then, she turned to me with wide, sad eyes.

"She still doesn't answer, Lee-yum?"

I shook my head, a certain sadness engulfing me. Ellie turned and bit her lip. She took Lena's hand in hers.

"Lena, please don't make Lee-yum sad anymore. Wake up, okay? He loves you very much and I love you too," said the little girl. Her voice had so much emotion, making me remember how much I loved her. I turned her body so she could face me and supported her tiny frame with my hands.

"How was school?" I asked. Ellie's eyes brightened and a huge grin appeared on her face, showing the missing front tooth.

"It was great! I got a star, because I could count to 50, see?" she said, pointing to the golden sticker on her hand.

"Good job, El," I mumbled, kissing her forehead. Ellie smiled softly, and then pouted her lips.

"Lee-yum?"

I knew she was up to no good, with that expression on her face. "Hm?"

"Will you sing?"

I raised my eyebrows, and chuckled. Ellie and I had a tradition of me singing to her and it was mostly when she felt tired and wanted to sleep.

"What song?" I asked, already knowing her answer.

"The one that goes like: "*I just wanna hold ya, hold ya, hold ya.*"

I nodded knowingly and said, "All right."

She put her hands together and then placed her head on my chest. She looked at me expectantly. I cleared my throat and took a deep breath. I hummed the piano solo in the beginning and then started singing Nina Nesbitt's song:

You're far away tonight
Haven't seen you in a while
It always feel like a climb
On this never ending hill

And I keep saying, wait just one more day
Days slowly drift away
And I can hold to the memories

But they won't hold me in the same way
As you

And this distance between us
Has come and cut us clean as
A sharp blade
And this distance between us
Has made my heart as weak as
Silk that's frayed

I started gently swaying, as if rocking Ellie to sleep. I realized I had been staring at Lena. That song described perfectly how I felt at the moment, about everything.

And I just wanna
Hold ya, hold ya, hold ya now
You're the one that
Keeps me, keeps me on the ground
I just wanna
Hold ya, hold ya, hold ya now
Can we turn this knife the blunt way around?

I feel empty, my eyes are closed
It's getting dark and I'm alone
And I sleep next to my window
In case you decide to come home

And I keep saying, wait just one more day
Days slowly drift away
And memories I have begin to fade
'Cause you're so far away

This distance between us
Has come and cut us clean as
A sharp blade
And this distance between us
Has made my heart as weak as
Silk that's frayed

And I just wanna
Hold ya, hold ya, hold ya now
You're the one that
Keeps me, keeps me on the ground
I just wanna
Hold ya, hold ya, hold ya now
Can we turn this knife the blunt way around?

And as I sang that verse, I looked down at Ellie, who was tenderly snoring. Her eyes were shut and she had an absent smile on her face. I was so lucky to have that little kid. She was the only person who gave me a little joy and the only other person I spoke to, besides Lena, of course. I shut my eyes, and sang the bridge, my favorite part of the whole song:

And I can only stay
One more day
It's like waiting on the rain
In a warm summer day

And this distance between us
Has come and cut us clean as
A sharp blade

And this distance between us
Has made my heart as weak as
Silk that's frayed

And I just wanna
Hold ya, hold ya, hold ya now
You're the one that
Keeps me, keeps me on the ground
I just wanna
Hold ya, hold ya, hold ya now
Can we turn this knife the blunt way around, now.

Finally finishing the song, I decided that I should go to the cafeteria, as my stomach was growling with hunger. I leaned over and placed a gentle peck on Lena's forehead.

"I love you," I murmured.

I walked into the halls and reached the cafeteria. It was almost empty, except for a couple of nurses and doctors, eating or drinking coffee. What was abnormal, though, was that Annabelle was sitting in a corner, an untouched sandwich in front of her. I went her way and tapped her shoulder.

"Oh! Hey, Liam."

Her cheeks had dry traces of tears on them. She looked like I'd taken her away from deep thought.

Good.

Overthinking while being in a depression never did nothing but make your mind explode, believe me.

I took a seat in front of her, carefully holding Ellie in my arms.

"Sandwich?"

I nodded, mouthing, *"Thank you."*

Taking the grilled cheese sandwich in my hands, I stuffed it in my mouth, savoring its heavenly taste with speed. When I was done, I wiped my mouth with a napkin. Belle's eyes were glued to her phone, which was placed on the table. I took out my phone and typed something, showing it to her.

"What's wrong?"

My cousin bit her lip and hesitantly looked at me. I could tell that she wanted to spill everything but she was scared of me judging her. Then, she waved her arms around in an *"Oh, what the heck"* way.

"Leo's been calling and texting me non-stop."

I sucked in a breath. Leo had spent two nights in jail and was fired from the restaurant. I haven't seen him since that damned day and I didn't want to. I'd sworn to myself that if I ever saw him, I'd beat the crap out of him.

"He says that he's sorry, that he misses me and that he loves me and a whole load of bullshit."

I typed a couple of words, letting my curiosity show on my face as I showed her my phone screen. She blanched a little and gulped. A fire appeared in her eyes and she locked them with mine.

"What happened with him?"

"We started going out in 12th grade. He was the perfect gentleman and I was completely in love with him. We were named the Golden Couple at school. He was also Adam's best friend. Adam was fine with us going out, he trusted Leo with his life. During the whole winter vacation, Leo was in France. And when he came back, he'd completely changed. He started smoking, drinking, and flirting with everyone. I felt like absolute shit, but I still loved him. When we were alone, he was the Leo I used to know.

"But with time, we started disagreeing and having fights. At one point, he...slapped me. I was scared, because he had this crazy look in his eyes. We soon forgot about it. But he started snapping at me for the little things. He'd physically hurt me every time, because every single time, we'd be alone. Slapping and kicking me."

Annabelle took a deep breath and continued. I could see how hard this was to say.

"On our graduation night—which was also his birthday—there was a huge party and everyone was there. Leo had gotten completely drunk. I wasn't completely aware of my actions, because I was a little tipsy. He took my arm and dragged me to his bedroom. We started kissing, but he went too far. When I pushed him away, he got mad. I didn't want to... you know. And I told him. He suddenly started uncontrollably hitting me, slapping me. That's when Adam came in and got him off. A couple of weeks later, Leo went back to America and I never saw him again."

By now, she was fully crying. I offered her a tissue from the box that was on the table. She gladly took it and wiped her tears away. I took my phone and tapped a few buttons and showed them to her. She smiled a little upon seeing them.

"I'm sorry for everything that happened. He's nothing but a complete asshole for hurting you that way. He doesn't deserve such an amazing person like you."

"Thank you, Liam. You're truly the best cousin in the world, no, you're like a brother to me. And I'm really sorry for everything that happened to Lena. It was all my fault and I'm sincerely sorry," she said.

"It's okay," I mouthed, patting her hand.

Belle glanced at the time and frowned. It was 7:00. Well, three hours could pass by like a blow of the wind.

"I've got to go. Mum's going to kill me if I'm late for dinner."

Just as she packed her bag and was starting to walk away, she turned to me with compassion in her eyes.

"Aren't you coming? She hates eating without you." Her eyes begged me to go.

"I'll be there," I mouthed, nodding.

"Okay, bye."

I looked down at Ellie, who was peacefully sleeping in my arms. She was so beautiful, innocent, and simply amazing. Her strength was inspiring, for someone her age. In the space of the last couple of months, we'd grown a lot closer.

We spent a lot of time together, other than the babysitting. Sometimes, when it would be snowing outside, we'd go to the park and dance under the snowflakes. It made me happy to see her laugh or smile. I tried to help her family as much as I could. Scarlett needed all the help she could get because of school, a job four days of the week, taking care of her sister, and doing everything her mom used to do was too much. Her dad helped, but not as much. He worked a full-time job, trying to drown the sorrow of losing his wife.

From time to time, when Ellie was asleep, she'd wake up crying. She had dreams of her mom and nightmares where "her mom wouldn't answer her." It broke my heart to see her like that, but there was nothing I could do than hug her and sing to her. My voice seemed to soothe her and she would sing along. She had a pure personality and I knew that she would grow up to be a strong woman.

I blinked several times to regain focus. I stood up and got out of the hospital, pushing my thoughts away. I put Ellie in the back seat and buckled her safety belt. As I started the engine, I reached for my pack of cigarettes, but almost immediately refused to take one. I wouldn't let any smoke infiltrate her lungs.

As I drove, I thought about something.

These days, I realized that there was another reason for my attachment to that little girl.

Serena.

My younger sister, Serena, who died. She was only five. I was the one who could calm her down, other than my mom. I loved seeing her smile or laugh. She was ticklish. At that time, I imagined an older version of myself threatening boys to take care of her and to never hurt her. I was excited for her to grow up. I used to actually *look forward* into having silly fights with her. Because hey, that's what siblings do, right?

Stop thinking about her.

A single tear ran down my cheek.

I lost my sister for a birthday gift.
I lost my parents in an airplane.
I murdered them.
I killed them.
It was all my fault.

The words resonated in my head, as my heart ached. Another tear escaped my eyelids, but I wiped it away. I didn't want to get into a car accident.

Suddenly I remembered the words Lena had said to me a few months earlier. They were vague, yet so clear in my mind:

"It isn't your fault. Your mom, your dad, Serena, and Grandma Darla are looking down on you right now, guarding you. They will always be in your heart. They wouldn't want to see you like this."

I remembered her promise that she'd never leave me.

Oh, how I hoped that promise wouldn't be broken.

26

Legos and Kisses

"Death leaves a heartache no one can heal,
love leaves a memory no one can steal."
~From a Headstone in Ireland~

Liam Christopher Black

February 14th.

Valentine's Day

  I ran a hand through my hair, perfecting it. Taking a look in the mirror, I smiled a little. I was wearing a new gray sweater, that had been lying in my closet for ages now, and dark blue jeans. I slid my jacket on, finalizing the look I wanted. My hair had been impeccably combed to look a little messy; I knew Lena liked it better when it was down. She had taken a certain liking to ruffling it and laughing at my frustrated expression while trying to fix it. I found myself smiling at the thought of her.

  I remembered buying the bouquet of red roses, her favorite kind of flowers, this afternoon from the florist so I could bring them to her. They were currently in the car though, waiting to be by a certain beautiful girl's side.

I patted the pocket of my jacket, sensing the *Tiffany's* box. The box held a beautiful necklace with a silver snowflake as its charm. Without a doubt, it was that day with the first snowfall. I could've gone with just an ordinary heart charmed necklace, but I chose this one because it reminded me of one of the most memorable days in my life and the day she and I had almost kissed for the first time. That day was the one I'd realized that I liked her. I realized that she could light up my whole world with just one tiny laugh or smile.

I had this tiny speck of hope that maybe, *just maybe,* she'd wake up today.

You watch too many movies, bro.

Shut up, don't ruin my mood. And don't call me bro. I'm *you,* idiot.

You do realize you just called yourself an idiot, bro.

Ah, sometimes, I had this urge of repetitively banging my head against the wall; my thoughts could get *really* annoying.

Even though she was in a coma, I wanted to make her happy and render this day special somehow. All I knew was that if she were awake, she would smile joyfully and hug me. My heart ached at the thought of her, wrapping her arms around me once again, something I've missed so much. I wanted to hold her in my arms, with the feeling of knowing that she was safe and sound. I wanted to listen to her talk to me about her day, or rant about how she was going to ace that test or—

You're only hurting yourself by thinking about her. Stop.

Unexpectedly, my phone vibrated and started ringing. Ed Sheeran's voice was blasting in my ears.

"But if I kiss you, will your mouth read this truth, Darling, how I miss you, strawberries taste how lips do, And it's not complete yet, mustn't get our feet wet, cause that leads to regret, diving in too soon, and I'll owe it all to you, oh, my little bird, my little bird."

Wait a second.

This was Ellie's house's ring tone; she would call me from time to time, when she wanted to talk or when she couldn't sleep. She was the only one who ever called me; the others saw no purpose in doing so since I never actually *talked* to them. Whenever Adam, Belle, Catherine or even Tori needed something, they simply texted me. But the thing was, it was 7:45 and it was dark outside. And that I know of, Scarlett was home today. The private high school she attended had given her vacation today and she refused my offer to take care of Ellie. So it's abnormal that Ellie's calling *now,* it's also almost her bed time. It was Tuesday, I had no school because they decided to give us a free day and I was determined to spend the night with Lena. A few extra pillows have been always available and I would just sleep on the chair, by her side.

I took one look at the screen and affirmed my hypothesis upon seeing a smiling picture of Ellie. I pressed the green button and held the phone to my ear.

"Hello?" I said expecting Ellie's smiling voice to talk on the phone.

"LEE-YUM!" exclaimed her voice, but instead of it being bubbly and giggling, worry and fear were written all over it. I furrowed my eyebrows in concern.

"Ellie, what's wrong? Are you okay?"

I heard two hiccups in the background, signaling that she had been crying.

"Scar's scaring me! She's not walking properly and she's screaming weird things!" She sniffled, her voice shaking. I took the keys and turned all the lights off, except one lamp in the living room, which faced the door.

"Okay, calm down. What else?"

"She's holding a weird bottle and she's drinking a lot of it and she keeps on crying and saying mean things! She's also saying bad words, like fu-"

"Okay, okay. Where are you now?" I locked the front door and headed towards the car.

Her voice trembled and I could literally *feel* how scared she was. "I'm hiding behind the couch."

"Is your dad there?" I asked, trying to keep my calm. I started the engine, and was already out of the driveway. The phone was placed on my lap, on speaker mode.

"No, he's at work."

"Uh-huh. Ellie? Stay right where you are, love. I'm coming, all right?"

"Okay, Lee-yum. Are you going to hang up now?" she questioned and I could see her clutching Mr. Teddy, who, ironically, was her favorite teddy bear.

"No, just stay on the line until I'm there. If anything happens, you tell me."

"Mhm. Lee-yum?"

"Yeah?" I said, concentrated on the road and mentally cheered at how empty they were at the moment. At this rate, I could reach her house in less than five minutes.

"Will you be my Valentine?"

This brought a small smile to my lips. Only Ellie would ask you such a question in the middle of a situation like this.

"I'd love to, you beautiful little girl."

She giggled a little and I immediately felt better knowing that I made her smile. I finally reached her house, and pulled in the driveway. The roses were on the seat beside me. I bit my lip and shook my head a little.

I promise I'll see you tonight, Lena.

I took one rose from the bouquet and held it with my left hand. Afterwards, I locked the door and took the phone off speaker.

"Ellie, I'm here," I said, possessing a bad presentiment about this.

"Good, I'll open the door for you."

I opened my mouth to prevent her from doing so, but the dial tone signaled that she'd hung up on me. I walked to the front door and waited, impatiently tapping my foot on the *Welcome* carpet. I just hoped everything would turn out to be okay. If my theory was true and Scar was wasted, this could get into a very long night. I knew I couldn't leave without making sure they were both okay. I might even take Ellie with me for the night.

Click.

The door opened to reveal Ellie, in her pajamas, with tear streaked cheeks. Just as I had predicted, her teddy bear was being tightly held by her left arm. She immediately hugged my leg as I ruffled her hair.

"Lee-yum," she mumbled, barely audible. She was obviously very sleepy as this was *way* past her bedtime. I picked her up, and supported her body with one arm. She wiped her eyes tiredly with her fingers and then nuzzled her face in my shoulder. I kicked my shoes off, leaving me in my favorite white, yet thin socks. As I walked into their living room, I scanned it to find Scarlett.

Normally, I would be happy to be right, but this was a very bad situation.

There she was, her legs spread on the floor and her hair messier than a bird's nest. My eyes widened at the sight of five empty bottles of beer sitting by her side, a sixth one being chugged down. Her cheeks were blotchy and a tinge of red in her cheeks. She was obviously crying and swinging the bottle to her mouth from time to time. I felt pity and sadness. Scarlett had always been calm and collected, and I had always admired her for being so strong. But it seems like she decided to let everything out the bad way.

I turned to Ellie, who had already started sleeping on my shoulder. Grateful for Scar not noticing me yet, I crept upstairs. I entered Ellie's bedroom, which was no stranger to me. Butterflies were glowing in the dark on the ceiling, right above her bed. Ellie said that they make her happy and make her feel like a butterfly. Other than that, it was a normal, seven-year-old's room. The walls were a pale pink and purple, with soft flowers and vines randomly appearing on a couple of parts.

As I was heading towards the bed placed in the middle of the room, I stepped on something that could be a needle, a spike, or a bear trap. I jumped in the air, close to tears.

"OWW, OW, OW, OW! SHIT!" I howled, the pain in my right leg almost unbearable.

Ellie shifted on my shoulder and mumbled something that sounded like, *"Bad word, hmmm, unicorns"*. I bit my lip to keep myself from saying anything that might enter that little girl's vocabulary. And plus, for her age, she already knew *a lot.*

I tasted blood on my lip and looked down to whatever was under my foot. I licked my lip and clenched my left fist, the one holding the rose, at the sight of the devil itself.

A Lego piece.

I did nothing but flashed my middle finger on it. Legos were created to do nothing but make children happy and murder anyone who stepped on it. Even when I was young, I hated those stupid creations. Sometimes, we would have fun together, but all of that would dissipate into dust from the moment I stepped on them. I had a weird habit of forgetting to put one or two back and that resulted in me crying my eyes out because of stepping on one of them.

Scanning the floor in the darkness, I felt relieved to find no more of it. Mentally cursing, I walked towards Ellie's bed. I held her tiny waist with my hands and carefully laid her on the bed. I froze for a moment as she twitched and held Mr. Teddy closer to her. A small smile appeared on my face as I put the covers up to her shoulders. I placed my lips on her forehead.

"Sleep tight, my Valentine," I whispered, tenderly placing the rose in her hair. She was truly a small angel.

I tiptoed my way out of the room and left the door open a little bit. Ellie hated sleeping in complete darkness. I cracked my fingers and took a deep breath.

It was time to console a drunken teenage girl.

I went downstairs and found Scarlett in the same position I'd left her in. Although, now, she had finished the sixth bottle and was opening another one. I rapidly took the bottle from her hands, averting her attention to me. Her eyebrows furrowed and she pouted a little. She reached for the bottle, but I walked further away from her.

"Give it to meeeeee," whined Scar, standing up and getting closer. I shook my head and threw it in a small trash bin in the corner. Her face fell and her jaw opened. She stared at me, completely bewildered.

"W-why did youuu do that, huh?" she slurred, sobbing. I took her arm and made her sit on the couch. An awkward silence settled in, apart from her crying. I had to talk to her, but that meant having to speak.

No shit, Sherlock.

I cleared my throat and took a deep breath.

"What's wrong, Scar?" I asked softly. She turned to me, her eyes full with sadness and pain.

"Y-you wanna—(hiccup)—know what's wrong? You wanna know what's wr-wrong huh?" she said, deeply breathing. I nodded, praying that she would see the honesty in my eyes. Her eyes flickered to a family photo on the wall and she averted her eyes to me. I saw a fiery glint in her eyes.

"What's wrong is that I lost my mother. She left me here, all freaking alone. She was m-my only friend, my sister, and my best friend. She knew what to say to help, but w-what about now, huh? Every Valentine's day, w-we'd make Dad go out, we'd buy a box of—(hiccup)—chocolates and watch sappy movies and cry. W-whaaaat about now, huh? She abandoned me and it'sallherfault. She shouldn't have- she shouldn't have-" She hesitated, and then finished her sentence, "Yeah, she shouldn't have died."

"She never meant to leave you, Scar. She loved y—"

"NO! Don't you dare say that she loooooved me. (Hiccup). She meant to leave me here, with the weight of everything on my shoulders. S-she left me with a little sister whom I have to act like a mother to and take care of and my d-dad who cries every night. Everyone expects me to be strong and all of that bullshit, but I-I just can't. It's just so damn *hard*—(hiccup)." She started crying again and put her head in her hands.

My heart ached, because in a way, I knew how she felt. She didn't really have anyone to talk to and coping with this was hard enough for her. The wound was still fresh and bleeding, but no one was caring enough to clean it and bandage it. Scar was one of my good friends, so I had a duty of helping her.

And so I did what I had to do and what was a hundred times better than "I'm sorry for your loss."

"Come here," I mumbled, offering her a hug.

She obliged and soon enough, my shirt was getting wet. Her shoulders softly shook, as she let every little emotion bottled up inside come out. I rubbed her back soothingly, and her breathing got better. I could smell the alcohol on her breath though, and I knew that she needed rest. In the morning, a massive hangover was waiting to greet her.

After a few minutes of staying this way, she lifted her head up and pulled her body away from the hug. She sniffled a little and rubbed her eyes, resembling Ellie.

"Better?" I asked, feeling better myself. It felt good to know that I helped someone. She nodded and had a strange look in her eyes.

"Thank you, for everything," she said delicately, smiling.

"There you go! There's that smile!" I exclaimed as she chuckled a little. Her eyes met mine with a deep look in them. I recognized it as the one Lena gave me when she had something on her mind. Nervousness, courage and...love? But, there was no way there was *love* in Scar's eyes. We were just friends, absolutely nothing more. That thought seemed to comfort me a little, but the back of my mind was very suspicious.

"You know, Liam, there's something I-I've always wanted to tell you."

I held my breath and mentally cringed.

Please, don't say what I think you're about to say. *Please, please.*

"I-It's just the waaay you smile and how your eyes light up and I've always thought you were really, really nice and cute. A-and you just knooooow what to say when I'm saaaaad and you give the *best* hugs. Liam, I—(hiccup)—really like you," she stuttered, giving me a sincere smile.

My legs were suddenly really interesting. I had no damn idea of what to say. I scratched the back of my head uneasily.

"Hum, uh, well, I don't-"

Scarlett cut me off by lifting my head up and kissing me.

Kissing me.

I felt like stone, I couldn't move at all. I also didn't feel anything at all; this was absolutely *nothing* compared to kissing Lena.

"LEE-YUM! WHY ARE YOU KISSING SCAR!" screamed a voice that could only belong to one girl.

Ellie.

Scar pulled her lips away from mine, as a giggle escaped her lips. I looked at Ellie, who was crying and shaking her head disapprovingly at me. The rose in her hair was still in place, making her look angelic.

"Lee-yum, she isn't Lena," she whimpered, tears freely escaping her eyes.

I know.

"Look, I'm sorry. I don't see you that way, all right?" I blurted out in a rush, standing up. Scar shook her head, smiling sadly, and lay her head on the corner of the couch. She closed her eyes and soon enough, snores were filling the house.

I turned to Ellie, who looked disappointed in me.

"I don't, I swear. *She* kissed *me*, I swear. It'll *always* be Lena. Scarlett and I are nothing more than friends."

"Really?" said Ellie in a small voice. I nodded fervently and squatted down to be at her level, as she attacked me in an embrace.

"Well, promise me you won't ever kiss anyone else than Lena." She offered me her pinky, with an extremely serious expression on her face. I linked her pinky with mine, slightly squeezing it.

"I promise."

Suddenly, my phone started vibrating and ringing in my pocket. I pulled it out and stood up. Confusion flooded all over me as I saw that it was Adam. He *never* called. I answered, holding the phone to my ear.

"Hey, mate. You need to get your bloody ass in the hospital right *now,* do you hear me?" he said, his voice shaking.

Strangely enough, Ellie was already at the door, reaching for her winter jacket which was on a small shoe closet by the door.

"Why?" I managed to croak out, fearing his answer.

"Lena's dying."

27

Omnia Vincit Amor

"Love is composed of a single soul inhabiting two bodies."
~Aristotle~

Liam Christopher Black

"Lena's dying."

All breath caught in my throat and suddenly it felt as if all my senses had gone numb. My vision got fuzzy, but my ears were still glued to the phone. I blinked a couple of times, trying to process what he had said to me. The temperature had dropped to -100 degrees. Part of me wanted to laugh and praise Adam for that prank, but the other part of me was certain that he wasn't lying. After all, he knew how I felt about her and Adam wasn't dumb enough to lie about something so big.

"How?" I whispered, barely audible, but loud enough for Adam to hear. I heard someone, possibly a girl, hysterically crying and someone saying, *"Sh, it'll be all right, Tori."* After a little shifting around, my cousin's side seemed quieter.

"We don't know exactly, but about an hour ago, the doctor called. Her heart's failing and her breathing's slowing down. Plus, at the rate it's going, I doubt that we have more than an hour and then she'll-"

"Don't you even dare finish that sentence. She's not going to die, do you understand me? I won't *let* her die," I cut him off with a stern tone. I had no idea if I was convincing him or myself. Maybe I was just dreaming, maybe I was going to wake up and realize that none of this had ever even happened. The kiss, the coma, Lena on the verge of dy-

Stop.

"Yeah, I understand, but you need to get here, *now*," said Adam, the tone of urgency in his voice doing nothing but worrying me even more. I nodded fervently, but then remembered that he couldn't see me.

"I'll be there in less than five minutes," was all I said before hanging up. I clenched and unclenched my fists, trying to steady my breathing. I took in my surroundings. Scarlett was sleeping soundly, her mouth slightly open and a little drool rolling down her chin. The smell of alcohol filled the air and I felt my stomach uncomfortably churning. My whole body felt on fire and beads of sweat were forming on my forehead. I took one look at the door and a thought suddenly knocked on my head with an incredible force.

What are you waiting for? Go, NOW!

I took the car keys in my hand and was in a flash at the door, which was already strangely open. I was already walking outside, ignoring the feeling of my socks getting wet under the snow. Who cared about shoes at the moment? There wasn't a second to spare. Time was running out and Lena was on that god damned bed in the hospital, dying. Heading towards my car, I saw a small figure standing beside it. She was fully dressed for the weather, half of her face covered by the pink Hello Kitty scarf wrapped around her neck.

Ellie.

Upon seeing me, she lowered her scarf so she could speak. She looked completely pale in the moonlight. She pointed to the back door, with a *duh* expression. I ushered my hands in the air, waving them around, exasperated. Ellie rolled her eyes and knocked on the window of the back seat, folding her arms stubbornly.

"Ellie, please go inside, I need to leave," I pleaded. This was definitely the last thing I needed at the moment.

"I'm leaving with you, Lee-yum," she stated, stomping one foot in the snow, making a little snow rebound further away.

"Go inside, *now.*" I adopted a strict tone, which I never used with her; she was always obedient.

"*No.*"

At that moment, something inside of me snapped. All the bottled up anxiety, worry, and fear just exploded out.

"*JUST GO INSIDE, ELLIE! I DON'T NEED THIS RIGHT NOW,*" I yelled angrily.

Ellie cowered away a little, but the fiery look in her eyes didn't even falter. Her bottom lip came out a little, forming a pout. Her eyes widened innocently. She knew exactly what she was doing, and she knew it was going to make me surrender. Guilt immediately washed over me and I groaned tiredly.

I felt bad for screaming at her, but at least I knew that she understood. "I'm sorry. But you can't—oh, who cares? You know what? Just get in," I said, unlocking the door.

She got in and buckled up her belt and smiled with satisfaction. I got in the car and started the engine, not waiting a second to get out of the Jones' driveway. Ellie hit the belt with her hand, reminding me to wear it. I buckled it and kept my hands firmly on the wheel, slightly turning it when needed.

The road was empty, and I had to restrain myself from going on full speed. I struggled taking deep breaths to keep my concentration on the road ahead of me. I had to control myself from screaming at the slow car that had suddenly appeared in front of me. It was like walking behind an old lady who took tiny steps to go down the stairs. I simply changed lanes and tried to calm my nerves.

I didn't want to get pulled over by a cop, or worse, get into an accident. I couldn't risk another life lost, especially Ellie's. At the rate I was driving at, we could arrive at the hospital in less than ten minutes. I just hoped I wasn't late. I couldn't bear the thought of her dying. I had to see her, I had to see-

Lena.

She couldn't die. I wasn't going to allow it. I've had enough of this; *people leaving me.* I wasn't going to lose her. Somehow, a goal had been set. I wasn't going to let her leave me. How? No idea. Why? Because I love her. Lena Rose Winter was the only person who mattered to me and she had to stay.

Glancing at the fuel gauge, I groaned. The indicator was on "E", signaling an empty gas tank. I cursed under my breath. If this car broke down in the middle of this situation, I would personally put it up in flames. This vehicle has been with me through a lot and if it abandoned me at the moment, I would despise it forever.

I looked straight forward, sighing with relief upon realizing that this was the hospital's street. I've seen it in movies,

the hero's car runs for at least ten minutes and that's all I needed. The car would surely last two more minutes, was I right?

No, idiot, you're wrong again.

Halfway into the hospital's parking entrance, the car sputtered, coughing weakly and halting into a stop.

"Uh-oh," murmured Ellie, breaking the silence. I mentally agreed with her and grimaced. At least I could push it to be in the parking spot which was straightforward.

My mind was already set and I knew exactly what to do. I got out of the car and opened Ellie's door. I signaled for her to get out as well.

"Okay, Ellie, I want you to wait for me in front of this door, al right?" I asked, pointing to the entrance. She nodded obediently, going in the direction of the door.

I took several deep breaths, thinking of Lena. Frustration was running in my veins and I guess this was the way I had to let it out. I stood behind the car, and summoned every ounce of power in me. I put my hands on the car and pushed. It moved a little, but then almost immediately stopped.

Wrestling classes, huh?

"DAMN IT!" I screamed.

I decided on leaving the car here and dealing with it later. At the moment, *nothing* mattered more than Lena.

Just as I turned to leave, a bulky security guard was heading my way. Oh, come *on*. I expected him to force me to push the car in or go get gas, but to my surprise, he offered me his hand.

"Your keys, sir."

"W-why?" I asked, confused. He shook his head, amused, and pointed to Ellie, who shyly waved.

"The little lady told me you needed gas. I've got some in the ambulance garage. Give me your keys, and I'll park your car and fill it up," he said, nodded his almost-bald head towards me. Without another word, I gave him the keys and patted his shoulder gratefully.

I ran towards the door, seeing Trudy with Ellie. I rubbed Ellie's hair affectionately. She smiled a little, her eyes meeting mine. I saw a level of kindness and comprehension impossible for a seven-year-old girl to have.

"Come on, Lee-yum, you have a princess to save. I'll stay here with Mrs. Trudy."

I looked up at Trudy and she only ushered with her head to the left, where the hospital halls were at.

"Thank you," I said, already running towards room 173, the one Lena was in.

My legs did me a favor and ran at full speed. I ignored the people trying to stop me from running in the halls, only one name in my mind. I didn't get tired, even though Lena's room was on the other side of the hospital. I earned confused and angry stares, but I couldn't care less about what people thought right now. The most important person in my life was dying and I had to see her.

I halted to a stop upon seeing Adam, Tori, Catherine, Belle, and Mrs. Winter in front of her room. I was close enough to see them, but too far to see Lena through the glass. Adam was sitting on a chair beside Tori, whose head was buried in his chest and shoulders were shaking. He acknowledged my presence with a small nod, as his eyes poured pity on me. I hated the way he looked at me.

Catherine was comforting Mrs. Winter, softly rubbing her shoulder, and offering her tissues. Her eyes met mine with the same expression as Adam's. Lena's mother was devastated. Her hair was disheveled and her face was completely red, or at least what I could see of it. She blew her nose with a tissue and sobbed quietly, her gaze directed to the ground. Seeing her that way broke my heart, because she'd always been a funny woman who'd tease Lena and me with silly jokes. She looked up to me with sadness and put her head down again.

Belle, on the other hand, was as stiff as a stone. She was leaning against the wall, her eyes empty and completely dry. Her expression was sullen, as if she were staring into nothing.

I took a deep breath and turned to the glass revealing Lena. My heart almost stopped upon seeing her. She had somehow become thinner than the last time I'd seen her, which was only two days ago. Her face was as white as a sheet, her features as delicate as snow. Her eyelids were still firmly shut, framed by full eyelashes, as they hid her chestnut brown eyes which I yearned to see again. A tube was connected to her mouth, for the first time, looking as if it was plastered into them. She looked peaceful, as if she was having a nice dream.

My eyes watered and in only a few seconds, a waterfall of tears freely streamed down my face. Looking at her hurt, everything hurt. Seeing how frail she was and the fact that I could lose her in a matter of seconds had now fully dawned on me. My eyes flickered to the heart rate monitor and I cried harder seeing the line weakly going up. The beeping wasn't as fast or normal as usual, it could be estimated to 30/second. It seemed to me as if it kept on slowing down.

Lena was dying.

Dying.

I looked at the doctor, who had just arrived, looking flustered. It was Dr. Morrison, the same one who had dealt with

Grandma Darla. Running a hand through his disheveled gray hair, he sent me an exhausted smile, while clenching his clipboard.

"How long?" I questioned, fearing his answer.

"A couple more minutes." He shrugged helplessly.

"Can't you do CPR?" There *had* to be a way to save her.

"The doctors, or rather technicians, are on their way. They're just preparing the equipment and should be here any second now."

"Can I go in?" I asked. He shook his head.

"There can't be any contact with her right now. We have to preserve every second. CPR, or more specifically, defibrillation, only works within seven minutes after the death. If they come a second later, she'll be gone."

I felt goose bumps appear on my arms at the way he'd so casually said "death." I turned to the glass again and kept my eyes on her. Staying in that position for about ten minutes, which seemed like an eternity, I willed with all of my heart for her to open her eyes and that the heart rate monitor beep faster.

We all stayed in complete silence, except for the sobbing. I had stopped crying and my heart felt numb.

I felt numb.

All of a sudden, memories flashed in my head.

The first day I saw her, the way she'd awkwardly thanked me for catching her, the day at the park, the sunset, the way she'd slept on my shoulder, the way I felt truly happy with her that day, the way she laughed about everything, the way her eyes lit up at the thought of winning against me, the way she danced out of happiness, the way she loved Ed Sheeran, the way her eyebrows scrunched up when she was in deep thought, the way she cried, the way we danced in the snow on the day of the dance, the way we kissed, the way she made me feel over clouds, the way she enjoyed every bite of ice cream, the way she let me cry and didn't judge me, the way she understood, the way she jumped in front of me and took the hit, the way she made *every simple, little thing so damn **beautiful.***

My heart beating and her heart barely making the machine beep were the only noises I could hear. Her heart was slowing down, too fast. I knew what was about to happen, there were only seconds left.

"Please, don't," I murmured repeatedly, my hands on the glass separating us. Her chest went up for the last time, almost as if letting out her soul.

Beeeeeeeeeeeeeeeeeeeeep.

The machine let us hear the last heartbeat and announced the **end**. Lena's body went limp, even more than it already was. Bereaved, my head lowered, I could still see her. The tears did not fall; my desiccated eyes already pained excruciatingly from crying. My throat was parched from all that blubber.

"LENA!" screamed Mrs. Winter to my side, crumbling to the ground.

Convulsive sobs racked her body. Looking at Tori, I saw that she was in the same state as her mom. Well, almost. She was on the floor, holding her knees and moving back and forth, her face completely hidden by the redness and the tears. I locked my eyes with Adam, whose eyes were betraying by letting a few tears escape. The only person who wasn't crying was Belle. She was standing beside me, directly looking at Lena.

"Why are you all crying, huh? She's not dead, okay? SHE'S NOT FUCKING DEAD! STOP CRYING!" I screamed at the top of my lungs. They stayed in the same positions as before, as if they didn't hear me at all.

I turned to Dr. Morrison, who was looking at me with pity. I didn't know what came over me at that moment. I took his collar in my hands.

"DO SOMETHING! SHE CAN'T DIE!"

He shook me off, pointing to about five doctors/technicians/nurses. They rolled a small table with a machine on it into the room.

The next moments were a complete blur to me. As the technicians prepared the defibrillator, I felt my whole body tremble. As soon as the two blocks-like defibrillators touched Lena's chest, her body shook, but was still motionless. She made no sign of breathing and the heart rate monitor still wasn't emitting any sound. They did the same action three times, and each time, my heart shattered even more. Imagine seeing the only human being who has ever made you feel loved being electrocuted in order to come back to life. I knew that she wasn't being electrocuted, but that's what it seemed like to me.

After the fifth time, one of the technicians looked at Dr. Morrison and me and shook his head a couple of times before telling the others to pack. He took the tube out of her mouth and then hid what could still be seen from Lena by the white covers. He got out of the room and patted my shoulder, leaving.

"N-no, no, no, no," came out a stuttering voice. I watched as Dr. Morrison mouthed an, "I'm sorry for your loss." Just as he turned to walk away, I grasped his shoulder, forcing him to look at me.

"Can I try something? Please? Can I go in?" I begged. He nodded, an obvious thought displayed in his eyes. *"Poor boy."*

I walked into the room, my heart beating a billion times per second. I sat beside her and uncovered her face and hands, revealing her beautiful features. I felt tears spring into my eyes at her sight. She looked simply in a deep sleep. Her mouth was slightly parted and her lips were a pale pink color, which was better than any lipstick in the universe. Her hair was the same, a waterfall-like chocolate brown mass of hair, softly flowing on the pillow.

I took her hand in mine and put my knees on the floor. I didn't have the time to take a chair or what not. Keeping my gaze on her face, I did what I was supposed to do and what felt right. I leaned in her ear and said a few words.

"Lena, listen to me, and *please* come back to me," I said, my voice thick with emotion.

I imagined the opening verse of the song I was about to sing in my mind, as its melody escaped my mouth. There was no one else in the world, but Lena and me. I closed my eyes and let every memory of us into my mind and they seemed to be playing inside of my head like a movie. I put every emotion I had into that song. *Our* song.

"Settle down with me
Cover me up
Cuddle me in
Lie down with me
Hold me in your arms"

The day she tripped over her bag, and I caught her before she fell. That same day she hugged me for the first time. The other day when she affirmed my theory of her being a complete klutz by tripping on the bucket of water I was sweeping the floor with.

"Well, Liam. Thank you for saving my life, again."

"I'm Lena and you're Liam, aren't you?"

"Your heart's against my chest
Lips pressed to my neck
I've fallen for your eyes
But they don't know me yet"

"Thank you, Liam. You're the best thing that's ever happened to me in a while."

"You know, my dream is to be a bird. They fly in the sky and seem so free. They're almost never alone. Would you like to be a bird with me, Liam?" she asked dryly, now looking at me. Her eyes were spilling tears, they seemed unstoppable.

"Willyougowithmetothedance?Justasfriends,ofcourse,lik eduh ehem," she said, barely coherent.

"Well, I just...will you go to the dance with me, as friends of course?" She asked shyly, never taking her gaze off me this time.

"And the feeling I forget I'm in love now," I croaked out, tears wetting the covers.

The way she told me that she loved me.

"Yeah, she was right. Because one, your voice is the most amazing and beautiful thing I've ever heard in my life— because I might, possibly be in love with you too."

"You're not just a star to me, you're my whole damn sky, idiot."

"Kiss me like you wanna be loved
Wanna be loved
Wanna be loved

This feels like I've fallen in love
Fallen in love
Fallen in love

Settle down with me
And I'll be your safety
You'll be my lady

I was made to keep your body warm
But I'm cold as, the wind blows
So hold me in your arms"

I belted out the note, a flood of emotions drowning me.
The way the simplest of events could make her smile and dance around like a little child.
"It's snowing, Li! That's what I wanted to show you!"

**"My heart's against your chest
Your lips pressed to my neck
I've fallen for your eyes
But they don't know me yet**

**And the feeling I forget
I'm in love now"**

The way she laughed and giggled while being tickled and yet not so adorably kicked in every direction.
"S-Stop p-please!"
"L-Liam s-stop," she managed to gasp out between giggles.

"Kiss me like you wanna be loved
Wanna be loved
Wanna be loved
This feels like I've fallen in love
Fallen in love
Fallen in love

Yeah I've been feeling everything
From hate to love
From love to lust
From lust to truth
I guess that's how I know you
So hold you close
To help you give it up"

The way she saved my life.
"NO!" screamed Lena in alert.

"So kiss me like you wanna be loved
Wanna be loved
Wanna be loved"

I continued on singing until I finished the song. By then, my voice was barely audible. I felt the whole world collapsing upon me. It was over. There was no hope of her waking up again. No miracle could save her. It was over.

"I love you so much, Lena. I'm so sorry," I spoke softly, kissing her hand while gently, yet tightly clutching it. The tears kept on escaping from my eyes and there was no way to stop them. The indescribable amount of guilt that had built up in me for the eternity that I had lost in everything, everyone, had come out. I kept my stare on her hands, refusing to let go of her. My heart ached already at the thought of losing her.

Suddenly, my heart skipped a beat. Was I imagining things or had this just happened?

The hand I was holding squeezed mine.

I shook it off. The probability of me hallucinating at the moment was huge. Although, a light flickered in the back of my mind.

Squeeze.

Nope, this time was real. I saw it with my own eyes.

My ears realized that a noise had started in the distance and looking at the monitor, I felt my heart leap at the sight of the lines going up at a perfectly normal rate.

I lifted my gaze to her face and couldn't help but release a gasp of joy at the sight before me. I sensed a tide of happiness wash over me.

Eyelids fluttered and blinked a couple of times and then opened, revealing a pair of confused, but breathtaking chestnut brown eyes. They met mine and a certain kind of hope appeared in them. That familiar sparkle of recognition and love that she wore when she was with me, was there.

Lena was alive.

28

Ice carved Love

"We loved with a love that was more than love."
~Edgar Allen Poe~

Lena Rose Winter

A huge weight had laid itself upon my entire body and I began to slowly process what was going on. I felt literally numb, incapable of using any of all five senses or moving any body parts. I had no idea what was going on, as it felt as if a fog had ruled over my brain and thoughts. I couldn't decide if seconds or hours had passed by feeling like this, but my mind screamed; *moments.* I tried moving my toes, and thankfully, that worked. I felt my sense of hearing came first to me, but my ears took a few seconds to adapt to the sounds surrounding me.

I could only pinpoint one out of many, *someone crying.* Soft sobs shook their body, vibrating against mine. The mystery person's hand was clasped to mine and I recognized a certain familiar softness in them. The face was also close to my hips, where I felt whatever clothing on me got moist. Feeling myself getting stronger, I squeezed the hand holding me for comfort.

They, or should I say he, froze. I repeated the action, putting more emotion in it this time. He gasped, lifting his face.

With all the power I could muster in the world, I tried to open my eyes. I blinked several times, trying to get my vision to adjust. A bright light was shining in them, but with every second that passed, its strength lessened. The first thing I saw was *his* face. Bright, blurry blue eyes were staring down at me with happiness and it took me a few moments to process who it was. The tear-streaked red cheeks, defined features, and red lips helped me remember.

Suddenly, memories came rushing to me. They were all connected and *he* was in all of them. His eyes always stood out, a certain emotion appearing in them. Anger, sadness, happiness, disappointment, courage, confusion, and **love.** They made me realize who it was faster than you could click your fingers together.

Liam.

I kept on staring at him, as a small smile formed itself on his angel-like face. That action immediately spread happiness in my veins. And with every second that passed by, he became clearer to my eyes. With every second that passed by, he looked even better to me.

"Lena?" he asked, his voice raspy and barely audible. He seemed hesitant and confused, yet somehow on the point of jumping up and down in joy.

"Hey," I managed to blurt out, as my voice was scratchy. As soon as I spoke, my throat felt dry. "Water," I whispered.

Liam immediately stood up and took a bottle of water that was messily lying on the floor. Someone must've dropped it.

He brought the edge to my lips and frankly, the cold water felt like heaven in my mouth. I gulped the biggest amount I could and shook my head, signaling that I'd had enough. He placed the bottle on the night table beside me and sat again, keeping his gaze on me.

That moment was interrupted when came in Annabelle, Victoria, and Adam, running towards me. They had a bewildered look on their faces, as if shocked. Puzzled, I turned to Liam with a questioning stare.

"What happened?" I asked, just as it all came back to me.

Leo, the fight, Liam, me running in front of him to prevent two full bottles of wine crashing on his head. The bottles crashing on *my* head. And then, absolutely nothing.

"You...were in a coma," said Tori, holding my other hand. She shared a look with Liam and he nodded in agreement with whatever message that passed between them. Belle and Adam apparently understood too, because they bobbed their heads as well.

My heart fell. *A coma?*

"How long?" I murmured, oblivious to the stares they were giving each other.

"Two months," said Adam, rubbing Tori's shoulder. My mouth parted slightly as I absorbed that information.

"*Two* months? Oh my god, I missed so much in school, I might even fail my year and-" I was cut off upon the sight of Mom staring at me, but she was on the other side of the room. Her eyes were wide and she seemed as if she'd seen a ghost. But I was alive, wasn't I?

"Hey, Mom," I said, giving her a smile. I expected her to cry, or laugh or even hug me, but no, she stayed glued like that. I looked at Tori, but she just ushered for me not to worry about it. I gave her a small smile, although something was twisting and turning inside of me.

Pain came rushing to me and I felt my chest ache miserably. I gasped from the agony. The people around me seemed more alert.

"I think one of my ribs is broken," I said.

Tori's eyebrow rose. Liam simply squeezed my hand, worry literally radiating off him. His face slackened; his brow furrowed—eyes darting about in concern as if he was searching for a place to hide.

"It's normal," said Belle hesitantly.

I was confused. "Why?"

They stayed silent. "Come on, tell me!" I urged, wincing at the pain the effort to say that took.

"You needed CPR," spoke Mom for the first time.

And it was the way they stared at me that made me know. I took in a sharp intake of breath.

"I…died?"

Trying to remember how to breathe, I felt my chest tighten. I didn't understand, as if my brain became short-circuited and needed to be rebooted. It was like my mind had gone blank, that single announcement stunning me.

I had died.

And now I was alive.

"And…how did I come back?" I breathed shakily, taking my trembling hands away from Liam's. He flinched.

"CPR," said Adam, a hidden look in his eyes. It was certain that there was way more to it than CPR and I wanted to know. I didn't want any more secrets, hidden in the shadows.

"And?"

"I-I sang to you," murmured Liam, almost ashamed. Belle smiled at him.

"Really?" I asked, truly surprised. He nodded.

To find out that I died was something, of course. I would've been with Dad. Although, I didn't want to. As much as I missed him, I wanted to see him again when the time came, when I was old and wrinkled. And I partly had Liam to thank for the fact that I was alive. I was aware that CPR had done the major, main role of *reviving* me. The concept of dying had been one of my fears and I was happy that I wasn't. To be perfectly honest, I didn't mind. I was alive now and that was all that mattered.

Liam singing to me was something else. It proved to me that he truly did care, and he didn't want to give up on me. He didn't want to lose me, and he had made sure to be by my side no matter what. He didn't let me go, even though some people said that it was better to. In a way, he had fought for me, to keep me alive.

"Liam?"

He turned to face me, expressionless. I leaned in and put my lips on his, hoping that the gratitude and happiness I felt would be transmitted to him. Pulling back, I gave him a smile.

"Thank you."

"Oi," called out Tori. "Don't go all lovey-dovey. There are other people here too."

I chuckled, looking at Adam's hand holding hers.

"Mom? You okay?" I asked, looking at the blank look in her eyes.

She suddenly walked towards the bed and Tori moved to give her space. She reached out and wrapped her arms around my head. I could feel her crying.

"I thought I lost you," she mumbled repeatedly through tears. I felt my eyes prickle as well and I let a few tears fall.

"I'm here now," I reassured her.

She held me like that for a long time, and for the first time, I realized just how much she cared. It dawned on me; the people here, they all cared about me.

I smiled.

***

"Goodbye, dear," said Nurse Trudy, tightly hugging me. I smiled at how close we'd become in the short space of a week.

That old lady sat with me for hours after my awakening from the coma, simply talking to me. She told me about how Liam came to see me almost every day and would sing; about Ellie, whom I haven't exactly met yet; about Annabelle, who apparently came every Monday and Friday and wept by my side. I had gained a huge amount of respect for that girl, especially after the day she came to visit and poured her heart to me. We both cried together and I realized that Belle was one of the strongest people I knew. I did my best to comfort her, as she blamed herself for the incident at the restaurant.

"Now, I want you to take care of yourself and do me a favor; don't go to any more restaurants. All right?" the nurse said, chuckling. I nodded obediently, giving her a sly grin. She put her hands on my shoulders, her expression turning serious. Black strands of hair flecked with white fell into her face, her bun on the verge of breaking loose. Her hazel eyes, piercing mine, contrasted on her cinnamon-colored skin.

"I want you to know, that boy loves you more than anything in the world. Take care of him, just like he took care of you, because he deserves it. He deserves love and so do you. Promise me to do everything you can to make him happy," she said, warming my heart at the mention of *him*. I saw a small glint in her eyes, as if she knew something I didn't.

"I promise." Although, I knew that deep down, I would never be able to repay Liam for standing by my side during the coma. For not leaving me.

For loving me when I was at my worst.

"Oh dear," said Trudy, glancing at her watch, "my break was over fifteen minutes ago."

"Go, it's okay. I promise this won't be the last time I see you." I gave her a cheeky grin, making her chuckle.

Trudy smiled, pecking my cheek. She walked away, leaving me alone with my mom.

"Let's go, Lena." Mom patted my shoulder, signaling that these were officially and hopefully my last moments in this hospital. I turned to her and she put one arm around me as we made our way out of Sainte-Catherine's hospital. I gave small waves to some friends I'd made over the last week. I didn't have the right to go outside, but the doctors said that it wouldn't do me any harm to walk around the halls. The nurses gave me slight smiles and I returned them back.

Opening the entrance doors, I almost cried of contentment. As I hadn't gone out of a building in more than two months, well, it had felt like having a deep sleep, feeling the wind in my hair and the sun's light on my face felt like heaven. We were in February now, but the piles of snow in some corners of the parking indicated that spring wasn't coming by for a long time. I smiled upon seeing freshly fallen snowflakes glittering at the contact of the sun, making them appear like diamonds.

After a thirty-minute drive, Mom stopped the car and I pulled my headphones out of my ear, stopping my train of thoughts. Surprisingly, she gave me a small smile that held childish mischievousness. She led me to the house and stood beside the door, as if waiting for me to open it. I raised an eyebrow as she handed me the keys.

I gave her a confused look, but she pointed at the door. Removing one of my incredibly soft mittens off, I inserted the key in the hole and twisted the knob. I pushed the door and it opened wide.

Weird.

There was a strange smell: perfume and cake. The lights were out, the curtains were closed, and even though it was only 4 in the afternoon, I couldn't see anything. I put my hand on the wall to my side, patting it to find the switch.

'WELCOME BACK HOME!" screamed about 20 people as the lights turned on. I nearly jumped out in fear. But, realizing what was going on, a grin was immediately plastered on my face and I felt joy rush through me at the sight in front of me.

Decorations were placed literally everywhere in the living room: colorful balloons, garlands hanging from random spots. Our small dining table had been moved from the kitchen and was filled with pizza, soft drinks, and a huge chocolate cake. A banner reading "WELCOME BACK, JACK" was hanging from the wall, but the Jack part was scribbled on and beside it, there was a messy *Lena.*

Belle, Tori, Adam, and a couple of school friends were present there too. They all rushed my way, each giving me a hug. I searched for the brown, almost black tall head, but found no one.

After about an hour of chatting with people, eating, and just plain old celebrating, I sat on the couch taking small sips of my Coke and watching others socialize. A small, dry chuckle escaped my lips as I overheard Kevin from science flirting with

Belle, but she replied, "Listen, Reddie, I'm not really in the mood for this. So go, flirt your silly bum with some airhead, okay?" And that's when the poor boy blushed as red as his hair and shamefully walked away.

Boy, was she good with boys or what!

A small girl came towards me and sat next to me. She gave me a small smile. Long blonde hair framed her face. She had blue eyes that shone with curiosity and wonder.

"Hello," she said.

"Hi?"

She stuck out her hand to me, "I'm Ellie."

My mouth dropped a little, but I gladly shook her hand. "I'm Lena. I've heard a lot about you."

She grinned. "Lee-yum talks about you a lot, too." I felt my heart get warm at the mention of him.

"You're an amazing little girl, do you realize that?"

I thought back to what Liam had told me about her.

She nodded. "And you're very pretty."

"Can I hug you?" I said. She answered by attacking me into a hug. I laughed a little.

"Don't ever hurt Lee-yum again, please. Don't go to sleep."

She was talking about the coma.

"I promise I'll take care of him," I said.

"Good," she said, eyeing the plate full with chocolate cupcakes hungrily. "Do you want a cupcake?"

I shook my head. "No, you go get one."

She smiled at me again and went to take one.

At the same moment Ellie stood up and left, Tori plopped herself next to me and gave me a one-sided hug.

"Hey there, *pretty brown eyes*," she sang the last part. I gave her a half-heartened smile, hoping she'd buy it. Her eyebrows instantly furrowed and she switched from *happy* to *worried.*

"What's wrong?" she asked, her brown eyes shining with curiosity and concern.

"Where's Liam?" I answered instead.

Her expression changed, from confused, to giddy, to excited, to mischievous. When Tori was mischievous, *something* was about to happen.

"I don't know," she said, shrugging. I rolled my eyes at her subtlety. Nudging her a couple of times, I tried to get it out of her.

"Tell me, please?" I whined, ignoring the fact that I sounded like a baby.

"I-I don't know, I swear." She giggled, as the poking turned into tickling. I gave up, slumping back to the couch.

"I officially hate you," I declared just as Adam called her over. Tori gave me a sly wink and walked, or technically ran into her lover's direction.

I sat alone for a couple of minutes, glad that everyone had forgotten about me. I kind of needed the peace and quiet. Actually, I really wanted to see Liam right now. You know that feeling when your heart's all fidgety and sending butterflies everywhere? Yeah, I had that.

Bad.

Belle, Adam, and Tori were now walking towards me, but that wasn't what scared me, it was the freaky smiles on their faces. It was the kind of smile that made them seem as if they had won the lottery or murdered someone and hid their body in an unknown island in the middle of the Antarctic Ocean.

They kept on getting closer and then each sat beside me.

"What's up?" I asked, slightly nervous. "Guyyyys," I trailed off, not really knowing what to expect. Adam gave Tori a thumbs-up sign and she nodded in determination. She turned to me and grinned.

And suddenly, I was blindfolded by my favorite scarf that smelled like strawberries. My vision went completely *black*. I automatically reached to un-tie it, but one of them held my hands together and clutched them tightly.

How fantastically wonderful.

"What's going on?"

I received no answer. I was helped up and my sister was pushing me to walk in an unknown direction. It seemed as if no one noticed the kidnapping going on.

"Stairs, be careful," muttered Tori. I went down the stairs, which made me understand that I was going into the basement. The door behind me closed, signaling that I was left alone.

I took the blindfold away from my eyes and opened them to be met with complete darkness.

There was a slight shuffling. I felt a fear creep on my arms. I was not a fan of the darkness. "Um, hello?"

As if by magic, a dozen candles or so lit up and cleared my vision. They formed a gigantic rectangle. In the middle of it all sat Liam with a small smile on his face. He sat on a picnic blanket and stood up upon seeing me.

He bowed a little and took my hand. He placed a small kiss on it that made my heart skip a beat. "M'lady."

I laughed. "Liam?"

"Please, do sit." He offered a pillow that was on the ground. I sat on it and watched as he sat in front of me.

"Are you mentally unstable?" I asked before I could help myself. He chuckled. There seemed to be a fire dancing in his eyes because of the candles.

"No," he said, taking a small basket from behind him. He gave me a plastic bowl and took out a big *Ben & Jerry's* container. I let out a small gasp.

"Cheesecake brownie?" I asked, already knowing the answer. He nodded, took out an ice cream scoop. He put three large balls of the delicious looking ice cream into my bowl and did the same to his.

I took a bite of it with a plastic spoon and moaned in delight. "Oh, god."

"I know," said Liam, savoring the ice cream himself.

"So you invited me down here to eat ice cream, surrounded by candles—" I paused at him, pointing at the ceiling, "—under glow in the dark stars and a moon?"

He nodded. "Nothing but the best for you." He winked in an exaggerated way. I let out an unladylike laugh.

"You rock," I said.

We sat there for what seemed like forever, eating ice cream and talking. There was something different about the way he talked and the way he was. He was more carefree, yet I noticed the spark of fear in his eyes. He had developed strength.

I stared down at the empty bowl of ice cream and grimaced. He caught my look and offered the half empty box. I took a big scoop of ice cream and looked at it.

Liam seemed concerned. "You okay?"

"Other than a pain in my ribs and a slight brain freeze, I'm fine."

Liam's eyebrow rose.

"Can I put ice cream on your face, please?" I asked.

"Uh, sure?"

And so I did exactly that. He let out a small shriek when the freezing cheesecake and brownie flavored ball collided with his face.

"Why?" he asked.

I shrugged. "I wanted to see that." I stifled a laugh.

He scooped up a small amount of ice cream and put it on my face as well. "Liam!" I cried out, shivering. He slid a spoon on my face so that the ice cream was well distributed.

I started laughing hysterically. "Why?" I said, in the same tone he used earlier.

He grinned and his ice cream covered cheeks looked adorable. "I wanted to see that."

We looked like idiots, faces covered with ice cream and grinning like Cheshire cats, but it was a moment I wanted to capture and keep forever.

"Would you be mine?" he said. His eyes got wide at the question he asked. It was obvious that he didn't mean to say it.

I looked at him.

He sighed. "Would you be mine, Lena?"

I blinked.

"I can't risk losing you, not again. Please, be mine."

I leaned over and placed my lips on his. I pulled back and smiled.

"It would be my pleasure. And I'm not just saying that because you give me ice cream and you taste like it."

He smiled.

29

Euphoria

"But it wasn't about their love story; it was the way he looked at her. She was his savior, the one who helped him get up after the world pushed him down. He thought she was the most beautiful human to set foot on Earth, and made her believe it. I, personally, hope to find a love as strong as theirs one day."
~The Author~

Lena Rose Winter

Staring out the clear window, I admired the view before me. The gravel-gray skies were bare today; there was no storm. A beautiful layer of snow lay on the ground from yesterday's harsh storm.

"Mooooom! Please?" I pleaded, watching as my mother literally tucked me in the couch, as if I was a little kid about to go to sleep.

Except that it was 3 in the afternoon and I was far from being a kid now.

"NO! You're sick and you're not getting out of the house. I don't care if you have homework, you need to rest. It's all Liam's fault," she exclaimed, putting on her jacket and eyeing me disapprovingly. Although, faking anger was not her thing at all. A hint of amusement on her face betrayed her.

"Please, I was sick this week, I'm not sick anymore! And don't blame Liam," I protested. And it was true, I came down with a strong cold this week, but this morning, I felt just fine. The wonders medicine can do.

"Oh, don't smile like that!" she scolded, seeing the smile forming on my face. I shook my head at her, taking a sip of the hot chocolate in my hands. Sneaking a peek at her, I mentally praised her outfit. She wore a pale blue sweater that complimented her skin, black boots with small heels and a big, elegant white coat. Knowing her, she didn't usually dress up like that for nothing. So, there must've been something special waiting for her.

"Now, I'll be back at around six, okay?" she said, planting a small kiss on my forehead and heading for the door.

"Mom?" I said, stopping her for a second.

"Yeah?"

"You're going out with Roger, aren't you?" I asked, a small smile forming itself on my face. She nodded, affirming my thoughts. I stood up, the huge checckered blanket wrapped around me securely. I attacked her in a hug, feeling her body relax.

"Is he outside?"

She blushed, and that was enough for me to know. I hadn't seen Roger since the first date he had with my mom, the same day where I snapped at her. I never had the chance to apologize to him for my behavior. Besides, if my mom was going to start dating again, I was better off being on good terms with the luckiest man.

"I want to meet him, please," I said, smiling at her. Her face brightened considerably and she took out her phone and called him. In the span of seconds, the doorbell rang and I opened the door.

This time, instead of being too busy being shocked, I actually looked at him. He was handsome, still taller than Mom even when she wore heels. His black hair had a few gray hairs in it, but that suited him. He was heavily dressed up; I could see that he was someone who didn't like the cold.

"Hello, I'm Lena," I greeted, holding out a hand for him to shake. He smiled; a welcoming expression on his face. He seemed relieved.

"Roger Johnson."

"I'm incredibly sorry for being so rude and impolite the last time, I'm really sorry," I apologized. Mom squeezed my shoulder, gratitude for my actions evident.

"It's perfectly okay, I understand," he said, looking at my mom with a twinkle in his eyes. I could feel that this wasn't their second date and I was perfectly fine with that.

"I'm happy for you too, and please treat her well."

"Always," he said with a wink. "May I?" He offered his arm to my mom, who accepted happily. She blew me a kiss before heading out with him. I felt my heart warm at the sight of her staggering to walk in heels in the snow; she held on his arm tightly. She slipped, but he caught her just in time. The couple's laughter filled the air, and I smiled, chuckling to myself as I closed the door.

Mom was in good hands.

I let out a sigh, boredom already reigning over me. Tori was out for the whole day; Adam took her to a Winter Amusement park, something like that. Belle was occupied as well; she had work today. Liam, well, he had said that he was busy today for some reason that he refused to tell me.

Liam.

He was mine, I was his. I really did like the concept of that. Some nights I still pinched myself to make sure I wasn't dreaming. I knew I was still too young to be truly in love, but I was. This wasn't some kind of a silly high school crush. It wasn't about his looks or his shy attitude, it was about everything. I could've went on and on, but the fact that he was so sure of loving me back was one of the many reasons.

Oh, for God's sake, he came to visit me when I was in a coma.

I swear, he is like a perfect character coming out of a book written by a teenager, I thought, my heart fluttering at the thought of him.

I took out the movie Aladdin and put in the DVD player. To be perfectly honest, Disney movies never grew old and would always be my favorite type of movies. They knew how to blend romance, humor, action, and mystery in about two hours.

After about an hour into the movie, the doorbell resounded in the house. I stopped the movie, mad at Aladdin for lying to Jasmine again about "getting dressed up as a commoner to escape palace life" like her. He kissed her, that pose paused because of me.

I reluctantly stood up, groaning. I had no idea who it was, but I was disturbed by the fact that they interrupted the movie and my little moment. Opening the door, I instinctively pulled the huge checkered blanket tighter around me, the frostbitten wind giving me goose bumps.

"Hey there," said a voice that I knew too well. Liam was standing in front of me, completely obscured and safe of the frosty weather, except for his face. His scarf was messily covered around his neck, his lips barely showing. Blue eyes shone with excitement and mischief.

Ah, I guess Aladdin was interrupted with a good reason.

"Are you just going to ogle me all day and not let me in?" he said, smirking. I felt my cheeks get warm and ushered for him to come in. Upon closing the door, he placed a chaste kiss on my cheek casually before taking his jacket, hat, scarf, and gloves off.

"Ellie's coming in a few minutes, too. I didn't want your mom to kill me for being here," he declared. I simply nodded. Babysitting Ellie seemed really fun, and the idea of spending time with Liam was even more pleasing.

"I have something for you before that though," he smiled, taking a small box out of his pocket. My smile faded and I simply looked at him, shocked.

"Really?" I whispered, shocked. He simply grinned, although a spark of anxiety appeared.

"Merry late Christmas and happy late Valentine's day," he declared, putting the *Tiffany's* box in my hands. He suddenly froze, as if realizing something.

"What?" I asked, curiosity taking the better of me. He looked up at me, guilt written all over his features.

"I need to tell you something first, actually," he stated, taking my hand. His expression was cautious. He seemed afraid of my reaction, but ready to help right away.

"Is it good or bad? Or so bad I'll drop dead?" I said jokingly, trying to cast the horrible cloud that had set itself on him away. He didn't answer, silence being his answer.

"Come on, don't scare me. What is it?" This time, my voice was much softer. He led me to the couch, forcing me to sit down beside him. I was scared of his next words, Liam was unpredictable. He wasn't going to announce that he was going to die, right?

"You know the day you woke up from the coma?"

I muttered a small "hm," impatient for him to actually spill. How could I possibly have forgotten that day? It was the day I'd finally woken from my long, long slumber.

"Scarlett-"

"Ellie's sister?" I cut him off, a beautiful blonde coming to my mind.

"She sort of, kind of kissed me."

My heart sank. It felt as if someone had taken an exceptionally sharp needle and pointed it on the happy bubble that had formed itself around me and had taken pleasure while popping it. It seemed as if he was holding his breath, anticipating a breakdown or me yelling at him.

"But she was completely drunk and she was sad, and she just forced me to. I just—I'm so sorry! I didn't even kiss her back," he blabbered. I stopped him by putting my hand on his mouth, his lips now clasped shut.

"It's okay, I understand," I said slowly, taking deep breaths. He was trying to read my expression, but it was hard since I had put on an impenetrable mask. Instead, I forced a small smile and nodded comprehensively. I *did* understand, but the sharp pain in my gut would not leave.

He took my hand away and looked at me hesitantly.

"Are you okay?"

"It's fine! Don't look at me like I'm going to explode! And plus, you're not her boyfriend, right?" I said, more to myself than to him, feeling slightly better. I pecked his cheek, and he instantly brightened, but uncertainty was still haunting his face.

It was *okay though; he kissed her before we were officially together.*

"Thank you for telling me though, it means a lot."

And for the third time that day, the doorbell rang, making me clench my fists. The last thing I wanted at the moment was to be interrupted, again. Taking a deep breath to stabilize myself, I walked to the door and twisted the doorknob.

"Lena!" cried out a little blonde girl, throwing herself at my feet, hugging them. I couldn't help but smile, she was so loveable.

"I'll come pick her up at 6, if that's okay?"

I looked up at the voice and my eyes met Scarlett's blue ones. She stared at her sister with such love and kindness and I knew that I had no right to be jealous, even a little.

"Yeah, that would be just fine," I answered, feeling Liam's presence beside me. He had obviously stiffened, as did Scarlett when she saw him. Her smile disappeared, her lips pursed into a fine line.

"I told her," said Liam to Scarlett. She nodded. Ellie looked at all of us, a confused look adorning her angelic face.

"Are you mad?" Scar shuffled her feet, her cheeks getting warm despite the freezing weather.

"No, I really am not. I understand, it's okay," I reassured her, but she didn't seem to believe me.

"I'm really, really sorry, I was stupidly drunk and I just—what, El?" she was cut off by her little sister tugging on her sleeve urgently.

"Lena isn't mad at you, so stop saying sorry," moralized the girl, making me praise her incredible intelligence and ability to comprehend what was going on.

"Okay, bye, hon. Thanks again, guys, I'll see you later," she said, walking to her car. Liam closed the door and I watched Ellie take off the winter bundle she had on professionally, without needing any help. That girl was independent and strong and I loved her for that.

"What do you want to do?" Liam picked her up and put her on the couch. I knew that she was too old for that, but he just liked having her in his arms. He loved kids in general.

"Can someone tell me a story?" questioned Ellie, widening her eyes in wonder.

She knows that Liam's a sucker for puppy dog eyes, I thought, laughing. Liam turned to look at me skeptically, while Ellie joined me, her laughter ringing in my ears.

"What?!" asked Liam, feeling left out. We continued on laughing, even though I was pretty sure that we were laughing for different reasons. I waved him off, amused by his bewildered face.

"Lee-yum, can you tell me a story?" she repeated her question, pouting her lips this time.

"Only if Lena tells it with me..." he trailed off, looking at me expectantly. I rolled my eyes at him and nodded fervently. I was almost certain that this wasn't the typical "Cinderella" type of storytelling; this was the "make-up-at-the-moment" kind.

"Can you get us pillows, please? Three, if possible." I furrowed my eyebrows at his question, but ran upstairs and got the pillows lying on my bed.

I had to admit that I was frustrated by the fact that he never told me what the second thing was and he never gave me the chance to open the box. But I was determined to talk to him later.

Descending the stairs, I beamed at the sight before me.

Liam had taken the liberty of laying the blanket across the couch. He was currently concentrated on tying Ellie's hair into a ponytail, but her protests that he was tugging too hard made a grimace appear on his face.

"May I?" I said, throwing the pillows on the couch. Liam let her hair fall loose and handed me the elastic, sighing. I removed a part of the blanket, sat on the couch, and then covered my legs with the blanket. Liam put the pillows behind each of us and sat again.

"Lee-yum is horrible at making ponytails," stated Ellie, positioning herself to be close to me. Liam's face darkened and scooted himself further away. Ellie pulled her tongue at him. I took her golden hair in my hands, gathering all the strands to blend in, and gently wrapped the elastic twice around the tail I'd made.

"All done!" I exclaimed. Ellie touched various parts of her head, making sure that every strand was in the ponytail and kissed my cheek. She thanked me, and gave Liam a look.

"Lee-yum," whined Ellie, "come back here, I want all of us to be close."

Liam obliged, he came closer to Ellie.

"Let's start! Lena, would you like to start?" he asked and I nodded. Ellie averted her attention to me with a twinkle in her eye; I could tell that she loved stories.

"Once upon a time, a princess named Elizabeth lived with her mom, the queen. When Liz was a baby, a mean fairy cursed her to be forever sad. The princess never smiled, *ever,*" I started, gaining a shocked gasp from Ellie.

"The only way she could ever be happy was if she found true love," continued Liam. "The Queen made Liz meet every prince from all over the world. But every time, Liz would cry, because she knew that he was not the one for her."

"The kingdom was devastated. The thought of their young princess being so sad made them sad. Like every day, Liz went to watch the sun go down by the river Ohana. She would cry there and be sad for herself. After all, being sad forever was horrible." I stopped. The name Ohana had just come to me, I remembered that it meant *family* as soon as I had said it.

"Terrible," agreed Ellie in a hushed voice, her eyes wide with interest. She turned to Liam, realizing that it was his turn to speak.

"Uh, well, one day, she saw a boy sitting by the river too, at the same time as her. She had a strange feeling in her heart, but she gathered up her courage in two hands and said: *Hello.* He didn't answer, he was extremely shy, but she broke the ice. Liz talked to him about how beautiful the sunset was, and the boy knew in his heart that he was going to fall in love with her," he said, saying the last sentence looking straight at me.

Memories flashed in my brain and I remembered the day we had watched the sunset together at the park. The day I had talked to him and spent time with him for the first time. I couldn't believe he didn't forget about that day; it seemed to be an eternity ago, rather than few months ago.

"Liz, too. She knew that she found the one for her, because the second he told her his name, which was, uh, Ian, she smiled at him. For the first time in her whole life! She smiled at him and introduced herself too. And the curse was broken, because she found her true love," I went on, feeling absorbed in the story as well.

"And then?" whispered Ellie, rubbing her eyes.

"Liz and Ian were never sad again. They lived happily, ever after," finished Liam, a small, knowing smile on his features. Ellie closed her eyes and snuggled up against the pillow behind her.

Soft snores were being emitted from her and I let out a soft chuckle at her innocence. Liam took a pillow with one hand and picked her up with the other and pointed to the stairs. I nodded, not minding that he would put her on my bed to sleep.

When he came back down, he sat beside me and took my hand. I lay my head on the soft pillow underneath my head, feeling peaceful.

"Good story," I murmured.

"I couldn't have done it without you," he answered.

"We should start our own storytelling business. We're not just good; we rock!" I exclaimed in a hushed voice. He let out a laugh and offered a high-five, which I accepted gladly.

Silence reigned over, but the comfortable kind. I decided that it was a good time to open the box that was on the coffee table.

He took the box and handed it to me.

"Open it."

And I did.

There was the most beautiful necklace I'd ever seen. The pendant was a silver snowflake, the light in the room hitting it causing it to glisten. For the second time that day, a memory flashed in my mind. It was the day I had met up with Liam at the park, when we witnessed the first snowfall, signaling the start of winter. I was at a loss for words.

"You-you got me this?!" I exclaimed, tears welling up in my eyes. They fell on my cheeks, displaying my joy.

"As I said before, merry late Christmas and happy late Valentine's," he replied, grinning at my reaction. He kissed my cheek, causing it to burn.

"I love you!" I blurted out, instead of thanking him. His face brightened, if possible. The smile on his face lit up the whole room, it was infectious.

"You know I love you too."

And in my head, I had been happy dancing.

I got a spontaneous idea—the perfect way to pass time while Ellie was sleeping and to simply have fun together.

"Are you up for a snowball fight?"

He burst into laughter, making my heart flutter.

"Your mom would kill me; you know how sick you were last week. You could barely take any notes in class and you went out of class at least five times to freely blow your stuffed nose. And when Mr. Collins refused to let you out, your nose-cleaning made the whole class look at you." His comment caused me to slap his arm jokingly; it wasn't nice of him to make fun of me like that.

"But I'm fine now! Please, please, please, please," I begged, giving him a look that resembled the one Ellie gave him earlier. He let out a sigh and stood up. He started putting his jacket on and I copied his actions. When we were finally ready to *play* in the snow, we went out. I guided him to my backyard, where there was a fine coat of snow.

"What about Ellie?" he asked, suddenly stopping.

"She'll be sleeping for a long time and knowing you, we won't stay here for more than half an hour," I reassured him, poking him with my gloved hand.

I let myself fall in the snow, not caring about how my butt was going to freeze. The jacket I was wearing covered me to my knees, so my rear end was in safe hands. Pulling myself up, I took a handful of snow and formed it into a perfect snowball.

"Heads up!" I cried out, throwing the snowball at his hip. His lips formed an "O" and he started forming his own snow ball, hitting my back.

"It's on!" he screamed.

And soon enough, several snowballs were being thrown in the air. I didn't know how much time had passed by, nor did I care. Snowflakes were one of nature's most fragile things, but look what they could do when they stuck together; attack my boyfriend. I was creating warm memories in the cold of winter with Liam and that was all that mattered.

"Boo-ya!" A ball crashed into his head, making him laugh heartily.

Throwing another snowball, I grinned, satisfied by the fact that it directly hits his heart.

"Oh no, I am dead!" he exclaimed dramatically, falling in the snow-covered ground with a *thump*. I giggled, running to him, every footstep seeming to cause my leg to be pushed further into the snow.

"Oh no, my prince is dead! Maybe a true love's kiss will save him!" I said, pecking his lips. A few wisps of my hair fell to my face in the process, as I tried to blow them away. Liam's fingers tucked the lost strands behind my ear, smiling.

"What?" I asked, lying beside him in the snow. He took my mitten-covered hand in his and we both stared at the sky.

"We have such a sappy love story, do you realize that?" he wondered. His blue eyes were glued to the heavy, swollen clouds above us. A snowflake landed on my cheek; it was snowing, and I couldn't feel warmer.

"Yeah. But it was all worth it in the end. We're here now, aren't we?"

And it was true. We were happy.

"No, but I mean our love is different, I think."

"Good different, or bad different?" I thought out loud.

"Definitely good. Of all the books I've read and the movies I've watched, I've never felt anything like this. I guess you could say that our love is just-"

"Unique?" I finished, happiness settling in my heart. I had a feeling that it would stay there for a long time.

"Yeah, definitely."

Year 2025

Narration

Lena went through two years of a photography course. She now owns a small shop called ForeverTogether in Times Square, which, throughout the years, had been making a lot of progress and becoming more and more known. During Liam's first year of University and Lena's first year of the photography course, they mutually agreed to take a break. They both needed to concentrate on their studies, it was their priority. And in their hearts, they knew that they would be together again.

She had invited Liam to the opening of ForeverTogether and that was how they reconnected again. Two years later, upon finishing University, Liam gathered up the courage to ask Margaret for her daughter's hand in marriage and proposed to Lena in the park—the same place where they formally met and where he asked her to be his girlfriend.

As for Tori and Adam, they broke up after two years of being together. Adam went back to Australia, and was a businessman now. Tori got married to a guy she'd met at University, Ian.

Belle graduated from Princeton and became a high school teacher. She was engaged to Christopher, a family friend her mom had introduced her to.

Lena admitted that she didn't mind being engaged to him while Liam had Med School starting. She was willing to wait a few years before getting married, she was just happy to be linked with Liam. And to be perfectly honest, Liam was the happiest guy on Earth. Margaret, though, refused to let Lena move in with him. She insisted on her principle: you don't live together until you're married.

On the 1st of May 2019, the happy couple finally got married. The wedding was small and private, and it had everyone they had or needed in their lives.

On the 24th of August 2021, the world was introduced to Jake Adam Black, brown eyes and black hair. He had Adam's cheekiness, Liam's sweetness, and Lena's impatience. He was his parents' world and was loved by everyone. Liam and Lena were both terrified at first; they both had messed up childhoods. So, they vowed to do everything they could and be extra careful to stay there during Jake's life.

Today, on the 21st of April, after about nine months of waiting, a fourth member would finally be joining and complete the Black family. Lena refused to find out what gender it was, but was rather sure it would be a boy. Liam, on the other hand, had a gut feeling that he was about to be the father of a beautiful baby girl.

***

Liam Christopher Black, 29

"Liam? Please wake up. Liaaaaaaaaaam," said a distant voice. I felt someone poking me repeatedly, so I lifted the covers over my head and turned away from the voice, groaning. I closed my eyes, savoring the seconds of silence and drifting away to sleep.

What did anyone in the world want in the middle of the night?

"Liaaaam! Come on, babe, wake up!"

I opened my eyes, annoyance growing towards whoever was trying to wake me up. I recognized Lena's voice and stayed still for a couple of seconds, trying to process what exactly was going on.

Shifting my body towards her, I snuggled my head against the pillow and looked at her. Her hair was messily put up in a bun and her brown eyes shone with fatigue and determination. I was immediately alert when I noticed that she was lying down to the side, her bump brushing my lower back. It was a bad position for her, especially during the ninth month.

"Yeah?" I said, a yawn escaping my lips. "What's up?"

"I really want some orange juice."

I straightened my position, sitting up a little. Looking at her with incredulity, I scoffed.

"Are you serious?" I asked.

"Do I look like I'm joking?"

I raised an eyebrow at the way she'd said that, but then again it wasn't surprising.

"I really feel like drinking orange juice and all we have is stupid apple juice."

"B-but you hate orange juice!" I exclaimed, sighing.

"Well, now I like orange juice and I really want some. Please go to the store and get me some," she pleaded.

"So, you woke me up at-" I stopped to look at the red clock on the wall, "-4 am for orange juice?"

She eagerly nodded, tucking in a wild hair strand.

"Can it wait?" I asked, anticipating the answer.

"No."

Running a hand through my hair, I groaned with frustration. "Lena, please, just wait until morning, all right?"

"I want orange juice," was her only response.

"Lena, it's the middle of the night. You won't die if you don't get the damn orange juice. Please go to sleep now, 'kay?"

She gave me no answer, but slowly stood up and started patting the pair of jeans sitting on the wooden chair beside our bed. A jingle was heard and she stopped searching. Lifting the keys up, she opened the closet and took her pale green coat out.

I stood up, blinking several times to clear my vision. Taking a few steps, I placed my hands on her waist. A sniffle came from her and she slid my hands away with her free hand. She put on the coat, still not facing me.

"Lena," I urged, grabbing her hand and tugging her towards me. She turned towards me, tears in her eyes. I lift her chin up, so that she could properly look at me.

"Where are you going?" I asked, even though I already knew the answer.

"To the all-night store to get myself orange juice," she replied, sniffling.

"Daddy?"

We both turned to the voice simultaneously. Jake stood there, holding his stuffed turtle, Rave, tightly, looking at us with innocence and wonder. Lena sighed and walked over to him. She wiped her cheeks with the tip of her sleeve.

"Why you up, sweetie?" she asked, lifting him up with difficulty and setting him on the bed, since she couldn't kneel down.

"I heard you and Daddy being mean. Please don't be mean to eachothah'. Even Rave hates it when you're mean," said Jake, pouting and holding up the turtle. Lena looked up at me, her expression unreadable. It was obvious who had won here.

"We're not being mean, we're just talking. Now, Jake, let's go to sleep, all right?" I said, picking him up and supporting his back.

I entered the room beside ours. Star stickers glowed in the dark and a green nightlight was my guide in the room. I was careful not to step on any toy Jake had forgotten to put away. I walked towards Jake's big, dark red bed. I held his tiny waist with my hands and carefully laid him on the bed.

"Daddy? Sing to me?" he asked, holding the covers closer to himself. I tucked him in, watching as that caused him to laugh.

"Sure," I replied, fully knowing that he'd be asleep as soon as I started to sing Ed Sheeran's *Where We Land*.

Soft snores came out of him. He looked incredibly peaceful, and my heart warmed at the sight. I froze for a moment as he twitched and held Rave closer to him. A small smile was on my face as I placed my lips on his forehead.

"Sleep tight, buddy," I whispered.

I tiptoed my way out of the room, and left the door open just a little bit. Jake always said that the light from his nightlight would chase the monsters away; the door not being completely closed would scare them, because they'd know that his Daddy, the superhero, would protect him from anything.

I went back into our room, rubbing my forehead in hope to get the starting headache away. Lena was in bed, the beige covers hiding her body. I shook my head, knowing that she was awake. I opened the closet and took out a black big hoodie I wore every now and then. Sliding it on, I took the keys that were on the nightstand beside her.

"Where are you going?" a small voice asked, so low I barely heard it.

"To the damned all-night store to get orange juice."

***

"Lena! You're going to be late, your mom's waiting outside!" I said, watching her grumpily munch on a cucumber. After placing the apple in Jake's lunch box, I put it in his Spiderman backpack.

"Oh, let her wait. After all, I've been waiting eight damned months to grow a baby and bring it to life," she grumbled, putting the vegetable down.

"Lena, if you don't stop, I won't get that box of cucumbers after work today," I said, reminding her to stop being so grouchy. It was a deal we decided to do after her first pregnancy. Whenever she would get snappy, or rather hormonal, I would threaten her with something. Unfortunately, it wasn't entirely efficient at all times.

"Yeah, yeah, I'm sorry blah," she mumbled, walking over to our son and petting his soft brown hair.

"Mommy! I'm not a kitty!" exclaimed the little boy, scrunching up his face into a grimace. I chuckled at how their expressions were so alike.

"You look like a cat," said Lena, pinching his cheeks while smiling.

"Daddy! Mommy has a kitty moment," yelled Jake, running towards me and wrapping his tiny arms around my legs. I let out a laugh, Lena's cheeks got red.

"I'm not sorry! You're just really cute, okay?" exclaimed Lena, sliding her feet in the black flats she loved so much. She pulled her hair up in a messy, high ponytail, obviously disrupted by the weather. The problem with her being pregnant was that the weather seemed to get much hotter or colder to her. So if the weather was perfectly hot, she would complain about her body being on fire.

A buzzing noise was amplified by the wood in our small, oak dinner table. I gave Lena a look, perfectly knowing that it was her mom. Plus, Margaret obviously didn't feel like knocking on the door and coming in. That meant she was cranky.

Just as I opened my mouth to make her go out, she cut me off: "Don't. I'll be out."

"Bye, Jake. Have a good day, sweetie. I love you and?" trailed off Lena, watching as Jake got up on a bean chair to be at her level as she couldn't bend down.

"And I love you, mommy," said the boy, hugging his mom, or rather, her balloon-like stomach that contained his future sibling. He giggled, making me smile.

"What made you laugh?" I asked, taking a bite of a recently washed grape. Jake laughed again, his head glued to her stomach.

"The baby kicked Mommy's tummy, it knows I'm here! It likes me!"

Lena laughed as well, putting her own hand on her swollen stomach. I walked over to them, an idea in mind.

"I think I can find out if the baby really likes you!" I said, ushering to Jake to move his head. The little boy gasped, his face covered in pure shock.

"You talk to babies?! You are..." He stopped, stroking his chin thoughtfully.

"The baby whisperer," I offered in a hushed tone.

"Go, Daddy! I wanna know if it likes me!"

"Don't call the baby 'it', say 'he'," said Lena. I raised an eyebrow, mentally correcting her. The baby wasn't a 'he', but rather a 'she.'

I put a finger on my lips, demanding silence. Jake copied my actions, eyes wide with curiosity. Putting my head against her stomach, I made an exaggerated surprised face.

"Mhm, I see. Well, she loves Mommy a lot. I think she loves me too. As for you, Jake, she doesn't like you."

"SHE DOESN'T?!" shouted the kid, looking terrified.

"No…she loves you more than she loves Mommy and me!"

"Yay! Sowwy, Mommy, I'm too loofable," said Jake, huffing his chest with pride.

"Lovable, sweetheart, loov-able," corrected Lena, her face glowing. Her phone buzzed again and she groaned.

"Bye, babe. Have fun, be careful. Love you," I said, placing a kiss on her forehead.

"Always, love you more. Bye, Jake!" She waved, closing the door behind her.

Looking at Jake, I found him giving me a toothy grin.

"Woof," he uttered, putting his tongue out like a dog.

"Tongue in," I warned. He obliged. "Come on, we're going to be late. I don't think Tori will tolerate you being late again."

So we headed towards Guardian Angel, the fabulous kindergarten that Tori owned.

***

A few hours later

"Cinderella married the prince and they lived happily, ever after," I said, closing the book. The girl lying in the bed smiled at me, a toothy grin brightening her angelic face. She suddenly frowned, appearing to be deep in thought. I braced myself; questions from a six-year-old were, strangely enough, tough to answer.

"Does everybody get a happy ending?" asked Julia, looking up at me with curiosity shining in her blue eyes.

"Yeah, they do. You just have to be patient enough and be able to wait for it, because everyone has a happy ending," I answered, my mind drifting. I knew that I lied to her, because a lot of people die unhappy. For example, victims of war, or victims of suicide or victims of crimes.

"Okay, Julia, you ready to go to sleep now?" I asked, shaking the thoughts away. She eagerly nodded, her eyes already drooping. I sighed, pulling the covers over her, careful not to hurt her leg or neck. Julia had a quite eventful ski day, but she fell and damaged several parts of her body. Thankfully, she survived the fall and would be out tomorrow.

Blonde hair spread on the pillow, she had the same mischief Ellie used to have. Speaking of Ellie, she was coming over for dinner tonight with Scarlett and Scarlett's husband. Ellie's dad had passed away about two years ago; ever since, Scarlett was the head of the house and was way too busy to do anything that was related to her personal life. Lena came up with several arguments to force her to start dating again. The result of that was us being invited to her wedding a year ago.

Standing up, my eyes fell upon a crooked drawing of a sunset I'd drawn a few months earlier. I fixed it straight, smiling at the memory. It had been our fourth wedding anniversary and Lena insisted on planning the evening out. She prepared sandwiches, a fruit salad and, of course, there was a small chocolate ice cream container we had shared.

She had brought my guitar, and played a soft melody while watching the sunset from my side. I had decided that the moment was too precious to not be drawn and I took my sketchpad out of the picnic basket. She had put it in there, knowing that I'd use it at some point.

"You're so predictable," said Lena, laughing, her concentration not breaking.

"No, you know me too well," I had answered, smiling.

Shaking my head, chuckling at the memory, I left the room, but not before making sure that Julia was in fact asleep.

To be honest, being a pediatrician was the best choice I had ever made. Kids and I just went along really well. Yes, the process of fully learning everything was long and hard—almost 11 years. Although, I didn't regret a second of it. My first year here was one of the best years I'd ever had, especially having Lena and Jake by my side. Plus, of course, a fourth member was finally joining our family.

A petite woman was running in the hallways, muttering a few excuses to the people she bumped into. I recognized her as Kayla, one of the nurses and one of Lena's close friends. Upon seeing me, she halted to a stop, a few beads of sweat forming on her forehead. Dark brown eyes shone with excitement.

"Dr. Black!" she exclaimed, taking deep breaths to recompose herself.

"What is it?" I answered, worry beginning to settle in. Kayla was very calm and collected; this was the first time I'd seen her in a state like this.

"L-Lena's water-her mom-third floor-room 364," was all she managed to say, still huffing and puffing. I drew in a breath, my heart suddenly beating fast. The few words Kayla had uttered were enough for me to understand what was going on.

Running as fast as my legs could take me, I reached the maternity section within a few minutes. My hands were clammy, and I couldn't think straight. One thought stood out from the others: Lena was having the baby. Jake was going to get a sister—or a brother—but that was highly improbable. I was almost a hundred percent sure the baby would be a girl.

Stopping before the emergency room, I took deep breaths. Lena was in there, but she wasn't pushing yet. I knew that because no screams were heard.

"Liam!"

I turned to the owner of the voice and was attacked in a bear hug by Lena's mom. Her eyes were red from all the excessive crying, but her smile was blinding. Gray hair tainted the short bob of black hair she had.

"Is she okay?" I asked.

"She's fine, but go take care of her, she needs you."

I nodded fervently.

"Where's Jake?" I asked, worrying about him, my mind becoming blank.

"He's at the kindergarten, he's okay," my mother-in-law answered, waving me away.

"Okay, good, good," I mumbled, slightly trembling. Pushing the door, I entered the room Lena was in. A few nurses surrounded her and I knew that Dr. Clara was getting ready to get the baby. Rapidly putting a mask around my mouth and sliding the blue coat on, my eyes scanned the room for her.

There, lying on the bed, looking exhausted, was my beautiful wife.

"Lena," I whispered, taking long, steady strides towards her.

"Li-AHHHHHHM," she let out a scream caused by a contraction. Her eyes were weary, tears leaking from them. Beads of sweat were on her forehead. She gave me a small, grateful smile. I put my hand in hers and she squeezed it.

"How are you, babe?" I asked, watching as she took deep breaths.

"Fin-AGGH!" she shouted, crushing my hand by the way she squeezed it. Tears fell on her cheeks as she tried to steady her breathing.

"Okay, dear, you're ready to push," Dr. Clara, giving Lena a small, pitiful smile.

"Oh god," said Lena, her voice barely audible.

"It's going to be okay," I mumbled repeatedly. Even though, I was aware that the pain Lena would be going through during the next minutes would be unbearable.

"Liam, you-you were right. It's gonna be a GIIIIIRRRL-GAHHHHHHH! GET OUT, YOU, BABY, YOUR TIME IN MY UTERUS IS OVER!"

A smile formed itself on my lips and I squeezed her hand again.

Everything *was* going to be okay.

***

"Hush, little baby, don't say a word, Papa's gonna buy you a mocking bird…" I mumbled, reducing her cries into whimpers. Eventually, her whimpers settled into slow breaths. Her chest raised softly, her face as lovely as a primrose. I felt tears form in my eyes again, but blinked a few times to keep them in.

I held my *daughter* in my arms.

And she looked so pure and beautiful.

The angel I held in my arms had *my* eyes: blue, striking ones, looking at the world with a certain confusion.

"Liam," whispered a weary voice I recognized. I turned to her and rushed to her side while carefully cradling the baby's head.

"Hey there, sleepy head," I said softly, sitting by her side. She blinked a couple of times, staring at the bundle of joy I held in my arms. She offered her arms to me and I placed the baby girl in her arms. A smile appeared on her face, and her pale face brightened.

"How is she?" she asked.

"She's fine. It's normal that she's tiny, since she came two weeks earlier than expected. Beautiful, isn't she?" I mumbled, eyes glued on the newborn. Lena nodded, agreeing with me.

"Have you decided on a name?" she asked, never once taking her eyes off the baby.

"Yeah, the one on top of the 'names' list."

She chuckled and looked up at me, her eyes shining with happiness.

"Meet Lucy Evelyn Black, our daughter," I said, a grin appearing on my face.

"Her name means *light,*" said Lena, looking over Cloud Nine.

At that particular moment, she woke up, her lids revealing her eyes. Lena gasped.

"She has your eyes."

"She has your features, though," I replied. It was true. Lucy had Lena's light caramel-like skin. She had a small, button nose. Her mouth was heart shaped, and it opened and closed in wonder. I got an idea, remembering what made Jake laugh when he was as tiny as her. Putting my hands on my face, I said, "Peek."

"A-boo!" I cried out, removing my hands from my face. A short giggle escaped her mouth, making my grin widen. Lena chuckled, tears of joy freely streaming down her face now.

The door opened, revealing Tori and Jake. Tori held Jake's hand, her five-month bump showing in a gigantic sweater.

"Lena!" exclaimed Tori at the same time that Jake shouted, "Mommy, Daddy!"

He dropped his backpack, running towards me and hugging my leg. I ruffled his hair and lifted him up and set him on my lap. He giggled, although that stopped when he set eyes on Lucy. Hugging his stuffed turtle, his eyebrows scrunched up and he observed her very cautiously. Hesitantly, he poked her stomach, making her attention go from Lena and me to him. Lena cradled her softly, a motherly expression displaying how much she loved and appreciated this moment.

"Who's dat, Mommy?" he asked, eyes glued on her.

"That's Lucy, your new sister," announced Lena, watching him with a knowing smile. Tori walked by her side, placing a soft kiss on Lucy's head. She didn't say anything, knowing that this moment was very important. She put a hand on Lena's shoulder, her face emitting joy.

"So she came out of your tummy?" he clarified, pointing to Lena's now non-existent bump. Lena nodded, holding Lucy a little closer to Jake, so he could see her.

"No! I don't want her to see me!" He covered his face, turning his body so he could face me. I supported his waist, aware that he could've fallen on the ground.

"Why, bud'?" I questioned, slightly confused myself. He took his hands away from his face, slightly pouting.

"I wanna be happy when she sees me! And I need to say hi!" he exclaimed, his eyes wide. He put a big smile on his face and shifted his body towards Lucy. He bent down a little, so he can get closer to her.

"Hullo, Lulu! I'm your bro-zer, Jake. I'm three." He offered his hand to her, waiting for her to shake his too. Lena held up Lucy's minuscule hand and put it in his. Jake closed his fist and let out his index finger, realizing that her hand was too small to fit in his "big" ones.

Lucy looked at him with wonder, and wrapped her hand around his finger. Jake's face lit up, taking her gesture as her way of accepting him. He suddenly turned to me, a sparkle in his eyes.

"Daddy? Can she meet Rave?" he asked, holding Rave up to me.

"Of course!" I replied.

He held Rave in one hand and placed him above Lucy's head.

"Hi Lucy! I'm Rave, Jake's friend! You look like a cute, big po-ta-to!" said Jake in a deeper voice, impersonating Rave. My heart warmed at the smile Lucy had on her face. I laughed, mentally debating whether to scold him for calling her a "cute, big potato" or not.

"She's gorgeous, a perfect mix of you two," mumbled Tori.

"Yeah. Aunt Tori," teased Lena, nudging her. Tori grimaced.

"I'm a double aunt now. You will be one too, soon enough."

I immediately looked up at her, my eyes widening. Jake was completely oblivious, still bringing Rave and making Lucy laugh.

"You're serious?" I blurted out, completely shocked.

"Wait a second, so that means..." trailed off Lena, looking utterly confused and lost.

"I'm having twins," Tori finished for her, raising her eyebrows at the exhausted Lena.

"Twins?" exclaimed Lena, her mouth dropping. Tori nodded, patting her five-month-old bump.

"When did you find out? And why didn't you tell me sooner?"

"Yesterday. I was going to tell you today, but well, Lucy here came to life," said Tori, pointing accusingly, yet jokingly at the baby girl.

Lena congratulated her and they shared a quick conversation about how Ian, Tori's husband, would have to suffer from double the expenses, since two kids were on the way. Tori left for the coffee shop in the hospital, her craving being hot chocolate.

I averted my gaze to Jake, who had fallen asleep in my lap. Lena and I looked at each other, both of us grinning like Cheshire cats. We had two beautiful children, two human beings who belonged to us.

"I think I'm going to sleep too," announced Lena. I stood up and put Lucy in the crib beside Lena's bed.

Kissing her cheek, I said, "Don't let the bed bugs bite, baby girl."

Jake was beside his mom, soundly sleeping. Lena gave me a small smile, ushering for me to come by her side.

"Can you believe this?" she whispered, looking at our kids. I shook my head, feeling like the luckiest man in the world. She closed her eyes and drifted off as well. Every member of my family all looked so happy and peaceful.

My *family.*

"And my heart has been divided into three different hearts, without them, I wouldn't be able to live," I thought, looking at them.

THE END

Can't get enough of Lean and Liam? Make sure you sign up for the author's blog to find out more about them!

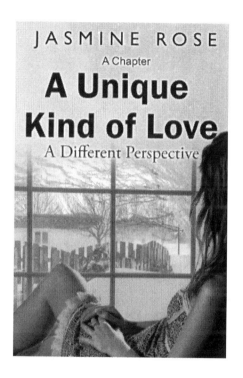

Get this bonus chapter and more freebies when you sign up at http://jasmine-rose.awesomeauthors.org!

Here is a sample from another story you may enjoy:

1

Love Doesn't Die

Did you ever even really love me, Ethan?

I think, my heart tightening at the sight of him laughing at something June had said. His eyes twinkle at her, just as they did once, to me. Why wouldn't he love her anyway? Everybody does. She is the epitome of a perfect girl. Beauty, brains, humor; what didn't she have?

"Amy?" A hand pokes my cheek, breaking my concentration and envy. "Amaryllis?"

My head immediately turns to the owner of the voice, the sound of my full name immediately sparking an annoyance within me. Jenna sits there with a clear look of distaste. Her dark brown eyes pierce through me.

"What?" I snap, watching as she twirls her perfect honey-colored hair around one finger.

She sighs wearily. "You were staring at him again. You're only hurting yourself by doing this, you know?"

I look down to my half-eaten sandwich, feeling ashamed. The muffin I bought suddenly seems ugly and mushy. I push my tray away, keeping my eyes on it.

"You can't keep doing this to yourself," mumbles Jenna, and I can feel her eyes on me. I want to tell her to shut up, to turn away and ignore me, but I can't. She knows how I feel, because a few months ago, I knocked on her door at 4 a.m. in tears. She knows because she stayed up with me that night, rubbing my hair and handing me tissues.

"I know."

And the conversation ends there. Her boyfriend of five months comes beside her and kisses her cheek.

"Hey, babe," says Ryan, hugging her. She turns from me, a glow appearing on her face. They share a kiss that's movie-worthy. All of a sudden, I feel sick. The half of the hamburger I ate is coming up. I swallow my saliva and stand up, my legs feeling wobbly.

"Amy? Don't go," says Ryan, his arm around Jenna's waist. I give them a small smile and pick up my tray.

"I have to study for the science test," I answer, already walking away, ignoring Jenna's voice calling my name.

Jenna and I both knew that wasn't true, because there is no science test.

I turn in a split second and find that Ethan is listening to June talk about something that captivates all of his attention. She flashes him a bright grin, and he gladly offers it. They share a high-five. And I cringe at the sound the collision their hands must've made.

***

I walk to my locker, and search it for my iPod. Thinking too much never helps me, which is why I always keep my mind busy, one way or another. Panic rises as I realize that the pockets of my old, teal-colored coat don't have the iPod.

"No, please don't tell me I dropped it," I mumble, looking in my school bag. I know that there's no chance of it being in there because I listened to music that morning and shoved the iPod into my pocket. I keep on looking, even though I know that my iPod isn't there.

Maybe Jenna took it? It happens a lot. I close my locker and take long yet quick steps back to the cafeteria. I want to run, but I see one of the teachers talking to the principal in the hall. Ms. Mathers seems to be flirting her way to another raise with Principal Jenkins.

And apparently, I look at them for too long. I don't have time to avoid bumping into whoever I hit. I look up, my mouth already forming the I'm sorry. My heartbeat is nonexistent for a few seconds.

A boy with smiling brown eyes looks down at me. His lips are slightly open, looking like he is about to form the same words as me. I can see the dimple on his cheek, the one I liked to see so often, the one spot I liked to poke a lot. There's a small, almost unnoticeable scar on his smooth chin from the time we went roller-skating and he fell on a rock.

"S-sorry, I didn't see you there," I say, my voice barely audible. I start walking away from him. My mind is fuzzy, and I can't seem to think straight.

A hand grabs my arm, and I freeze. "Wait," he says, but all I think about is how strong his grip is on my arm. I turn to face him, my heart beating loud enough for the world to hear.

He puts something in my hand. I look, and it's my iPod. My eyes go to him again, this time in confusion.

"I found it on the ground, beside your locker," he says, scratching the back of his neck. And I know he only did that because he feels uncomfortable.

I nod. "Thanks, Ethan."

"Anytime, Mars." He walks away.

All I can think about is the fact that he called me by the nickname he created himself, this time of last year. I press the power button to reveal the lock screen on my iPod. My breath gets caught in my throat.

The background is an old picture of us, when we'd just started dating. The picture captures me, laughing, and him smiling at me. Jenna took that picture.

Ethan had changed the background to a picture of us.

Why, though? Doesn't he know how badly I miss him already? How hard it is for me? Does he miss me? No-he doesn't. So why change my background?

A tear rolls down involuntarily on my cheek, and it splatters on the picture of us.

I close the iPod.

If you enjoyed this sample then look for **Mars.**

Other books you might enjoy:

Forever Night Stand
Ysa Arcangel
Available on Amazon!

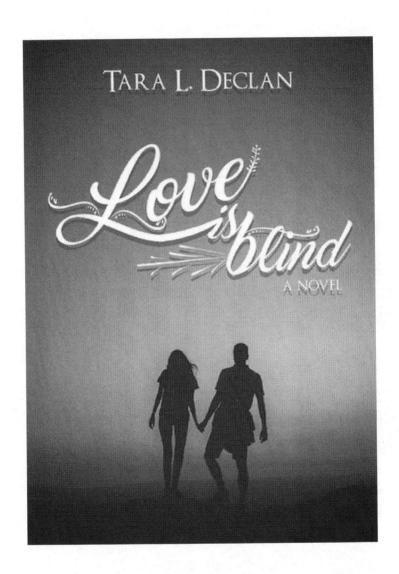

Love is Blind

Tara L. Declan

Available on Amazon!

Introducing the Characters Magazine App

Download the app to get the free issues of interviews from famous fiction characters and find your next favorite book!

iTunes: bit.ly/CharactersApple
Google Play: bit.ly/CharactersAndroid

Acknowledgements

First and foremost, this is a work of pure fiction. Everything in this book was created by me; the characters, the plot, etc.

Mom, Dad and Ahmed, I love you with all of my heart. I will never forget the fake interviews we made when we heard that this would be published. Family's forever and I couldn't be happier that you are my family. You are the biggest pieces of my heart and seeing you happy makes me the happiest girl alive.

I would like to thank Luciana Jhon Carpena, for always standing by my side and being the sister I never had. I hope this makes you cry over and over again, smile and love me even more than you do now.

Dananeele Jean-Baptiste, thank you for everything. You are the one who pushed me to start writing, and now, I think this will remain a part of my life forever. I hope you enjoy this book and we celebrate about this until our teeth fall out.

All of my friends; Shivany, Marcheli, Henia, Sarah, Nikita. I want you all to know how grateful I am to have you guys. Without your encouragement and help, I don't think I would've been able to do all of this. And how can I forget; my fake managers! Thank you for giving me hope that this story would be published one day!

Grace Perral, my agent, thank you for finding my story and me! Without you and your help, this would've forever stayed a little story on Wattpad. You changed my life.

And a huge thank you to Dhalia A. for the extraordinary book cover!

An extra thank you to Edward Christopher Sheeran, for being such an inspiration. Without him and his songs, I don't think I would've been able to write the book. I listen to his songs, most of the time while writing. So, thanks Ed.

Most importantly though, I would like to give a huge group hug to every single person who has started reading this story ever since it was a little story with a few views on Wattpad! You have survived this emotional rollercoaster with me, and you have been with me all the way. Without you, I don't think I would've ever been able to finish this story, much less publish it!

Special thanks to my greatest fans!

Aaliya

Abigail Lawver

Abril Rivera

Adelle Robson

Adilene Garcia

Adrienne

Ajisha K.

Alexa

Alexandra

Allie Flame

Allie Morley

Alma

Alyssa Howitt

Amanda Bennett

Amber Malhi

Amelia Howell

Amineh Rastandeh

Andrea del Mar Flores

Andrea Mendoza

Angela Tran

Anna

Anna Ã˜ihusom

Annie Wood

Aqilah Salim

Ash Friedrichs

Ashini (Ashi for short)

Ashley Felix

Autumn Hoy

Avonna Simmons

Bailey Hawkins

Barbara

Bella

Breanna Renee

Brianna Lynn

Briarley Coppens

Briayla Bowlen

Bridget Curley

Britney Walsh

Brittany Weeks

Caitlyn Flood

Catelynn Rios

Cecilia

Cecilia Andersson

Celeste Delgadillo

Cherry Baby Blue

Chloe Jones

Christian Guzmain V

Ciara Halton

Claudia Kearns

Damilola Fakoya

Daniela

Destiny Gerber

Devin Twitchell

Ella Brickman

Elory Dale

Emilie D.J.

Emily-Rose Macdonald

Erika De Leon

Fatema Soyatwata

Ffion Jackson

Florentia Natalie

Hailey

Hannah Caldwell

Hayley Muller

Huimin Yeo

Iana Makokha

Ismary Jaime

Jack Paolacci

Jeneffer Shamon

Jessica Au

Jocelyn Ott

Juliet Deleon

Kamelia

Katie Newton

Kativon

Kaycee

Kaylynn Witltshire

Kelsey Garcia

Kheyl Nicole Eugenio

Kiley Parke

Kim Nguyen

Krissy

Lamia Bushra

Leilani O.

Leizyl

Lexy Loo

Lindsey Ellen

Loraine Baral

Mackenzie

Maddi

Madeeha Ahmed

Madeleine Johnson

Madeline Rostmeyer

Madi Healey

Mariam Tohmey

Maura Kitto

Melisa

Mich Long

Mikee Lopez

Natalie Yanez

Nha-Thi Luu

Nicole Miller

Nicole Tao (Raven)

Nikki Pham

Nora Santos

Olina Goodman-Viereck

Olivia Vaughan

Paola G. Flores

Patricia Pingul

Paula Dukalska

Phoebe Unsworth

Princess Jazmyn

Rachel Lynn

Rayn

Rebecca Prieto

Rogaya Alhashemi

Rosalina Santiago

Rose

Rushna Tubassum

Rushna Tubassum

Ruth

Sabrina D.

Samantha Arce

Samia Salemohamed

Sarah Torres

Sarah Waliczek

Sasha Louise Durance

Savannah Grace Bison

Shannon Barker

Shannon Cucchiaro

Sierra Davis

Sophia Doyle

Stacia Baughman

Stephanie Linley

Stephanya Maszczakiewicz

Symone Bear Smith

Tamara Yatim

Taylor Lynn

Unique Richardson

Victoia Faria

Ysabel Evangelista

Yvonna Fuentes

Zainab Abdullahi

I couldn't have done this without you…And for those who aren't mentioned here but have been with me through this journey, I thank you also. You guys made my heart swell 10x its normal size.

Author's Note

Hey there!

Thank you so much for reading A Unique Kind of Love. I can't express how grateful I am for reading something that was once just a thought inside my head.

I'd love to hear from you! Please feel free to email me at jasmine_rose@awesomeauthors.org and sign up at jasmine-rose.awesomeauthors.org for freebies!

One last thing: I'd love to hear your thoughts on the book. Please leave a review on Amazon or Goodreads because I just love reading your comments and getting to know YOU!

Whether that review is good or bad, I'd still love to hear it!

Can't wait to hear from you!

Jasmine Rose

About the Author

Author of Fiction Romance book "A Unique Kind of Love" Jasmine Rose is a young girl from Montreal, Canada who dreamed of becoming a professional writer. She started writing on wattpad, a free site for budding writers who wanted to be heard and readers who appreciate a great piece of work.

In a very wonderful twist of events, one of her stories got over 11 million reads in total which launched her career as a Teen Romance Author.

Like her on Facebook: http://bit.ly/JasmineRoseFB
Follow her on Goodreads: http://bit.ly/JasmineRoseGR
Follow her on Amazon: http://bit.ly/JasmineRoseAmazon
Sign up on her blog for freebies: http://bit.ly/JasmineRoseWeb

Made in the USA
Middletown, DE
07 October 2017